PRAISE FOR A.M. DAVIS

"The Mourning of Leone Manor is a beautifully woven Gothic mystery. This book took me by the hand and led me down darkened corridors where I had no idea where I would end up..."

— L.V. RUSSELL, AUTHOR OF THE QUIET STILLNESS OF
EMPTY HOUSES

"A.M. Davis has woven a lush and terrifying tale, set against a perfectly desolate backdrop. Remi and Benoit are beautifully flawed characters who, despite their foibles, seem destined for one another. I couldn't stop turning the pages until the final terrifying twist!"

— LILLAH LAWSON, AUTHOR OF MONARCHS UNDER
THE SASSAFRAS TREE

THE MOURNING OF LEONE MANOR

THE MOURNING OF LEONE MANOR

A.M. DAVIS

THE MOURNING OF LEONE MANOR
By A.M. DAVIS
PUBLISHED BY QUILL & CROW PUBLISHING HOUSE

Edited by Tiffany Putenis and Cassandra L. Thompson

Cover Design by Fay Lane

Printed in the United States of America

ISBN (ebook): 978-1-958228-23-4

ISBN (print): 978-1-958228-24-1

Publisher's Website: quillandcrowpublishinghouse.com

For my family. For myself. For the readers who find and fall in love with this story.

This one is for you.

PROLOGUE

*S*he never thought love would be her demise.

Matters of the heart had never been her strong suit, but her father assured her she would make a lovely wife for any young man. She felt the opposite. Her suitors were few and far between, and the only boy she ever spent time with was her younger brother.

"You don't need anyone else," her brother would say. "You can stay with Father and me. We'll take care of you."

But it wasn't enough. She wanted what the other young ladies in town had, and when she saw them strolling with their beaus, it made the yearning worse. Perhaps it was the reason why she grew so desperate, why she set her eyes on *him*. It was that first glance at the door, with his pretty bouquet and bright gifts, that caught her like a fly in the spider's web.

Willingly, of course.

For days, he would go away on business, and a letter would arrive. It would spell out his yearning, his heartache, his *need* for her. But there was always a stipulation, a hint that he was bound to another, that he could not escape without money for the both of them to leave together.

If only I was not bound by a life here. I would have made you into my queen. A jewel in my crown, one letter read.

In another, he would lament, *I am miserable, my darling. Sitting in the dark, thinking of your lips and your skin. How much longer until I see you again?*

In most? He would rage.

It was a pleasure to be present when all three letters made up the man she loved.

In the heat of their affair, coiled like ravenous snakes around one another, they fed into the other's desires by night. She who wanted love, and he who wanted everything she could give him, her desperation bending her easily into his will. Until she wanted his daylight.

"I can't."

"Please," she begged. "Take me with you to Paris. Just once."

But his decision held firm. Then he would be off again, leaving her destroyed and determined not to let him back into her heart. But the letters would resume, pulling her back into his web.

Romantic words became honeyed apologies, promises of what would never be. She stored those thoughts away in some secret part of her heart, convincing herself that he would follow through someday, that he only needed money. But her fear sent her spiraling into madness. Time away from the manor, away from her, became agonizing loneliness.

So she told him she would find her family's treasure.

His eyes lit up. "Find it, and I will whisk you away to Paris forever."

And she believed him.

But there was no family treasure, no rumored gold—it was just a story. There was only her father and his growing suspicion. His scrutinizing stare as his daughter, once so bright and full of life, wasted away with frantic apprehension.

Then, one morning, she overslept and missed the post.

Her father's fury filled the household.

"You will cease this foolishness," he demanded. "How dare you bring shame upon yourself like this!"

She refused to listen. "But he is miserable, Father! He doesn't love her like he loves me."

Her father refused to hear it. He locked her in her room at night and had her chaperoned during the day. Not seeing her lover tore a hole in her heart, and she poured over his letters, broken by the loss of him.

It was weeks before she finally managed to dodge her chaperone, meeting *him* on the cliff overlooking the beach behind her home. But his demeanor toward her had changed. He went stiff in her embrace.

"Please," she begged. "You must take me with you. My father won't let us be together."

He shook his head. "No. I told you that there is no us without money. You promised me something you could not give. We can no longer continue this way."

"But I love you!" she cried. "I want us to be together, just like you promised."

His expression did not change. "I do not have the money, and neither do you."

"But we can make do! Surely you have some meager savings."

"Enough!" Anger flashed across his face. "It is time for you to move on."

She took a step back, startled that he had shouted at her. She did not like the look in his eyes. The sound of the waves rushed up behind them—a storm was brewing. Her lips trembled, but not from the chill of the breeze. She felt small, and her next words spilled from her lips without a second thought.

"I'll tell your wife," she cried. "I'll show her your letters! I will tell her everything."

Perhaps it was the way his face twisted into something hard, unfamiliar. He became someone else entirely, and it frightened her. But when he grabbed her shoulders, she couldn't have known he would throw her over the edge.

She couldn't have known her brother would be at the bottom.

She couldn't have known that love could be so painful.

A STORM IS BREWING

REMI

THE BLEUE ISLE / MAY, 1898

Remi blamed her mother's pearls the morning they found her husband dead in his office.

"You shouldn't wear pearls on your wedding day. It's bad luck," Tante Beline had said, her brows furrowed with practiced worry. "A dear friend of mine wore a string of them to her wedding some years ago, and the next day, her husband was nowhere to be found."

Remi had heard the story before, but she was always skeptical of its assumed truth. Yet it was easier to agree with Beline, for it would have been unwise to confess her true opinion. Ignorance was bliss for the folk on their island.

She understood its comfort now. She wanted to let herself sink into the blinded crowd, to believe that some unobserved superstition had killed her husband—not something *else*.

Remi sighed deeply, covering her face with her hands.

"Madame?" A small voice chirped. *"Les gens d'armes* are here, as is your family."

"I will meet with them." Remi looked up from her seat in the parlor, meeting her maid's questioning gaze. "Thank you."

Truthfully, meeting with anyone was the last thing she wanted to do. She was too out of sorts for the morning, dressed only in her shift and a heavy dressing robe. Still, duty called; she pushed back her blonde braid and baby hairs with purpose, swallowing the bitter taste of saliva as she stood. Water did little to wash away the bile her stomach had emptied out earlier.

"You're quite pale, Madame. Shall I—?"

Remi quickly interrupted. "No. I'm well enough, thank you."

Sylvie nodded, her lip quivering. She was just as despondent due to the morning's events.

"Are you well, Sylvie? Perhaps you should find some respite."

"Are you sure, Madame?" Sylvie's eyes widened.

Remi nodded. "Yes, please. It will help to ease my nerves."

"Much obliged." Sylvie bowed her head, halfway out the door as she did so.

In truth, Remi was glad to give her time alone. Sylvie was the one who discovered Edgar, after all, and she was in worse shape by far. Her pale, doe-eyed expression burned itself into the back of Remi's mind, synonymous with the memory of the entire morning.

All the more reason I must be steadfast, she thought to herself. She was the Madame of the House, after all. It was her responsibility to set an example, though she felt lacking in that regard. Remi wondered how Tante Beline managed to keep her attitude as neat and precise as her cuticles.

The walk to the study was a short trek, and Remi did her best to hide the misery that lingered beneath her sunken mask. Already, she could smell the ripe, pungent scent of death in the foyer. It lingered, staining the air with its thickness. With a steadying breath, she clung to the vestiges of her composure as she approached a small group by the stairs. They were a bright spot in an otherwise darkened room. The foyer was dim, washed in dark wood, and decorated with ornate rugs and dying plants in ceramic pots. Remi only hoped no one would pay any mind to the cobwebs in the corners.

Or the dust on the mantle, she thought woefully.

"Oh, Remi, darling." One of the waiting guests was her Tante Beline; the other was her cousin, Elise, who held a bright kerchief to her nose. They both looked up from the gentleman speaking to them, diverting his attention. Remi felt her knees quake beneath her, one wrong step from collapsing altogether. The older gentleman with them was dressed differently from *les gens d'armes*, but he was all business just the same.

"You must excuse me," Remi started shakily. "I did not mean to make you wait."

"At least you're here now," Beline said, clearly irritated. "Monsieur, this is my niece, Madame Leone."

The blue-eyed gentleman appraised Remi for a moment as if itemizing every feature in the span of a few short seconds. Whether he was pleased, Remi could not say. "Inspector Marceau, Madame Leone," he offered. Up close, he was similar in age to Edgar, though his hair was snow white, and he kept his beard trimmed closer to his skin. "Your *oncle* informed me that he would identify the body for you. Is that correct?"

Remi nodded, though she was surprised to hear it. *Right to the point, then.*

"The maid told us what happened," Beline clarified, holding Remi's questioning gaze. "About your illness. He thought it would be best to take care of it in your stead."

Remi was accustomed to her aunt's brusque nature, but Inspector Marceau was not. It surprised her to hear him deliver a similarly harsh tone. "Traditionally, next of kin would identify the body."

"But she is clearly ill, Monsieur," Beline argued.

Elise, her cousin, rolled her reddened eyes and pulled at her mother's arm. "Maman, we must not interfere."

"But your father—"

Elise pulled her mother away as they bickered, giving Remi space to speak privately with the inspector.

"I understand it is difficult, Madame, but you are his wife," the inspector said, "and the inheritor of this estate. I must ask that you identify his body for our records."

Remi was silent for a moment. Her stomach dropped at the notion.

"I would be willing to accompany you inside, Madame." The inspector's blue eyes reminded her of the boundless kindness she often saw in Edgar's. It was comforting enough that she agreed.

"That would be most gracious of you."

"This way, then."

Inspector Marceau was a head shorter than Remi, but he was taller than most men she knew. He wasn't familiar to her, and the cut of his fine suit made her wonder if he was from the mainland. There was only one tailor on their island; the difference in craftsmanship was evident.

Remi did not have a chance to ask; they approached the study within seconds.

Somehow, she'd hoped it would take longer to reach Edgar. There wasn't time to prepare for the smell that waited; it still crept into the hall like tendrils of rotting ivy. Fortunately, it didn't surprise her as much as before, and she wasn't doubled over by the wall, emptying her stomach of her dinner from the previous night. Being in the company of Inspector Marceau made it easier to ignore the scent. Even if she was withering on the inside.

"The doctor and the lawyer are waiting inside with your *oncle*," he said, though it sounded more like a warning.

She nodded and followed him in, the creak of the door alerting the gentlemen in the room. Their voices hushed as Remi and the inspector entered, and she found herself facing down her uncle from the other side of Edgar's desk.

They looked like schoolboys caught in mischief.

"Did we interrupt, gentlemen?" the inspector asked.

"What in God's name…?" Remi's uncle said angrily, abandoning his post beside the doctor and lawyer. A white sheet stretched along the ground, covering the body that rotted beneath. "I told you I would identify the body."

"And so you have." The inspector nodded. "However, it is Madame Leone's responsibility to verify. She is, after all, his wife."

Remi's uncle turned red. As he opened his mouth to speak, the lawyer stepped between him and the inspector.

"Enough now, Arnaud," Lamotte said. He nodded toward Remi, acknowledging her presence. "The inspector is correct. We mustn't get in the way. It is the law."

"What is there to inspect?" her uncle argued. A vein popped bright red against his forehead. "He died of heart failure. Didn't you hear the doctor?"

Remi glanced past Lamotte to the man hovering over Edgar. He seemed distant, as if dreaming. The island's doctor was practically a corpse himself. She wondered how he could identify anything anymore; he'd bumped into every surface in the room upon his arrival. Surely, the thickness of his spectacles was no mere coincidence.

Edgar deserves a bit of peace before he is prodded like cattle, she thought sadly.

"Monsieur, I implore you," Inspector Marceau said loudly. "You must conduct yourself appropriately. A man has died here."

"I am aware of that," Arnaud snapped.

Remi sensed the growing tension, and seeing Lamotte's concern spurred her into action. "Uncle, thank you for your kindness. You spared me a great deal of grief. I only wish to be helpful to the inspector and perhaps have a moment with Edgar if you are willing to give us some privacy. I know how protective you are of me, and I am grateful."

Arnaud's mustache twitched. His gaze broke from Marceau's as he took Remi in. Her words appeared to calm him enough, and the relief that followed was instant. She'd never seen him so riled up before, though she imagined it was part of his own grief. She wondered if some small part of him felt responsible for her circumstances, given that the marriage was his idea.

"Very well," her uncle said. "I could use some fresh air."

"As could I," Lamotte added, his usual good temper replaced by somberness. They were good friends, Lamotte and Edgar. It didn't surprise Remi that he would be upset.

"Thank you." She nodded.

"Come along, doctor. Let's all have a bout of fresh air." Lamotte's voice startled the dreaming man. He looked around, confused, but followed the others from the room without question. He was quicker to leave than the other two despite his tendency to topple things.

Eager old man, she thought as the study doors closed behind them.

Inspector Marceau wasted no more time, already crouched beside the white sheet as he beckoned her to join him. She held her composure, gripping tightly at the closure of her dressing robe.

"I just need you to identify him. That is all," he reassured her. His voice was gentle, like a father speaking to a child. "Are you ready, Madame?"

"Yes." Her stomach disagreed.

When the sheet moved, Remi swallowed the sickness that climbed up the back of her throat. It burned all the way down.

She croaked, "Yes, that's Edgar."

It was startling to see him up close. His eyes were glossy, and his hair was wildly out of place. Edgar's skin sagged in death as if what kept him full and lively fled his body. It was surreal to see his liveliness snuffed out so completely. She'd seen him the day before, rosy-cheeked and happy on his way into town.

"I'd never have thought," she said quietly, almost under her breath, "that a quick goodbye a day ago would be the last time I would see you alive." Remi blinked, her eyes prickling with fresh tears as she pushed herself to her feet. Before she could faint, she escaped to one of the armchairs at the center of the room. Bracing herself against the back, she gripped the cushion until her knuckles were white. The horrible ringing in her ears that followed took too long to subside as she tried to calm herself.

"I'm terribly sorry for putting you through that, Madame."

Remi shook her head weakly. "Please, don't worry over me. I'm well enough." She'd said the same thing to Sylvie before, but this time, she could hear the lie.

Inspector Marceau said nothing as he waited, patient to a fault.

"What will happen now?"

"Well, Madame, I had hoped to ask you a few questions." He sounded sheepish as he spoke; while it was a simple request, it startled her all the same.

"Questions?" She turned to level with his gaze. "Am I under some sort of investigation?"

He coughed. "No, Madame. I cannot imagine you would have anything to do with your husband's death, and believe me, I have seen many a murder committed by an angry wife."

Remi did not find the sentiment as comforting as he intended.

"May I?" he asked, producing a small ledger and pen.

"I'm an open book, Monsieur."

"Very well." He cleared his throat. "When did you last see your husband, Madame?"

"Yesterday afternoon. He was on his way to town," she said. "But I have no knowledge of his reason for visiting. We don't—rather didn't —keep the other informed of our daily activities. He was quite private."

The inspector made a note. "And did you see him return? Or did you retire before?"

"I retired well before he made it home. Sylvie usually alerts me."

But Sylvie had been indisposed with chores the night before, leaving Remi to bathe and dress herself before bed.

"And she didn't this time?"

"No. She had other duties."

He nodded his acknowledgment and closed his notebook. As he tucked it away, he asked her one final, yet strange, question. "Did your husband have any enemies? Any sour relations with locals that might stir up trouble?"

The question caught her by surprise. "Not that I am aware of, Monsieur. His family was known for its reclusiveness, but he was nothing but kind to everyone he came in contact with. You can ask the staff."

Marceau nodded. "I shall, Madame. In the meantime, I thank you.

Feel free to call upon me should you have questions or are in need of company. I do enjoy a cup of tea."

"Of course. My home is always open to you," she said sincerely.

He summoned a small smile and tipped his head. "Then I shall take my leave."

"I'll escort you out." It was a meager offer, one she didn't need to make, but the thought of spending one more minute alone in the study with Edgar's corpse made her stomach turn. In truth, she was terrified to be there. The inspector must have suspected the same and accepted her offer cheerfully.

As they left, she noticed there were two other officers and the doctor waiting outside. She spied a stretcher among them and sucked in a breath. They were going to take him away, and she felt guilty for feeling relief.

Edgar Leone was well and truly dead.

"You may hear from me in the coming days," Marceau warned, though his voice was kind.

Remi nodded, and they parted. She moved into the open dining room and closed the doors behind her softly. The cool touch of the door against her forehead told her that not every part of her body was numb.

"Now what?" She choked on a sob, silencing herself so that the voices outside would not find her.

"The audacity of that girl." Remi heard Beline's raspy, uptight voice in the foyer beyond the door. "Your father is quite upset."

"Maman, please," Elise pleaded with her, their voices turning to hushed tones.

Remi closed her eyes. She thought back to a time when she was younger, when there was a boy on a beach, and their chance meeting led to something stranger yet sweet. It was simpler then, easier to pretend that all was well and that her loneliness was just an echo. After all, they were only children when they first met. His countenance would have changed in their time apart, but a small part of her hoped that in writing to him about his father's passing, there might be comfort. Some reconciliation that might mend the dam breaking in her heart.

But that was just the wishful thinking of a widowed woman.

The truth was that Ben would be angry, and any visit from him would bring more thunder than the island's wild spring.

NIGHTMARES

BEN

A terrible nightmare woke Ben, pushing him from slumber as he careened toward the floor.

He landed with a loud thump, still tangled in sheets from the waist down. Behind him, the two slumbering women on the bed didn't so much as budge, completely unbothered by his wild awakening. He'd learned early on that they slept like the dead. One tended to learn these things if they stayed overnight. The brothel was always alive, even in the quieter hours of the morning.

Ben stared at the ceiling and sucked in a deep breath.

Normally, it would have comforted him to know he'd woken in a safe place—somewhere warm and familiar—but he felt gutted, the thick scent of perfume suddenly unbearable.

He choked back a gag as he untangled himself from the sheets and searched for his clothes. Neither of the women stirred, which made freeing his trousers from beneath their sleep-heavy bodies difficult. Once dressed, he stumbled groggily into the half-lit hallway, keenly aware that the nightmare followed him, a parasite that attached itself to his wakefulness. The sting of its grip was wretched with the memory of images that tormented him as a boy.

His heart raced like a bird beating against a cage. The fear was still raw inside him despite the passage of time. *I can still feel her,* he thought miserably. Her eyes still watched him long after waking. Murky and wide, they bore into him, unblinking.

He stopped for a moment to catch his breath. The nightmares always stole his peace. *Ignore it. Just ignore it, and it will go away.* Ben stumbled as he rubbed his eyes.

"Watch it, you drunk!" a man cried out in passing.

Ben grunted, stifling the man's protestations when he stood to his full height. He was taller than the average man, built sturdier than most of the gentlemen of Paris, and he often used it to his advantage. Not that it would matter if he couldn't find his footing. If the man didn't back down, Ben would be at a disadvantage. He could hardly breathe how his heart raced, let alone throw a singular punch.

Thankfully, the gentleman reeled backward and mumbled, "Sorry."

Ben pushed past him and rounded the corner of the hall into the salon. It was hard to see in the smoke and low candlelight. The madam kept the windows covered with thick curtains from dusk until dawn. Whether it was to protect her patrons' identities or preserve the ambiance, or both, it made it damn difficult for him to make out anything.

"Jacques?" Ben called. "Jacques? Where are you?"

Some patrons looked up, but no one said anything.

Among them, he could still see her. Everywhere he looked, the horror of her figure followed. Tattered dress, pale face, and matted hair…a halo that lent light to the petrified terror of her yawning face. Beads of sweat slipped from Ben's hair to the collar of his shirt, shaking as a chill gripped his body.

Am I still sleeping? Is this part of the nightmare? He pressed his hands to his eyes and breathed in deeply. *Go away, go away.*

After a moment, he lowered his hands from his face. From across the room, a shadow extricated itself from a corner, bringing momentary relief.

Jacques was unmistakable among the other patrons—a sickly

fellow with cheekbones sharp enough to cut a diamond. He wasn't one to partake in the same delights as Ben, so he was surprised to see a second shadow emerge. A young woman disappeared through the front door, but not before Ben recognized the exposed upper half of the baker's daughter.

"Oh, ho! What's this?" Ben leered at his friend, ignoring the nightmare. "Satisfying your sweet tooth?"

"Nothing different than what you do." Jacques frowned, swiping back his mostly silver hair behind his ears. His severe expression aged him considerably, but Ben was older by two years. "Only I don't pay."

"You say that, and yet..." Ben crossed his arms and chuckled. "You don't recognize the cost."

"I know the cost." Jacques rolled his eyes and made for the bar. "Spare me another lecture, lest I die here from the weight of your condescension."

"It's not such a bad place to die, my friend." Ben took a seat beside Jacques, bristling at the feel of long fingers brushing the back of his neck. Shakily, Ben waved down the barkeep.

"You jest." Jacques sighed. "And it is always in poor taste."

The barkeep approached with a tired look. "What'll it be?"

"I'll have whatever, monsieur," Ben said, licking his dry lips, "so long as it doesn't come in a green bottle."

The barkeep nodded and reached for a half-full bottle of gin. Ben had enough of *"la fée verte"* and her knack for mischief. The first sip of absinthe he ever drank should have been the first and last time, but he'd spent many nights wrapped in its warmth, sated and drunk. But his nightmares were all the worse for it.

"A little early for you," Jacques said, raising a brow.

Ben pulled his arms in toward his chest as he leaned in closer to the bar. The nightmare was still there, practically breathing down the neck of his collar. "I know."

"I recognize that look. You've had a nightmare, haven't you?"

Ben watched the barkeep pour his drink. He shivered.

"I'll take that as a yes."

Ben tipped the drink back and slammed the glass down, indicating another. "It was awful."

"Care to elaborate?" Jacques straightened.

"My sister."

Jacques hummed. "Ah. The enigmatic sibling."

"Yes. Soleil." Saying her name aloud after so long felt strange, like ash on his tongue or cotton rubbing against his teeth. It conjured up her visage—a countenance they shared in equal measure, although Ben's complexion was darker. In his memories, Soleil was finer. Her features were sharper, her cheeks rosy. The nightmare of her was quite the opposite, and it scratched endlessly at the back of his skull now, begging to be seen.

Jacques continued his inquiry. "What was it this time?"

"The same as always." Ben drummed his fingers nervously against the grain of the bar. "She falls, she dies, and then she's crawling toward me. Begging for my help."

"And?" Jacques asked. He was all too familiar with the story. It was part of how they'd met: both of them high in an opium den, writhing over nightmarish hallucinations. It was the purest form of torture Ben had ever forced himself to endure.

"And then I woke up." Ben closed his eyes, afraid to open them again. "Only, she's still *here*."

Jacques eyed him and then the waiting glass of another pour of gin. One hand shot out and took it, downing the substance with a sharp hiss. "Then this won't get rid of her."

"I think it's a sign. She's trying to tell me something." Ben swallowed hard and forced himself—out of spite—to open his eyes.

"A sign?" Jacques commented, his voice bordering on concern. "What do you mean?"

Ben froze.

Two arms snaked around his shoulders, a pair of cold, wet lips brushing his ear. Soleil's breathing hitched and labored as she croaked his name over and over again.

Ben! Please, Ben! It hurts...it hurts.

"I don't know…but it's something."

"That's deeply unhelpful."

Ben shrugged, but Soleil remained, her embrace tightening. *Just tell me what you want,* he thought. *Tell me what you want, or just leave me alone.*

But just as she started to speak again, the door of the bordello burst open. The ruckus caused Ben and half of the occupants to jump to their feet. It was enough to dispel him of her grip, and just like that, the nightmare was gone. In its place was a red-nosed youth in tattered clothing with wide, reddened eyes. He took a moment to catch his breath before finally calling out, "I've got an important message to deliver! For Benoît Leone!"

Ben's own eyes widened as every head in the bordello turned toward him.

"Who's asking?" Jacques shuffled ahead.

"I have a letter for him, monsieur." The boy sniffed. "I was told he would be here."

"I am." Ben stepped beside his companion. "What's this all about?"

"A message for you." The young boy produced a small envelope. "Urgent news."

Ben recognized the penmanship, and his stomach dropped. His nightmare came back in a rush. The last words she'd spoken from crusted, decaying lips just before she faded into the dark corners of his mind.

"Come home," she'd said. *"Come home!"*

His palms, slick with sweat, stretched at his sides.

Absently, he reached into a pocket and produced a single coin. The boy took the payment and left the letter in Ben's care, racing back into the dewy morning. Distracted, Ben walked to one of the more well-lit corners of the salon and collapsed into a seat. Jacques joined him a moment later, patient yet inquisitive.

"Are you going to open it?"

Ben licked his lips. The last letter he'd received from home was a wedding invitation, and before that? A letter that still stung to remember. Both came from the same sender. He might have ripped it open with vigor, hungry for another reason to burn with hate, but its arrival was ominous. In his heart, he felt its message was more important than the anger he might have felt toward the person who sent it.

Wordlessly, he broke the seal and pulled from it the familiar stationery.

Dearest Benoît,

I hope you will forgive me, as I did not wish to write to you under these circumstances, and yet fate has forced my hand. I am writing to express to you my deepest sorrow: your father has passed.

I can only imagine what you must be feeling, for I am beside myself with grief as well.

His funeral arrangements are already underway. Your presence is requested—please come home.

With love,
Remi A. Leone

Seeing her name pulled at a once-dead cord inside of him. Her words were different than before. They lacked emotion, somehow. Had her marriage been as awful as he'd silently hoped? He shook his head. He didn't like the way his mind wondered if she still held some kind of fondness for him, even though he had rebuked her.

"What is it?" Jacques asked.

Ben brushed his thumb over her signature. "My father died."

"When?"

"This was posted two days ago." Ben handed the envelope to Jacques and rubbed a hand over his face to the back of his neck, finally feeling tired again. "I've been summoned."

A long silence followed. The static of the background filled in the cracks as they formed. Laughter, jeering, and glasses clinking as drinks were poured. The merriment for those sodden souls around them would end in a few short hours; for Ben, they ended the moment he'd read her words.

Finally, Jacques spoke. "I'll fetch a carriage and arrange for an early departure."

"I'll meet you at the docks in an hour." Ben sighed and buried his head into the palms of his hands.

"Make it two." Jacques countered, clapping Ben's shoulder. "I take it this will be a long trip, and I must say farewell. After all, I have unfinished business with Farine."

"You have two hours," Ben said.

Jacques left without another word. Ben sat down at the bar again, setting the letter on its polished surface. He pushed his hair back and blew out a deep breath. He would need to return to his relatives and give them the news. The thought of that conversation sent an unpleasant shiver down his spine. They were cold people, his father's family, and he was sure they wouldn't care. Still, the thought bothered him more than he would have liked.

He was still my father, Ben thought. He ached at the memory of the man who used to sneak him extra scones after tea, the man who used to sneak him to the beach during his lessons to skip rocks and wade barefoot in the cool summer water. That was who his father had been before tragedy attached itself to their family like a parasite. Father was never the same after his mother passed. Ben understood that grief, but with his sister, it was different. When she died, he'd been cast out and sent away to live with strangers. He was spared nothing, not even an explanation. Now, there was only the weight of the mystery his father left behind.

Ben smacked the bar, a glass sliding into his waiting grasp a moment later. He tipped it back, drinking it down with a hiss. *One for the man I knew.*

He signaled for another and held it to his lips. *And another for the man I never did.*

With that, he finished his drink and stood. Gin warming his belly,

Ben strode out of the brothel, tucking the letter safely in his breast pocket. It felt heavy sitting above his heart, the fresh pain of its news joining the hurt of years gone by. He never realized until that moment, as he walked the early morning streets of a sleepy Paris, that no one could ever really pocket the past. Not when the weight of it was carried in words unspoken.

HOME

REMI

Remi anticipated Ben's arrival poorly.

She woke early and took extra care with her ablutions, dressing as sluggishly as if she had been ill and bedridden for days. After picking at the rasher of bacon and eggs set before her on the table, she returned to her room and stared at her reflection, startled by how plainly she wore her tiredness. The sagging beneath her eyes spelled a lack of sleep.

"Will he recognize me?" Remi wondered.

It was an awful thing to put vanity before grief, though it only served to distract her from everything else. Somehow, appraising the sudden shift in her features made her feel older, and more experienced than before. The soft, roundedness of her once pink cheeks now stretched over angles she never knew existed. Remi frowned and pinched them with cool fingers to bring some hue back to her milky complexion. It added some color, though the same could not be done for her eyes. If not for their darkened state, she might not have noticed how brightly they used to sparkle.

Ben will notice, Remi lamented, dropping her head into her hands with a miserable groan. *He once said they were more brilliant than the ocean.*

She could have laughed at herself for being so selfish.

"Remi?" Elise rapped on the door from the hall.

"Come in."

The door creaked open. "Goodness, *ma cherie!*" Elise's nose crinkled. "Could you be any more pale?"

Remi frowned, a limp strand of hair falling from place to emphasize her deflation. She pushed it back and turned to face the mirror again. "You're right. I could be."

"You know what Maman would say," Elise said as she found her way to Remi's unmade bed.

"I don't care to relive those stuffy lessons any longer, Elise." Remi leaned forward and pinched her cheeks again. It did little to revive her, not enough to forgo the rouge.

From the mirror, she could see her cousin puff her cheeks. "What's gotten into you?"

"I'm nervous, and I barely slept," Remi sighed, twisting at the waist to see her cousin better. "Can you blame me?"

"Hm." Elise considered her words. "It is a bit of an adjustment. The silence is almost...too much."

Remi blinked. "It isn't just that."

"Then what?" Elise's brows rose in question.

"I can feel it," Remi said, cupping one hand in her lap with the other. She traced the lines in her palms with sore eyes.

Elise asked. "Feel what?"

"Him. I can feel him." Remi had kept herself still most of the night, surrounded by empty darkness, but she could not shake the nerves away. Her stomach twisted somewhere between midnight and dawn, unrelenting. "He'll be here soon, if he hasn't already arrived."

"You can feel him? How scandalous," Elise teased, attempting to lighten the mood.

"Elise, please," Remi begged. "Be serious, if only for a moment."

Her cousin frowned and eased back, extending her feet toward the floor like a child being punished. She looked ten years younger when she pouted. Finally, she asked, "Should his arrival be such a terrible thing?"

"He's angry." She might have felt the same if she were in his position.

"How could you possibly know that?"

"I just do. I have a terrible knot in my chest, Elise. It's been there since I married Edgar...he never came."

"He could have been held up," she offered. "Paris is a bustling city, and word has it he *is* a doctor now."

"No, he wasn't." Remi knew without a doubt she was wrong. She wasn't naive enough to believe he was held up, not when she suspected she knew the answer.

"I wrote to him before the wedding," Remi admitted. "Before the invitations were sent."

"You *what?*" Elise perked up. A juicy bit of information was all she ever needed to reignite her interest. "And you're telling me now?"

"I know I shouldn't have, but I felt so...afraid. Desperate for someone to save me."

Elise's eyes widened. "What did you say?"

"I asked him to come home." Remi flushed, half from embarrassment and half from guilt. "Though, it would be more accurate to say that I begged him to."

I said that I loved him still, she thought, not brave enough to mention it to Elise. "It was foolish."

"And he never came...Oh, Remi. How cold." She might have been frowning, but some part of Elise enjoyed the drama. "I'm so sorry."

"I don't hold any ill will toward him," she paused, "but I know, deep down, he's angry."

Elise brightened. "Perhaps he never received it! Did you have the right address?"

"Yes. I snuck into Tante Beline's room and found her list of invitees." Remi tried a smile but failed. "It was the right address. Tante Beline does not make mistakes."

"She does sometimes."

"No." Remi turned back to her mirror, unable to look at anything but her sinking reflection. "I thought that, but then I asked Edgar about his cousins and where they lived."

Elise was silent.

Remi continued, "When the invitations went out, and we received word from others, I checked for their reply. When it didn't come, I asked if the address was wrong, if we'd overlooked something —*somehow*. He assured me it was correct and that his cousins, Ben included, would have received theirs on time because he'd posted it himself."

"Oh…"

"He didn't seem surprised." Remi sighed. "He dismissed their lack of reply. Said it happened all the time, and Ben, being a spiteful boy, would not bother to attend either."

Remi recalled their conversation in his study, brief though it might have been. Learning the truth solidified the utter misery she'd felt at the ceremony. Guilt had washed itself over her; the feeling of betrayal he must have felt far exceeded her own hurt. And the anger? Well, there was no discounting him for that, not when his father thought of him as a 'boy' and not a grown man.

"How sad he must have been." Elise mirrored Remi's worries.

"And angry," Remi added again for effect.

Elise moved away from the bed and was behind Remi in seconds. She placed two hands on her shoulders and gave them a squeeze before dropping her face beside Remi's. They looked at each other in the mirror—one as white as the moon's light, the other as healthy and pink as a newborn baby.

"Be at ease, cousin," Elise said cheerfully. "I'm sure, given time, he'll understand."

"And if not?" Remi grimaced.

"Well, I don't think you'll give him much choice in the matter. Not when you're his—"

Remi stood abruptly, nearly knocking Elise backward into the bed. Her face burned with fresh heat. "Don't say it," she said, her voice steely, though thoroughly humiliated.

Elise laughed. "At least you're not as pale anymore!"

Remi groaned and hid her face in her hands.

A knock at the door interrupted them, drawing their attention to

Sylvie's thin frame. She looked surprised and somewhat nervous, her lip already red from being bitten. Her hands curled into her apron as she addressed Remi. "Martin's son ran ahead. He says the carriage is on the way."

Remi's heart fell. "So soon?"

"Yes, Madame."

Remi was petrified, rooted to the spot as the breath left her chest. If not for Elise, she would have fallen back into bed and remained in hiding for the rest of the day. But her cousin looped their arms together and gave Remi a tug.

"As Maman would say," Elise said with a grin, "if your corset is tight enough, they'll never see you bend."

Remi groaned. She hated to admit, but there was a modicum of wisdom to be gained from Beline's lessons. Unable to protest, she let Elise pull her through the door and down the stairs. Above the sound of their footsteps and Sylvie's quick pattering behind them, Remi heard the tremble of thunder. It was so loud that for a moment, she thought it might have been her heart plummeting to her stomach.

She was right.

He'd brought with him thunder.

BEN

The Bleue Isle, named for the brilliant hue of the water that surrounded it, felt unfamiliar as Ben departed the boat. He stood on the water-worn planks of the dock and breathed in deeply.

Jacques appeared beside him, looking refreshed. He didn't have the same aversion for seafaring that Ben did.

"Quaint," Jacques remarked as he took it all in. The docks were old and empty, the fishermen out catching their wares. A few buildings waited ahead, a carriage and driver on the small street before them. There weren't any other passengers on the little ship they came by, so Ben knew it was for them.

"It isn't much." Ben grabbed the little luggage he'd brought with him. He motioned to the carriage with his chin and started forward. "The Isle has been lost to time. I'm sure not many people outside of the little towns where the fishermen sell their catch even know about the place."

The driver, Martin, quickly introduced himself and went about stowing their baggage while Ben and Jacques chatted on. They climbed into the cool, stale air of the cabin and sat opposite each other on the low seats.

"Brave men making that trip every day. Those waters were choppier than the worst roads in Paris," Jacques said.

The carriage started forward with a sharp jerk, followed by a loud apology thereafter.

"It's a wonder to me that the Isle still exists." Ben tried to picture the old halls from his youth, the sunshine streaming in from the bay windows that faced the cliffs overlooking the sea. He jerked upright when his sister's solemn face and tear-stained cheeks cut into his memory. Thankfully, it was quickly chased away when their carriage pitched violently from a stray bump.

"Good gods, man!" Ben cried as he toppled to the side. He thumped the ceiling. "Watch it out there!"

"Apologies, *monsieurs*," their driver called back. "We're nearly there!"

Ben composed himself and peered out the small window.

The manor came into view, rising like a dark angel above the trees lining the bleak dirt road. It was the same stony face of his youth, aged by the growing weeds and moss-stained crevices from the passing years. Shrouded in the morning dew, it seemed to stretch through the mist, its gates yawning wide in welcome. It would have made him happy to see it, but its countenance was as bleak as the reason he'd returned. It appeared to wear a shroud of its own as if grieving all this time. A snap of reality twisted his insides, stoking the anger inside him. Like a phoenix, his resentment rose from the ashes, a new being made from the fires that had burned within him for years.

His family's legacy. His father's death.

"Remi," he whispered.

"You've been saying her name in your sleep." Jacques knew nothing beyond the superficial. To him, Remi was simply his father's widow. There wasn't much that Ben kept from the man, but he kept the truth of his family and his past prior to Paris locked up tight. It wasn't that he didn't trust him. Jacques was the first friend he'd made in the glittering city, but there were parts of himself that Ben kept close and hidden. Jacques respected that, for he, too, had secrets better left unspoken.

"Have I?"

He nodded. "Hers, your sister's, and your father's. You're a man haunted by many names."

"Names and faces," Ben agreed. His nightmares persisted during their travels, and there wasn't much comfort in the memory of his father. Not anymore. All that was left to his dreams were faded recollections of a starry-eyed girl with rumpled hair and wrinkled dresses.

"Who is she?" Jacques leaned back in his seat. "Other than your father's widow."

"No one of importance." Ben shrugged.

"No importance?" Jacques peeked out from one closed eyelid. He was like a bloodhound when it came to liars. "That's a lie if I've ever heard one. My mother's third husband was no one of import, but you don't hear me calling out his name in my sleep." Jacques was no defeatist. He pinned Ben in place with his objection and held him there until he relented.

"She was a… *friend*." Ben tried to keep the tenderness from reaching the confession, but Jacques was quick.

"A *sweetheart*, you mean."

Ben pressed his lips together and narrowed his eyes. Finally, he spat out, "Yes."

"And she married your father?" The pieces fell together for Jacques, and like a good game of cards, he found himself with a winning hand. Normally, he would delight, but the expression he wore showed his sympathy. "Your sour mood makes sense now."

Ben lowered his eyes to the floor of the carriage. It was muddied from their boots, and the wood slats were thinning enough that he could see the faintest light slipping through them.

"Why your father?" Jacques pressed on. "I thought he was already a widower."

Ben frowned. "It wasn't her choice."

"Whatever could you mean by that?"

"She wrote to me weeks before the wedding. About two months ago now." The letter arrived on the brightest day of spring, and he'd felt such joy at first receiving it. He also remembered how much he admired her boldness and how quickly he plummeted into rage when the wedding invitation arrived. "It was the first letter from her in years, and she begged me to come home."

Jacques, who never looked surprised, seemed utterly shocked.

"What?" Ben asked.

"And that's the first I'm hearing of this?" Jacques's incredulity hid the betrayal he must have felt.

"I was unhinged with grief and anger." Ben glanced out the window again. The manor loomed, the structure coming clearer into view. "I wanted to forget. So I holed myself up with as much drink as I could get my hands on and sunk into Lilly's bed."

"I remember that," Jacques said, scratching at his jaw. "Took nearly three days to sober you up and pull you out of her bed. You reeked, too."

"You needn't remind me."

"This will be an interesting visit," Jacques noted.

"This isn't a visit to the theater." Ben shook his head. "Remember, we're not strictly here for my father's funeral."

"Right. Your sister, too."

"I want to get to the bottom of these nightmares." Ben nodded, crossing his arms. "After that and everything else to do with my father, we can leave."

"Well," Jacques sighed, settling into the seat, "if there are answers to be found, then maybe your sister will finally be at peace."

If. That was the key.

It was the unknown 'if' that nagged Ben for years. Soleil had changed in just a few short months—happy and glowing one day, downright miserable the next. Sometimes, he caught her rummaging through old rooms and the attic, mumbling about money and needing more time. Their father had caught her on one occasion, sneaking off with a few stolen francs from his study, and sent her to her room for a few days. She stayed in there, hidden away—plagued by something Ben could not see. While he played with Remi and the others, his sister stayed secluded. He wondered why and what she could have been doing in there all the while.

If he was wrong about her death, and she had jumped as it was rumored, then why?

Even now, it didn't make sense. He was reaching, he knew that. But why else would her shade haunt him for so long? Her ghastly reappearance was an omen, without a doubt. Perhaps it was the reason she'd followed him for so long, always hiding in the shadows of his room or his dreams. Every nightmare was her, reaching for him from beyond the grave as if to say, *I didn't do it.*

"It's a gut feeling, Jacques," Ben said, rubbing at his tired eyes.

"Whatever you say, *Monsieur* Leone."

"Enough of that." Ben chuckled, grateful for the change of tone.

Seconds later, the carriage came to a stop. Ben wasn't eager to leave the cabin yet, but as the door opened and Martin peered inside, he found he couldn't hide. He climbed out of the carriage ahead of Jacques. His boots ground the dirt outside the manor as his eyes fell upon the familiar structure of his home. A crack of thunder sounded overhead at the same time, and a young woman with a head full of yellow hair appeared at the entrance. His heart nearly stopped.

A flash of blue-green against a pale, sullen face. The black mourning gown she wore accentuated her rigid posture, which tensed as they found each other's gaze. She mirrored the great manor rising behind her, a portrait of melancholy.

Not as starry-eyed as she used to be, Ben thought.

Whoever Remi was, she was not the same girl he remembered. He wasn't sure what he'd been expecting, though he'd done well to keep it from his mind while they traveled. Fantasy was not the same as reality, and imagining Remi in any other way would have conjured sympathy; he didn't want to feel anything.

Suddenly, his stomach coiled tight with nerves and the urge to look away. Instead, he held his eyes level with the young woman at the door, focused on her unchanging expression—a mixture of shock, fear, and something else. Her pale pink mouth twitched as if she meant to speak when a second figure burst through the door. At once, he recognized the brunette as Remi's cousin, Elise. They were two sides of the same coin—where one went, the other was always close behind.

"Oh!" Elise yelped, her eyes widening. She quickly leaned toward Remi's side and whispered something inaudible.

"Monsieur, my son and I will take the carriage around back," Martin said as he patted Ben's shoulder lightly. "We'll serve supper once you're settled."

"Thank you," Ben said, though he made no effort to acknowledge Martin. In fact, he couldn't find the will to move, even as the first drops of rain hit his forehead. Remi was all that he could see, and it took everything in him to keep from turning tail back to the docks, back to Paris.

Within the sea of her blue-green eyes and his raging fire, a chasm of doom lay wide open between them. Below the surface of their silence, sixteen years' worth of darkness laid itself bare.

Ever the brave one, Remi took a step forward, moving away from her cousin's grip. Unbothered by the rain, she said, "Welcome home, Ben. I'm glad to know my letter reached you."

He hadn't expected that.

Is this really the same woman who wrote to me before her nuptials?

Ben was silent, tormented by the rush of his emotions. The way his name left her tongue sweetly and the kindness in her solemn expression left him raw and gutted. She used to be an excitable thing, full of smiles and laughter. What happened to her? Where was the spark he remembered? The desperation in her first correspondence echoed in his memory. She was less than half of what she used to be, even less so than the woman who originally sent the letter.

Idiot! Remember, she still went forward with the marriage. She's reaped what she's sown—you shouldn't care if she's miserable.

But the fire wavered regardless.

"I know this is a difficult hour, but I hope that we can—"

The rain drowned out the last of her words as it picked up, soaking them both as the others ran inside to take shelter. The deluge came down, blocking her from his view, and his sympathy broke. The connection he felt, the confusion, all of it washed away. His anger and irritation renewed itself, hurtling him forward.

"Spare me," he sneered. "Gods, *spare me.*"

And then he was inside, blind to everything but the stairs where Jacques waited. His companion appeared surprised but said nothing as Ben passed. Soaked to the bone, he was numb to the chill in the house. All he could feel or would allow himself to feel, was the hate he'd built up for the sad, solemn woman he'd left in the rain.

Welcome home, Ben thought bitterly. *Welcome home, indeed.*

THE PRODIGAL SON

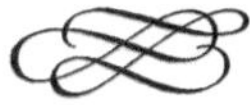

REMI

Remi stood in a shallow pool of rainwater.

She waited patiently for Elise to bring her a blanket as the drip-drop echoed in the empty, cool foyer, distracting her from the chattering of her teeth. Ben's dismissal had left her shocked.

"Ma cherie," Elise called out, winded as she rounded a corner. "I found you a blanket. Martin is in the kitchen warming some tea, as well."

"Thank you," Remi murmured as she wrapped herself tightly in the scratchy fabric. It was an old blanket, but warm enough.

"What a brutish thing to do," Elise offered, "leaving you out in the rain like that."

Remi pulled the blanket around her tighter. The fabric was coarse under her fingertips as if it had been made from Ben's anger. "It was my fault for standing out there in the first place. I was too...*eager.*"

"Hm." Elise crossed her arms. "I suppose I can't disagree with you now, can I?"

"No, you can't." Remi smiled weakly, glancing at the stairs. She needed to change, but bumping into him in the hall was a risk she did not want to take.

"It could have been worse," Elise said.

Remi stiffened. "He hates me, Elise."

"He might." Elise shrugged.

The sour taste on the back of Remi's tongue burned. "You're not meant to agree with me!"

"He's deeply serious." Elise ignored her cousin's alarm, answering her own question from earlier that morning. "Did you get a good look at him?"

"No." Remi pulled the blanket to her face and caught a trail of water dripping down her cheek. "It was difficult to make him out in the rain," she lied. Of course, she'd seen him. Her heart stopped the second they found one another. He was all angles, with sharp cheekbones and a distinct brow-line that dipped into a deep 'v' when he scowled. They were as expressive as his eyes, which were so dark they shone like polished onyx. They seemed to reflect more than the rain and lightning. Remi surmised they held a great deal more than just the surface of his disdain for her, and she wanted to know every thought that hid within his darkness.

"He's handsome," Elise started, circling her cousin. A hand fell against Remi's back as Elise ushered her forward. "And tall. Quite tall, in fact, and his hair is darker somehow, black like his...well, like his father's."

"Elise."

But she went on, the teasing in her tone hinting at mischief. "Such broad shoulders, and my stars, did you see his lips? There is potential there, if only he did not frown so much. They seem very soft."

"Is your corset too tight, Elise?" Remi snidely remarked as they approached the first step.

"You must have noticed." Elise pushed.

"It's indecent. Especially when you're already engaged." Remi broke away from her cousin, spearing her with a sharp look. It bothered her that Elise was so perfectly dry while she no doubt resembled a wet foal. Though, in truth, she was made more uncomfortable by Elise's loosened tongue than she was by the growing heaviness of her gown.

Elise rolled her eyes emphatically. "Hugo? He's dull, and his foul mood is as bad as his taste in suits."

Remi could hardly protest. Hugo was more than her fiancé, though; he was also her father's business partner. Over the years, he ingratiated himself with the family so thoroughly that news of their engagement never came as a shock. Except to Elise. She hated the idea as much as she hated Hugo. They weren't a match, but that didn't stop the ladies of the wedding brigade from joining Beline in her daughter's life and future planning.

"That doesn't excuse you." Remi chided.

"*Ma cherie*, please. They were merely observations." Elise waved her off. "You should try to make amends. Extend an olive branch during supper. I'm sure he'll be happier once he's had a decent meal."

"Supper?" Remi couldn't imagine having a stimulating conversation with him, not after he'd snuffed her so thoroughly.

"Yes."

"But—"

Elise's expression hardened. She looked like her mother when she was serious. "His father died—*your* husband."

"You needn't remind me."

Elise took the first two steps up, a gesture for Remi to follow. "Supper will be soon. Perhaps we should get you changed."

Remi responded with a shiver.

The thought of changing into something dry and drinking a cup of warm tea brightened her a little, but as they reached the second floor, Remi heard Ben's voice, and her earlier anxieties returned with a vengeance. It was warm and friendly, and it surprised her to see him conversing so easily with Slyvie, who was seemingly dazzled by him. So, he could be a charming gentleman. Neither of them paid any mind to the two women ascending the stairs. It would have been the perfect moment for Remi to slip by unnoticed if Elise hadn't stopped her halfway from retreat.

"Not so fast, cousin," Elise hissed, giving her a push in the opposite direction. "Go and talk to him. I'll gather your garments."

"I would prefer not to," Remi argued.

A devious smile curled along Elise's lips. "Remember what Mother would say."

Remi frowned. "You are a cruel torturer."

Elise batted her eyes and flipped her hair back dramatically. "I know."

An unspoken 'you'll thank me later' passed between them as Elise left her one step from the landing. Ben and Sylvie had moved further away now, closer to an open door down the hallway to the guest quarters. Their voices still reached her, though their words were muted.

He's just a man, Remi thought as she pulled her blanket tighter. It was damp from her clothes, its warmth completely lost. *I won't let him intimidate me!*

"A warm bath would be nice," Ben said as Remi came closer.

"Of course, sir."

"Thank you, Sylvie." He moved from her side and lingered in the doorway, turning at the sound of Remi's approach.

Elise was right—Ben was handsome. Sixteen years marked itself on him, and even Sylvie could not be faulted for lingering. He was unlike any of the other men on the island. He could sport any number of expressions, and still, his charm would make itself known. His jaw was strong, like his high cheekbones, and his nose was long but regal. The confidence he exuded was an undeniable part of his appeal. None of the hours and days she spent fantasizing about him could hold a candle to the man standing before her.

"Oh, Madame! I didn't see you there." Sylvie startled, nearly dropping the laundry in her arms.

Ben's thick brows raised with interest. In the slight glow emanating from his room, the dark complexion of his forever sun-kissed skin seemed to glisten.

"Sylvie," Remi addressed her with as much authority as she could muster. It was hard to keep her focus when Ben's attention focused on her heavily. "I just wanted to be sure our guest was settled. Does he have everything he needs?"

"Yes, Madame." Sylvie didn't move. "Monsieur was just asking for a bath."

"Before supper," he added, leaning against the doorframe.

"Then we should tend to that presently," Remi pressed.

"Yes, Madame. Excuse me." Sylvie's eyes widened, and she ducked her head as she passed.

A frigid moment of silence passed between them, his dark eyes hard and empty.

Remi tightened her grip on the blanket and opened her mouth to speak. "I hope—"

"Don't." Ben held his position.

Remi sucked in a breath. "Have I done something?" she asked. "I apologize if—"

"Madame." His voice was deep, a rumble in his chest that she could practically feel rattling in her breast. "I need none of your apologies. We are beyond such formalities. I'm not here for you."

The emphasis of his words was like a smack to her cheek.

"I was under no such impression." She never expected him to come back for her, not after he'd rejected her so thoroughly. If not for Edgar's death, she knew he might never have returned at all.

Ben straightened an inch.

"Let me make myself clear," he started, a trace of poison lacing his tone. "I do not care to know, nor do I have any interest in the relationship you had with my father. Your condolences and sympathies are unnecessary for me. In fact, they are most unwelcome."

She tipped her chin up in defiance. His eyes lit up, half-amused, though he was still visibly angry.

"If you intend for us to share in our grief, then you are to be sorely disappointed, Madame." The sound of footsteps on the stairs echoed as the last syllable reached Remi's ears.

"I haven't the slightest intention to share my grief, as it were," she said coldly. "You may not approve of the circumstances of our unique situation, but we can at least come to some sort of understanding." Wet and dripping a sizable river along the floor of the hallway, she refused to be dismissed again.

"And what sort of understanding is that?" Ben sneered, a mocking smile plastered on his face.

"Until the reading of the will, I am the lady of this estate." She paused for a breath. "And while you're here, you'll treat me with some modicum of respect."

Ben considered her, as though surprised.

She fidgeted but pressed on. "Of course, I will do the same."

"That's rather courteous of you."

"I only want you to feel," she paused, searching for the right words, "...at *home* again."

He pressed his lips together, his expression hardening. It felt right to say it, yet Remi regretted her words instantly. She'd never seen someone shut down so completely.

"Remi!" Elise called from behind.

Just in time, she thought. "I'll leave you to your bath then."

Quickly, Remi gave a polite nod and hurried down to the opposite hall. Elise did not take her eyes off Ben until Remi was pulling her along. It was hard enough to speak so plainly with Ben but harder still to get her cousin to stop ogling him.

"I don't know what you said to him," Elise said once they were safely in Remi's room, "but he couldn't take his eyes off of you."

Remi shook the blanket off and ran both hands over her tired eyes. Whatever Elise meant to imply, it was just the opposite.

"Just get me out of this dress, please."

Supper would be an insufferable affair.

REMI

"I wonder if he missed us," Elise said as she fixed Remi's damp hair.

Remi frowned. She was dry now, dressed in a fresh ensemble, but the chill of the rain clung to her skin, and she shivered. "I'm not so sure he did."

"We could ask him?"

"I very much doubt he wants to reminisce on memories long since past," Remi said.

Elise finished Remi's hair and slunk back towards the bed, sinking into its cushioned duvet. The look on her face was distant, almost sympathetic.

"I miss those days."

"You do?" Remi chuckled. "I find that hard to believe. You only ever complained."

If it wasn't about the dust or her ruined hemlines, it was something or someone else entirely. She would have a fit if Ben and Remi went off on their own, especially if Guillaume was not around to assuage her temper. Remi smiled to herself. She missed those days as well.

"I wasn't the best of companions, I know that. But I can't help but yearn for those early afternoons playing hide and seek." Elise crossed her arms, forlorn as she looked longingly toward the past. "Being here as a grown woman is an entirely different experience."

Remi nodded. "I know."

"That's why I wonder," she started, "if he missed this, too."

"What are you trying to get at, Elise?"

Her cousin looked up, sullen and small. "It won't ever be like it was then. The two of us will be in different places in a few short months."

"What do you mean? You'll be across town, not the ocean!" Remi laughed, but Elise did not. Her expression sunk further into desolace.

"Hugo means to move us overseas."

"What?" Remi asked. Their island was just off the coast, and though it was inconvenient at times, travel to the mainland wasn't hard to do. "Where to?"

"Somewhere far," Elise said. "He's mentioned the Americas, New York. I've argued the point, but he's reluctant to stay."

"I'll visit," Remi offered weakly.

Elise forced a smile. "I know you will—when you can."

Grieving a spouse lasted a long time. It would be months before Remi could travel outside her home again, let alone wear anything other than black. Her stomach plummeted then, subdued by the thought of ever leaving to visit Elise. As fanciful a thought it was, she knew deep down that she would never be allowed to leave the Isle.

"Madame!" A voice called from the other side of the door.

Remi and Elise turned as it opened.

"Madame! Monsieur Lamotte has arrived." Sylvie announced. She was red in the face, small hairs peeking out from under her cap. "He's waiting in the parlor to greet you."

"Thank you, Sylvie." Remi stood from her stool beside the vanity and smoothed her skirt. "Would you let Monsieur Leone know that we'll be having an early supper?"

Sylvie nodded. "He's already with Monsieur Lamotte, Madame."

Remi groaned internally. "Of course he is."

"Why don't Sylvie and I check on supper?" Elise offered casually. "You go on ahead."

"Yes, alright then." Remi rushed forward, forgetting how unlady-like it was to run. "Thank you!"

The parlor doors opened the moment she arrived and both men, accompanied by Ben's footman, stopped in surprise at her presence. She was at once skeptical of the company they shared prior to her arrival. Lamotte was flush, already a drink in hand, and a smile graced his lips. Remi tried not to glance at Ben but could feel his harsh gaze regardless. She pushed a stray hair away and swallowed her fear. Whatever was discussed, it could not have been more important than an exchange on the quality of the wine.

"Welcome, Monsieur Lamotte. Thank you so much for coming." She bowed her head and shifted to take the space between the two men. The third man, Ben's footman, seemed to slink away into the shadows. He was there, but she could not see him. "There's more wine in the dining room if you'd care to join me there."

"Of course, of course! So lovely to see you, Madame Leone." Lamotte announced as he looped his arm through hers with a little too much enthusiasm.

"Right this way." Remi guided their small troupe through the dark-ening foyer to the dining room. All the while, as they walked, she could feel the weight of Ben's gaze, boring holes in the back of her skull.

GAMES

BEN

*B*en followed Remi wordlessly to their meal. He had crept down earlier after his bath in hopes of finding a drink before supper. By the time he secured one, Lamotte arrived and took the drink for himself.

"Such good manners," the lawyer had said too happily. "It's as if you knew I was coming."

Ben did not, in fact, know Lamotte was coming at all.

"I believe Martin has prepared his special *Coq au Vin*," Remi said as she pushed open the doors to the dining room. "He says you once confided in him that it was your favorite. I hope it will be to your liking."

"He is correct! I shall eat it with the vigor of ten men." Lamotte took one of her hands in his ham-like fists and patted it with swollen fingers.

Ben watched her conceal a flinch with an easy smile. There was an undercurrent of caution about her that made him curious. *Lamotte is somewhat of an unpleasant fellow.* He tried not to notice how much more relaxed Remi was when Lamotte released her.

The dining room, bathed in flickering candlelight, was always a grand backdrop for any affair. It was a tribute to his mother's eye for splendor, featuring an imported ebony table that seated twelve at a time with high-backed chairs of the same dark wood. Their cushions were a deep plum, meant to match the papered walls. Ben once told his mother, during its renovation, that it made him feel like he was sitting in her jewelry box. It was purposefully beautiful, the highlight of past dinner parties that he used to peek in on as a small boy.

Inside, one occupant already waited to be seated. Elise glanced at Ben and held his gaze for a second longer than she must have intended, though her expression remained steely.

Lamotte pulled out a seat for Remi, his chattering turning loud as it commanded everyone's attention. "Goodness, when was the last time I enjoyed a meal under your roof, Madame?"

Remi frowned. "I'm unsure, Monsieur. When did you last visit?"

The lawyer took the head of the table, the spot where Ben's father used to sit at meals. For all his pomp and frivolity, he was a bold man to assume the master's seat with ease. Ben, on the other hand, seated himself snugly a few chairs down from Lamotte while Jacques found himself a corner tucked amongst the meager shadows.

"Why," Lamotte exclaimed, "it was your wedding!"

Across from him, both Remi and her cousin appeared affected; the former seemingly embarrassed as she tried to regain her composure, while the latter found humor in the old man's theatrics. Lamotte had announced it with intention, Ben was sure. All around the table, the wine glasses were filled, thanks to Jacques's quick hand. He was too good at reading the room.

Remi took a measured sip from her glass.

"It was the finest reception I'd ever been to, Madame," Lamotte continued. "Have I ever told you that?"

"On countless occasions."

He cracked a smile at her bland response. "Ah, well! What's one more time, eh?" Then he turned to Ben, his face red from excitement and drink. "Pardon my rudeness. I know you were absent from that particular celebration."

I ought to whack him with the wine bottle, Ben thought as he sipped his wine. *Spare us all his drama.*

"She was a vision!" Lamotte exclaimed, distracting from the meal as it was served. "Absolutely breathtaking in her wedding gown. Your father was so happy! You should have seen how he beamed."

Ben's jaw twitched. He didn't have to look at her to know that Remi was clearly uncomfortable with the exhibition. He would have enjoyed her wriggling if it wasn't also at the expense of his own comfort.

"A perfectly happy day," Elise interjected before Lamotte could carry on. "What a shame you missed it, Monsieur Leone."

"A shame indeed," Ben agreed, unsurprised by her audacity.

"I think it was to everyone's disappointment that you did not attend." Elise frowned. "Being that we were all such close companions as children."

"All children must grow up." Ben glowered at her.

"I couldn't agree more!" Lamotte laughed. "Though, if you don't mind my saying, Benoît would have been a much better drinking partner than *your* father, Mademoiselle Elise."

"You must accept my apologies," Ben managed. They were testing his patience, and there was no humor in it for him. "It surprised me to see my father remarrying at his age, especially as he was so much older than his bride."

Remi visibly flinched at his mocking tone, flushing a fantastic red as she brought her glass of wine to her lips and took a generous swig. Based on their earlier exchange, Ben expected her to rally and put up a fight. But she didn't. It appeared instead that she wanted to drop the subject of her marriage altogether.

"Tosh! What good reason does anyone have to marry?" Lamotte waved dismissively. "Your father lived alone, you know. Perhaps he wanted a companion."

Ben glanced at Remi.

She would not meet his eye.

"Our Remi breathed new life into the manor, into your father." Lamotte wagged a dogged finger at Ben. He had a fine sheen of sweat starting at his hairline, and his beady eyes could barely focus as he spoke. Still, the weight of what he said slammed into Ben. A seed of envy planted itself in his anger.

New life? Ben recalled her miserable countenance outside. She looked as pallid and pale as the faded wallpaper in the hallway. He thought back to the letter she'd sent him before the wedding. *How much life could she have brought with her when the woman who wrote to me was so desperate to be saved?*

"You must have been a great comfort to him, Madame." Ben snickered, fingering the neck of his wine glass.

"I was," she declared. Much to his surprise, she returned his irritation in kind. "Your father said as much himself, believe it or not."

"Oh, I do." Ben grimaced, a charge of tension passing between them.

"Come then, you two!" Lamotte trilled. "We are here to honor a great man, husband, and father!"

Ben scoffed and leaned back in his chair, extending his long legs outward until they reached under the table. His boot bumped into Remi's leg, and she shifted, scowling at him from across the table. He curled his lip, savoring the derision in her expression.

Clearly disgusted by his antics, she pushed her chair out and stood abruptly. Elise, though surprised, followed suit.

"I'm afraid I've lost my appetite," Remi announced stiffly. "I think I'll retire now. Thank you both for being here. I know Edgar would have been pleased."

"He would," Lamotte agreed, stumbling as he pushed out of his own chair.

Ben did not move, keeping his eyes trained on Remi.

"Good night, gentlemen." Remi bowed her head and took her cousin's arm, leading her from the room as they tucked their heads together in hushed whispers. No doubt, they would be discussing everything about the day and dissecting every single detail. He was sure Remi would have a few unsavory comments about his attitude; it was all he could do to keep himself from smiling.

The three men waited for the ladies' steps to dissipate into silence.

Jacques sat idly in the shadows while Ben ate his meal with the satisfaction of a child who'd successfully stolen candy.

"Well then." Lamotte sighed. "What an evening we've had."

"All by your design." Jacques's low voice grumbled from the corner.

The lawyer did not seem to hear the comment; he turned to his meal and then looked at Ben. The earlier humor was gone, replaced by a seriousness that sobered him.

"Now that the ladies have retired for the evening, I have some personal business with you." He reached into his breast pocket and produced a sealed envelope. "This is a letter for you from your father."

"My father wrote me a letter?" It caught Ben off guard, given that he'd received no word from him prior to his death.

Lamotte nodded. "I didn't want to present it until we had a moment alone."

Ben took the sealed envelope and turned it over twice. "What is it?"

The lawyer shrugged, forking an unfortunate pile of steamed greens into his mouth. "Instructions? Perhaps a goodbye? He gave it to me a few months ago. Just before his wedding, in fact. I thought that was odd."

"Very odd," Ben agreed.

The envelope read: *For Ben, My Son.*

"He was a good man, your father." Lamotte cut into his meat before shoveling it down. "I can be a bit tenacious, as you've seen tonight, but I am almost always sincere. You must learn to forgive him; he never meant for any of this."

"Forgive him for what?" Ben set the letter on the table and smacked his hand firmly over it. "Keeping me away for sixteen years? Marrying a *child?* What does a dead man need with my forgiveness?"

"It's not for him." Lamotte sighed, dabbing his mouth with a napkin. "It's for you."

Ben said nothing. His meal waited on his plate, but his stomach felt too heavy to consume anything else. After some time, Sylvie returned to gather their plates. Lamotte finished his last bite and stood to excuse himself. "Try not to stay up too late now, Ben. Busy day tomorrow!"

"This way, *monsieur*," Sylvie beckoned. "I'll show you to your room."

Lamotte bid them another goodnight and followed her into the foyer.

Jacques moved with quick feet to shut the doors behind them.

Ben realized how tense he was. "I miss the bordello."

"I hope you don't plan to seek one out," Jacques warned.

"You think I would?" Ben asked innocently as he flexed his fingers over the envelope. The paper was coarse beneath his fingertips. He'd received more letters in the last two months than he had in sixteen years.

"Obviously."

"You have so little faith in me." Ben forced a short laugh. "Trust me, my friend. I won't sully my good family's name with any debauchery. Now, why don't you sit down and have a drink with me? We still have plenty of wine left."

His friend took the chair across from him, a frown on his face. "You know I don't like to drink."

"Liar."

Jacques used to enjoy all spirits, but that was years ago when Ben discovered him in the opium den, fully intoxicated. Since then, he'd sworn it all off, claiming it made his bones ache. But the years of heavy imbibing had taken its toll on his appearance, making him look so much older than he was.

"Suit yourself." Ben didn't offer him another drink, finishing the bottle instead. "Speaking of the maid, did she prepare a room for you?"

"She did."

"Excellent." Ben tipped his head back and sighed. "Do you miss the streets of Paris yet?"

"No. The air is cleaner here."

Ben wanted to disagree but found he could not. The island's fresh air managed to clear away the stain of the city that had caked his lungs for years. His first deep breath of brackish air had done him good. "I'm afraid I can't argue."

"I'm shocked."

Ben ignored him. "Let's get some rest." He stood, grabbed the envelope from the table, and tucked it into the pocket of his vest.

Jacques stretched his arms in reply.

"Tomorrow, we send my father off to his final rest."

"And as to the other matter?" Jacques pushed out his chair and stood. "Regarding your sister?"

"It will have to wait." Ben stepped out of the dining room and into the foyer. "At least until everything with my father and *Madame* is settled."

"Shall I investigate while you're busy?" Jacques asked as they climbed the stairs.

The creaking hardwood steps echoed loudly underfoot. When Ben was a boy, wandering the halls during sleepless nights, he often trod carefully, afraid to wake anyone. But he was too grown to be stealthy anymore, and his boots were made much finer than a boy's slippers. If he woke anything up now, he wanted it to find him.

"You're welcome to. Be careful, though," Ben said as he stopped at his door. Already cracked, he could see the fire inside and the shift of a shadow. A play of the light? Despite himself, a cold sweat broke out along his forehead.

"Of the Madame?" Jacques asked.

"No." Ben swallowed. "The ghosts."

MOTHS & MAUSOLEUMS

REMI

APRIL, 1898

ollowing their nuptials, Remi was escorted to the second floor after the end of the short reception. Their exchange of vows lasted longer than the supper that followed. It was an awkward affair with minimal conversation, only a few quiet congratulations on their marriage. Remi was beside herself with disappointment but pushed herself to thank everyone for coming. Even if she wished she was anywhere but there, with the weight of her family's expectations bearing down on her.

Once Lamotte excused himself from the reception, the rest followed him eagerly. For that, she was grateful.

"Here we are." Edgar's gentle voice brought her back to the present. They had stopped at the end of a hallway with a single door. "I hope it's to your liking."

Dubious, she asked, "You hope what is to my liking?"

"The room." He gestured to the door again, and her heart thrummed uncomfortably in her chest.

Of course, she thought, swallowing as she reached for the brass. *Pull yourself together, girl. It is only natural that we would share a room.*

As the door opened, she gasped.

The spacious room was fully furnished and decorated in the classic style. The floors were a deep shade of mahogany, with a finely crafted fireplace of embellished marble with a carved floral mantle. Lively flames crackled in the hearth. From the wardrobe to the *escritoire*, everything matched, including the four-poster bed, which was draped in delicate shantung—the same fabric as her wedding gown.

"It is yours," he said happily.

"Curious," she muttered after a silent beat.

"What is?"

Remi licked her lips nervously, unable to bring herself to look him in the eyes. "When you say mine, I wonder if you mean that I will have my own room, apart from yours."

Edgar chuckled his reply, unbothered by her timidity. Instead, he ushered her forward with a wave of his hand. Remi took a steadying breath and towed her way in. With its round windows and cozy seats inlaid with plush cushions, she felt she could stay there for the rest of her days and be content. The finery decorating the room was made for royalty.

And perhaps she was royalty now. Becoming *Madame Leone* meant a great deal to those on the Isle, even if the inflection when speaking the family name implied death.

"I asked for much help. I'm afraid that home-making is not my forte," Edgar said from the hallway, a respectable space between him and the door.

"I'm grateful," she said, though her question remained unanswered.

"Then I shall leave you in Sylvie's care."

"Edgar?" Remi managed before he was gone.

He stopped. "Yes?"

"I don't mean to be a nuisance, but my mind is somewhat addled. Will you not…" she paused, willing her uneasiness to subside. "Are we not to share a room?"

Edgar was silent for a moment, his face unreadable, before he finally smiled. "I thought you might like your own private space. Are you not pleased?"

"No," she said a little too loudly, earning a short laugh from Edgar. "I couldn't ask for more if I'm honest. Thank you."

"Excellent." He turned into the hall and gestured to someone unseen. "Sylvie, if you please? I leave Madame's care to you now."

A young woman appeared then, the look of awe in her eyes the same as Remi's. They were both new, Remi could tell, and it comforted her in a way to know they would learn about the manor together.

"*Bonsoir,* Madame Leone. My name is Sylvie."

"*Bonsoir,* Sylvie."

After appraising their exchange with glittering eyes, Edgar nodded and excused himself. Remi wondered absently where he was going but did not think to ask.

"Monsieur told me that you might want a bath?" Sylvie grinned.

Remi's skin tingled at the mention of a bath. "That would be nice, thank you."

Remi unsteadily followed Sylvie down the hall. Her gown rushed behind her in a cascade of fabric, too heavy to bear for much longer without a bustle to hold it in place. She should have asked for an extra hand but was loath to bother Tante Beline for anything. Instead, Remi spent the rest of her reception carrying what bunched-up fabric she could hold onto until her hand was cramped and the festivities dwindled. Once they were safely in the washroom, a light gray room with green accents, Remi shed its weight, glad to be rid of it. From her first fitting, the disdain she'd held for the gown grew. She would be sure to tuck it away into some hidden space with the hope that it would be lost to time and eaten away by moths.

"The water is ready, Madame," Sylvie said.

Remi slipped into the clawfoot tub and sighed with relief. She'd felt like an outsider all day, misplaced in a story that wasn't meant for her. It was still hard to wrap her mind around the fact that the marriage was real, though there was no denying it when the proof was wrapped around her ring finger. Remi frowned and dropped her hand below the water's surface to hide the polished gold band.

"Sylvie, I suspect you are new as well."

"I am, Madame."

Remi shifted in the tub, leaning forward as the maid scrubbed her back. "Might I confide in you?"

"Please, Madame. Nothing would make me happier." She sounded sincere.

"Will I be…sleeping alone?"

"Monsieur said that you would be comfortable in that room."

"Yes, but will he send *for* me?" Remi swallowed her fear. She was not so naive a woman that she was unaware of what happened on the wedding night. She knew what was next, what was meant to happen. She'd been preparing for it, ready to move forward, but that seemed odd now that she'd been given her own room.

Confused, Sylvie said, "I was told you were tired."

"Oh, yes. I suppose I am."

Remi finished her bath in peace, dressing in a simple nightgown before Sylvie led her back to the ornate bedroom. On the duvet, a neatly wrapped box waited for her. As Remi opened it, Sylvie parted the sheets and waited patiently.

"What is it, Madame?"

"A wedding gift?" Remi beheld the gold locket inside, heart-shaped and embellished with an 'L' surrounded by little flowers—wisteria. She lifted it from its velvet pillow carefully. "It's a necklace."

She held it up for Sylvie to see. Her doe eyes widened, and she smiled.

"It's beautiful, Madame! Would you like to wear it now?"

"Tomorrow, perhaps." Remi held it for a second longer before putting it away. When she closed the box, she felt a shard of ice pierce her heart. It was a beautiful gift, but not one she felt ready to wear yet. Her marriage had been rushed, her relationship with Edgar stilted, if not altogether awkward. She was young, and marrying someone older wasn't unheard of, but she had reservations about the arrangement. Initially, when her uncle mentioned it in passing, she was delighted by the notion of marrying into the Leone family.

How foolish she felt when she learned the truth about her groom later on.

Remi climbed into bed and waited for Sylvie to finish tending the fire. She hoped that once her head hit the pillows, she would feel the day's exhaustion settle in completely.

"Goodnight, Madame," Sylvie said.

"Goodnight, Sylvie. It was a pleasure to meet you."

The maid nodded and bowed out into the hallway, disappearing as the door closed.

Almost an hour later, Remi tossed and turned in her bed. The mattress, like everything else—including herself—was new and untouched. Its stiff, cold shape did not cradle her figure like the one at Tante Beline's.

Remi threw the covers back, first too warm and then too cold. She could not keep her eyes closed long enough to grasp the edges of sleep as it evaded her. What she would do for a visit from Somnus, to be sent into baleful dreams as she wanted. But the house creaked as the wind blew, and Remi's mind wandered to far darker corners than those of a golden childhood spent with a boy whose hair was as warm as his eyes.

Remi moved the blankets from her legs and slipped on her dressing robe. A quick look through her bedside drawer turned up a matchbox, and she lit the candle Sylvie left behind. Grasping it with a shaking hand, she started down the hall from her room. She felt out of sorts, remembering at time when she was young and happily traipsing through the manor, rather than tiptoeing quietly through the night.

Like being in the belly of a great beast, she thought.

Time may have aged her, but the manor remained as large and expansive as ever. There were the family's quarters on one end and a partition on the other half dedicated to guests. In the days before it closed its doors, the manor used to welcome plenty of visitors. But that was years ago, back when his wife was alive. Their wedding was the first time anyone was allowed to step foot inside again.

An absolute privilege, she heard her uncle's voice echo in her mind. *I wonder what flowery words he used to convince my father to let me marry.*

Still, it was hard to forget, given that he'd delivered the line more than once to guests who were curious about their match. It made her ponder the question of whose privilege it really was to marry into the Leone family. Hers or her uncle's.

Creeping further down the hall, Remi observed paintings of landscapes and people as they stretched on into endless shadows. She did not dare go near the guest's quarters, knowing some were sleeping there. Instead, she headed for the stairs to the first floor. It was quiet and still, with no servants to catch her sneaking about. Still, a house as old as the Leone's, steeped in a troubled past, must have eyes watching from somewhere in the walls.

It would make for an excellent ghost story, she thought, shuddering at her own admission. It was curious enough behavior to wander the halls so late, but stranger still to imagine that something might be watching her.

Remi went past the cellar door, spying a light at the end of the hall, just beyond the kitchen. A golden glow beckoned from within; she hurried her pace as the floorboards creaked beneath her feet.

Two doors were cracked open at the end of the hall. Curious, she peeked inside.

Edgar sat behind a large desk, reading a stack of papers, his eyeglasses perched on the tip of his nose. He was as she remembered him so many years ago, though the silver in his hair chased away the darker roots. A few more wrinkles joined at the corners of his lips, and the crow's feet beside his eyes were deeper. He seemed at ease, though tired and weary. So much of Ben lingered there that it was hard to ignore her imagination and what fantasies it conjured.

Enough of that! Ben is gone; you are married to Edgar! Remi sucked in a deep breath but covered her mouth too slowly to hide it. Edgar looked up.

"Hello?" he called out. "Come in."

She pushed the door open and walked in slowly.

"Good evening," she said, concealing her curiosity. The room was spacious, a beautiful study with six rows of bookshelves parallel to her and an oak desk off to the right where Edgar watched her tentatively. There were few furnishings in the center: two armchairs and a side table, with an immaculate moth display as the focal point. A fire burned in the hearth to the far left of the study, with the same craftsmanship as the one in her own.

"I couldn't sleep," Remi said, ducking her head.

"No?" Edgar asked. "It was quite a long day. I myself am feeling tired."

"It was." She agreed. "But there is so much to take in, I feel I can't sleep yet. The house is...*new* to me."

"Ah." Edgar nodded in understanding. He laid the papers in his hands down and sat back in his chair. "If you find yourself wandering, please know my study is always open to you."

"Thank you," she said, slipping into one of the chairs as the floor creaked underneath the new weight. A clock somewhere ticked, beating easily against the sound of the wind outside. "I hope I'm not disturbing you."

"Not at all."

Remi hummed a reply, distracted by the moth in the glass case. It was much larger up close and so true to life that it could flutter away at any given moment, even though she could clearly see the pins that held it in place. She felt sympathetic to it, dead yet displayed for everyone to gawk at. In a way, it was how she felt standing at the altar, a pretty thing pinned down under a glass dome while prying eyes glittered from the watching crowd.

Distracted by her pitiable thoughts, she didn't hear at first what Edgar said.

"*Saturnia pyri*," he repeated. "The great peacock moth."

"It's beautiful," she said.

"There are nests of them around the Isle." His chair groaned with the motion as he stood, approaching the glass display. "I have a few other species, but none quite as eye-catching."

"Is it your favorite?" Remi asked, standing. She felt weak on her knees, but it was necessary to close the space between them. It was still curious to her that he would give her a room and leave her be on their wedding night. She wanted to ask if it was something she'd done or if he felt she was too young.

Edgar moved his hand away from the hardwood base of the display, evading her attempt expertly. "It is."

"Monsieur Leone…" Remi felt her voice tremble. "I want to ask…"

"About our arrangement?"

She found his eyes watching her. They were kind, just as they were so many hours ago at the altar. "Yes."

"My dear," he started gently, "I must tell you that I have only ever loved one woman in my life. Her portrait is there above the mantelpiece. Immortalized in all of her earthly beauty, just as this moth in its display."

Remi followed his gaze. The portrait he'd fixated on was subtle but large enough that she could make out the woman on the canvas. The late Madame Leone passed well before Remi's arrival, but the island was never without its stories of their romance. A traveling Romani woman wooed by an upstart young man with startling good looks.

Truthfully, everything she knew about their family came from gossip.

"How many years has it been?"

"Twenty long years." Edgar moved closer to the fireplace, distant from Remi as he spoke. "She fell ill after a difficult pregnancy. Benoît was six at the time, looking forward to having two siblings to look after."

Oh my. "To lose children… I cannot fathom it."

"We were deeply hurt by their loss." Edgar nodded. "My wife felt that wound deeper than the rest of us, as you can imagine. Her illness took her body, but I believe their loss took her much sooner."

Remi felt her chest tighten. She dropped her gaze from the portrait, unable to see the late lady without feeling the need to cry.

She never knew about two other children. The truth of her passing was hard to win through constant gossip and twisted iterations of the same tale. Ironically enough, the people preferred their tall tales and fairy tales about the Leone family over the truth of their tragedy.

When Remi's marriage was first announced, all anyone could discuss was the reception or the wedding colors. A handful of folks mentioned his first wife, but there was little else discussed past that. Even when Tante Beline hosted a tea party for the ladies on the island to celebrate the engagement, the only thing any one of them could think to talk about were the invitations and Remi's gown. Despite their surprise at Edgar's intent to remarry, they mentioned nothing else about the family's past or its dark tragedies.

Remi considered it odd since the backbone of their get-togethers was gossip.

Maybe Tante Beline had something to do with that. Beline would have wanted to keep everything "easy to swallow" for her benefit more than Remi's.

"My dear girl," Edgar turned and tucked his arms behind his back. "My hope is that you will find comfort here. You'll want for nothing."

But why? she wondered. *Why marry me? What about Ben?*

It was the question she couldn't ask aloud, as though asking would cross a line that laid bare at her feet. Edgar tapped her lightly on the shoulder and went back to his desk, returning to the papers he'd been studying earlier.

By leaving her there, conversation abandoned for busy work, he made it clear that their wedding night would be nontraditional. He would not touch her or share a bed with her. Though it relieved Remi, she felt utterly alone. Meeting the painted eyes of the woman above the mantelpiece, Remi stared long into their depths and wondered what it was like to be so loved, even in death.

"Feel free to visit my study whenever you like," he said as she wandered to the door. "I have plenty of books for you to read if you're interested. Borrow as many as you want."

Remi nodded. "Thank you."

"Goodnight," he said.

Remi left, suddenly tired, as she found herself back in her new bed. That night, curled in the warm duvet, she dreamt of moths and weddings and ghostly faces watching her from the portraits on the walls.

EDGAR'S FUNERAL

REMI

MAY, 1898

*R*emi tugged at her collar, tracing a light touch over the line of buttons down the front of her mourning gown. The lace on the cuffs of her sleeves stuck to the crushed velvet bodice of the dress, and she recoiled her fingers. Crushed velvet made her skin crawl, but every piece of cold-weather clothing she'd inherited from her cousin was made with it. She was not surprised that, when her cousin offered to have her dress made, it was in a fashion that suited Elise's tastes.

"I really shouldn't complain," Remi whispered under her breath as she appraised herself in the mirror. After all, it was the first dress she had ever commissioned for her body.

There have been many firsts lately, she thought solemnly, eyeing the locket at the base of her throat, polished gold against her black fabric collar. First husband, first funeral, first love—all contained within one place. It felt appropriate to wear Edgar's gift now, even if she wasn't supposed to wear jewelry.

"It's a tribute to his memory," she said aloud.

A moment later, just as she was pinning her hair, a loud knock came from the other side of her door. She hastened to open it, expecting it to be Elise, and her heart dropped.

Tante Beline stood in the doorway, her face pinched. Her tight lips barely moved as she spoke. "Remi."

You are the lady of the house, Remi reminded herself. *She cannot intimidate you.*

"*Salut,* Tante Beline."

Beline bristled at the greeting as she strode into the room. She sized it up soundlessly, her expression unreadable when she finally rested her eyes on Remi again.

What she lacked in natural maternity, Beline made up for in rigid etiquette. It was the reason their family was so well-respected and had earned Beline her place as the head of the Bleue Isle Ladies' Tea Society. The coveted role required a nomination and an election. The society was made up of the finest women on the island, and no lady with a good name was left out. Except for Remi, who suspected her invitation would never arrive. Especially now that she was a widow.

Unfailingly predictable, Beline sized Remi up and found her appearance lacking. "No jewelry. You're a widow now."

"I know, but I thought—"

"And your dress! Remi, it's far too gaudy for a funeral. What were you thinking?" Beline's nostrils flared, disappointment replacing the dour look from before. "No wonder your home is in complete disarray."

Remi opened her mouth to speak, then closed it.

"Regardless, the necklace must come off." Beline tapped the spot of her chest where the locket rested on Remi's.

"Thank you, Tante Beline." Remi unclasped the necklace and set it carefully on her bedside table. "Your advice is always welcome."

"It's clear that you are in desperate need of me. I should have come sooner." Beline approached the bed, scoffing at the state of the duvet. "Your maid is severely lacking in her duties."

"I hadn't noticed," Remi lied. Sylvie was slipping in her day-to-day work, but she was also the only one keeping up with the house.

"Where is she? The maid, I mean. There's plenty of work to be done yet." Beline did not linger in Remi's room a second longer and strolled out into the hall, followed by Remi.

"Tante Beline, she's busy," Remi tried to argue. "Perhaps if you told me—"

Beline scoffed. "Remi, you are the Lady of the house. Chores are not becoming of your station."

"Yes, but—"

It wasn't so unusual for her to lend a helping hand once in a while, but she would never admit that aloud. Not to Tante Beline.

"No buts."

Giggles and light-hearted chatter cut off the conversation. Beline looked sharply toward the sound, her ears perking up. She continued down the hall, the smug look on her face worsening the pit in Remi's stomach as they came upon Sylvie and Ben. His door was wide open, and she carried a pile of sheets in her arms.

"You were correct. She's *quite* busy, dawdling about when there's work yet to be done." Beline muttered.

In an attempt to save herself from another lecture, Remi called out, "Sylvie?"

Sylvie tensed, her eyes wide. She held the bedsheets closer to her chest and braced herself. "Madame, good morning."

"Sylvie, where have you been?" Remi asked, ignoring Ben's eyes on her as he walked past. She didn't have time for him, especially with Beline breathing down her neck.

"I've been cleaning the guest quarters," Sylvie stammered.

Remi tamped down her guilt at being so abrasive. Sylvie was the only one she'd been able to rely on for the past month, but having Beline there made the roiling nausea in her gut win out over her usual pragmatism. It worsened with every syllable that left Beline's lips, every pointed look that spelled out her disapproval.

"Goodness, Remi. Tell the girl to finish her chores," Beline sneered from behind her, taking advantage of the silence. "This place is filthy; it needs a good dusting, at the very least."

Sylvie looked to Remi, pleading. "Madame, I have so much to do yet. Master Ben has asked—"

Remi raised a hand to stop her. "Take your laundry to the wash-room, Sylvie," Remi said. "I expect *all* of your chores to be finished before you turn in for the night."

"Yes, Madame," Sylvie stammered, hurrying away.

"You should have her dismissed," Beline muttered loudly enough for Sylvie to hear. She brushed past Remi and ran one finger along the banister as she took the stairs, inspecting her dusty finger with a loud *"tsk."* Once Beline was out of earshot, Remi sagged against the wall. Squeezing her eyes shut, she sucked in a deep, steadying breath. There was a low throb in her temples and her chest felt tight.

It's just one day, she told herself. *She can't do more than what she's done already.*

But Remi was wrong. Raised voices traveled up the stairs to her, tugging her forward. Remi took the stairs quickly, joining her aunt, an apologetic-looking Elise, and the lawyer at the bottom.

"Inexcusable!" Beline cried out. "I don't understand why we can not *all* be present for the reading."

Elise spared an apologetic glance at Remi.

"I'm sorry, Madame Cuvilyé," Lamotte said carefully. "You are not the intended party."

"Yes, we are," Beline argued. "We have every right, don't we, Remi?"

Remi stopped short of her aunt by two steps. Lamotte caught her expression and relaxed.

"Good morning, Monsieur Lamotte." Remi bobbed her head. "Tante Beline, would you be so kind as to watch over the house while I am absent? Your guidance would be appreciated."

Her aunt's face changed three shades of red. "I will do no such—"

"As you said," Remi shot her a weary look, "there is much work to be done."

"Come with me then if you will." Lamotte spurred into action, interrupting the older woman as he put himself between the two. He offered his arm, which Remi took easily. "I have the young master waiting for us in the study."

"Ben?" Remi blinked.

"Go on, Maman and I will check in on the dining arrangements," Elise beelined for her mother and linked arms, pulling her around the corner before she could protest.

"I'm terribly sorry to do this to you now," Lamotte said as he led Remi to the study.

Remi nodded, focused on the end of the hall, unable to shake her nervousness.

Lamotte pushed open the study doors to reveal Ben dressed in black. He seemed to tower over everything in the room, a scowl on his face. She was hardly prepared to maneuver his terse behavior, especially when her aunt had thoroughly shredded her nerves.

Don't let him intimidate you.

"Please have a seat," Lamotte commanded.

Remi tried to ignore Ben as they sat, but it was difficult to do so when his legs stretched out far enough to graze the hem of her skirt. He took up so much space that the chair could not contain him. Despite his fists being balled in his lap, his elbows hung far over each side, and the top of his head reached over the backrest.

Lamotte shut the doors and rounded to the seat behind her late husband's desk. "Your father would have been overjoyed to see you in his study, Benoît," he commented.

"How unfortunate that he's dead now," Ben replied with a humorless smile. "Were he alive, we could all have tea and talk about the weather."

A moment of awkward silence passed between the three of them. Remi squeezed her hands together in her lap and swallowed a lump in her throat whilst Lamotte continued nervously shuffling papers.

"Then again," Ben went on, ignoring the obvious tension. "I wouldn't be here if he were alive, would I? You would have your husband, Madame, and I would have my dark little corner of Paris. So, we shall never truly know what sort of emotions I would elicit, will we?"

He's trying to get a rise out of me, she thought. *I won't let him get to me this time.*

"Nonetheless, it gladdens me to see you again after so long," she managed politely. "It is a terrible thing to grieve alone, but to be home after so many years? I'm sure the adjustment has been an enormous strain."

"Enormous, indeed." He scowled.

"Excuse me." Lamotte coughed, drawing their attention. "I do apologize, but I have another appointment approaching. Might we manage the task at hand?"

"Monsieur." Remi nodded her acknowledgment. "You may have the floor. That is, if Benoît is finished?"

"Quite." Ben sat back in his chair, folded his fingers across his stomach, and smirked, holding her gaze.

Heat bloomed in her breast, but she held her composure. He wouldn't best her today; she would make sure of it.

Lamotte cleared his throat and began to read.

As his voice droned on, Remi's eyes grew heavy. Edgar's statement was long and precise but written as an academic and lacking sentiment. She knew him well enough to glean that much about his character from the short time they'd spent together. He could be affectionate, but she only ever saw that when she caught him staring up at his late wife's portrait. Or on the rare occasions when he mentioned his children, Ben and Soleil.

"...finally, the award of my estate and all properties contained within shall be shared equally among my widow, Remi Leone, and my son, Benoît E. Leone."

Remi's back straightened.

Ben, to her immediate surprise, did not seem phased.

"And lastly, he makes mention of a hidden sum..." Lamotte peered at them hesitantly from the top of the paper. "A small fortune which he refers to as the 'family treasure.'"

"Treasure?" Ben asked, suddenly at the edge of his seat. His entire manner changed at the mention of it. "Not *the* treasure?"

"Treasure?" Remi inquired, her eyes falling on Lamotte.

"Yes." The lawyer eyed the paper again. "It has been long rumored that the Leone family has a stash of treasure somewhere on the island.

Though, for all it's worth, our dear Edgar makes no mention of its whereabouts. I suppose he meant to make it a secret?"

Ben groaned, sinking back into his chair. "He wouldn't make it obvious, no. Especially not in his will."

"But if he mentioned it,"—Remi sat forward— "wouldn't he have known where to find it? He's left it to us, after all."

Ben sneered at her from behind a curtain of dark hair. "Oh? Thirsty for my family's wealth?"

"Pardon?" Remi's eyes widened. She had never counted herself among the young women who might have been starry-eyed at another's wealth, but Ben's opinion of her person had soured over the years. "I am insulted that you would even suggest it."

"My apologies," he drawled with a roll of his eyes. "You seemed all too eager."

"I was not," Remi argued.

"Regardless, you will likely never see an ounce of it. That treasure has been lost to us for decades, *Madame.*" He spat her title at her, his voice dripping with derision. "The last person to look for it was my sister, and it drove her mad."

"What a cruel thing to say," she frowned.

"Now, Ben…" Lamotte tried to interject as politely as he could. "We can't know for certain why Soleil did what she did. We can only hope she is at peace now."

The fury in Ben's expression stretched, tensing him from head to toe

"You never knew her," Ben seethed. "She was miserable here. She wanted to leave—that treasure was her only hope."

Lamotte closed his eyes and pinched the bridge of his nose. "Benoît, please. That's enough."

But Ben wasn't finished, and all Remi could do was watch. "If my father knew all this time where to find this long-lost fortune and let what happened *happen*, then I have no interest in grieving the man."

"You have my sympathy," Lamotte bowed his head, "but dredging up the past will do no good here today. Your father would agree."

"You don't want me to dredge up the past?" Ben asked, his tone incredulous. "Monsieur, my father left us a fortune the likes of which I have never seen, a sum lost to time. One that drove my sister to the brink of insanity. I think we are well past the point of ignoring the past."

Lamotte tapped his fingers against the grain of the desk, moderately annoyed. "Point taken."

"All my father has *left* me is the past." Ben's eyes flickered to Remi for a moment, the anger deepening the ridges of his brows. She flinched away from his hard stare. "A home on the verge of collapse, crumbs of an inheritance, if you can even call it that, and a *widow*. It's a fine mess he's made, Monsieur."

A beat passed before anyone spoke, and it was Remi who found her voice again.

"We're stuck in an unfortunate predicament," she said. There was no denying that everything he said was true.

"Unfortunate for some," Ben said, a cruel smile playing on his lips. There was no humor in his dark eyes, just contempt. "Fortunate for one. You and your family gain the most from this little arrangement."

"My family?" Remi said, taken aback.

"Yes, *your* family." Ben approached her then, advancing like a lion prepared to pounce on its prey. He towered over her by a foot, and she strained to look up at him. He was close enough that she could scent his cologne; cypress and juniper. "Devious and money-hungry. I have no doubt that your aspirations are no different than your aunt's and that you've been cowed by her desire for status and wealth."

Remi felt herself still as her fury renewed.

"You took advantage of him," Ben said, his tone accusatory.

"You don't truly believe that." Remi couldn't wrap her mind around the image he painted. *Am I really as horrible as Tante Beline?*

"I believe you to be quite capable of anything." Ben spat.

How could she tell him that their marriage meant nothing? Because for Remi, it felt like a sham. She was as empty with him as she'd been living with her aunt and uncle; one cage exchanged for another, a moth pinned inside a glass dome. But she couldn't. It wouldn't assuage his temper.

"If I'd been here"—Ben leaned closer, his voice above a whisper—"you would have never weaseled your way into our family."

"That's enough!" Remi snapped. Her right hand connected with Ben's cheek. A second of silence spanned the length of an echo as the throbbing in her palm pricked with an unfamiliar heat.

Lamotte gasped, but Ben remained quiet.

Remi did not wait for him to tread on her further. She cupped her sore hand to her chest and summoned what composure she could muster. "No matter what odious opinion you might have of me, it does not change the fact that Edgar has left us both an equal share."

She turned on her heel and reached for the handle of the study door. It was cool on her palm as she pulled it open, letting it fall shut behind her. Tears pricked at the corners of her eyes, daring to spill if she did not blink them away. There were voices down the hall, a sign that guests were already arriving; she didn't have time to cry or break down. As if it was as simple as fixing a stray hair, she pushed back her wounded pride, and walked down the hall.

THE WAKE

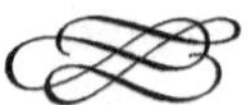

BEN

"That...was a pleasant surprise." Ben rubbed his cheek where it still stung from Remi's hand.

"Was it really?" Lamotte was skeptical. "What a foolish thing you've done."

Ben considered his words. "I suppose I underestimated her."

"You do her an injustice then," Lamotte grumbled. "I had hoped your father might have talked some sense into you, but I suppose I was wrong."

"What do you mean?"

"The envelope I gave you last night." Lamotte arched a brow. "Curious of you to forget it so soon."

"His letter? No, not forgotten," Ben said. The truth was, he wasn't sure what happened to it. He'd left it on the bedside table before turning in, and by light, it was gone. He asked Sylvie to keep an eye out for it that very morning, but in all of the disorder of the day, he had forgotten.

"Watch your temper and mind yourself around her." Lamotte paused before adding, "Lest she raise her hand in opposition again."

Ben didn't disagree. It was a warning he would do well to heed.

She could certainly hold her own, he was now certain, and that put him at odds with the emotions warring inside of him. He wanted to be mad at her, to blame her for everything, but his cheek was still buzzing with her reply. Her passion excited him in ways he didn't want to admit.

As Lamotte packed up his things, Ben milled around aimlessly and stopped to observe a moth under its dome. One of his father's many victims and prized possessions. A dead thing encased in glass, a dark reminder that he would be seeing his father next.

"I'm off." Lamotte tottered toward the door, an austere look on his face. "Do behave yourself with Madame Leone around."

"Safe travels." Ben said, feigning interest in the moth.

"And Ben," Lamotte said, already halfway in the hall. "While he was my good friend, I will always disagree with his decision to send you away. It was sad to see you go, but I'm very glad that you are home."

The door to the study closed softly, ending the conversation.

He would be on his own the rest of the day, forced to entertain and supply condolences to people he didn't recognize or remember. But then, so would Remi. Both of them were forced to comply when either would prefer silence and solitude over chatter and empty tears.

We are stuck with each other.

His father's will be done.

Moments later, a knock sounded at the study's door. It creaked open lightly and Jacques peeked in. He looked vexed.

"What's your face about?" Ben chuckled.

Jacques frowned. "You've been asked to join Madame's family in the dining room."

Ben felt the humor leave him. "I don't think so."

"*She* insists."

"She?" Ben's brows drew together in confusion, but then it struck him. He snickered. "I see you've met Beline then."

Jacques's eyes rolled emphatically as he crossed his arms.

"My employer," said a second voice, "commanded it. She'd like to speak with you."

"Who are you?" Ben asked as a young man entered the room.

"Guillaume." The young man bowed, his curly brown hair falling forward. "Can't say that I blame you if you've forgotten me. Elise and I were good friends, once upon a time. We used to play together as children."

Oh yes, he thought, *now I remember him.*

If he recalled Elise as the bird, then her childhood friend turned footman was most certainly the worm she pecked at. Elise's life was the gilded type, with the finest gowns and the most popular toys at her disposal. Meanwhile, Guillaume was a pauper, clothed in the scraps left over by such extravagance.

"So you're still around?"

"I am." Guillaume nodded.

"Traded rags for a uniform then? Hard to imagine that you'd stick around." Ben crossed the room, one hand extended. "But then, you and Elise were always attached at the hip."

Guillaume took his hand candidly and grinned. "I can't seem to rid myself of her."

Or her, you. Ben thought. He wondered how someone so vapid as Elise could hold the attention of one doting man for so long.

"It's been a long time," Ben said.

"Likewise." Guillaume smiled. "It's good to meet you again, despite the circumstances."

"Yes. Very unfortunate."

"My condolences to you and your family."

"That's very kind of you." Ben glanced at Jacques, who made no move to excuse Guillaume from the room. Sagging slightly and unprepared to meet anyone before the wake, he relented his privacy. "Now then, I'm famished, and there's food to be eaten. Madame Cuvilyé wants to meet with me, you said?"

"This way." Guillaume led him down the hall and to the dining room. It was a short walk, and there were already a few guests milling about. It gave him a small measure of strength to see some surprised expressions, especially when the head of the Cuvilyé's finally laid eyes on him.

Beline was a tight-lipped woman draped in a simple gown, somehow able to look down at him with her pointed nose despite his obvious height.

"Good morning," Ben said, acknowledging her and Remi.

"Come and sit." Beline waved her hand, gesturing toward an empty seat across from Remi. There was a covered plate waiting for him there. "I thought we could enjoy a quiet moment together before it's time."

Ben bowed his head and sat down, avoiding Remi's eyes as they drifted toward him.

"How thoughtful of you," Ben said plainly. "Though I was told differently. You wanted a word with me?"

"Yes, but business can wait." Beline smiled, though it hardly reached her eyes.

"So then it is business?" He asked.

Beline ignored him. "It's so good to see you. I speak for my entire family when I say that you've been missed."

Ben bit his own tongue. Missed him? It was an absolute lie—Beline never liked him or his father. And her husband? Well, he made himself scarce whenever Ben was around. It made the mystery of Remi's marriage that much more compelling.

"It has been more than a decade, Madame," Ben said as he moved closer to the table, purposely scraping the chair loudly against the grain of the floor planks as he went. "I was certain I'd been forgotten."

"Not at all!" Beline forced a small, polite laugh. "We missed you at the wedding, though I'm sure you were quite busy then—"

Wanting to avoid another conversation about the wedding, Ben leaned forward and glowered. "Madame, I mean to be plain with you. We should skip the pretense of this—whatever *this* is—and move on to your business."

"Excuse me?" She started, her cheeks reddening.

"My father cannot be any more dead than he is," Ben laced his fingers together on the table, encircling his meal with his arms, "but still, I would like the opportunity to say my piece before he is gone."

"As would we all." Remi chimed in and shared a pleading look with Ben.

"Now then, what's this business you wish to discuss?" he asked again.

"Fine." Beline adjusted her hair, though there was not a strand out of place. "I am curious about your intentions. Do you mean to visit for very long?"

Ben shot Remi a look, who appeared just as annoyed by the woman as he felt.

"Visit?" Ben uncovered his dish and began to eat. "I intend to stay."

In truth, he didn't intend it at first. But with half the estate now in his name, he needed time. Jacques would be miffed, but he would understand, and his sweetheart on the mainland would have to wait for his return a bit longer.

"Stay?" Beline's voice rose in pitch. "Where?"

"Here." Ben cut into a slice of ham and brought it to his tongue. "This is my home, after all."

"Surely that would be inappropriate."

"Not at all." Ben swallowed, bringing another bite to his mouth, and chewed. Slowly.

"What about Remi?" Beline asked, as though horrified by the notion of them living under the same roof.

"What about her?"

"If you were to stay, she would be forced to leave! Would you truly put her out on the streets?"

Ben nearly choked. "*Force* her? Put her out on the streets? Madame, certainly the reaches of your hospitality would not end at family?"

"Of course not!" Beline's eyes bulged. "But I—"

"The estate is shared, Tante Beline," Remi announced.

It was almost humorous to watch the one-woman drama unfold.

She gasped. "Shared? But surely—"

"According to my father's will." Ben set his utensils down and reached for his croissant. "Remi, as my father's widow, is entitled to this estate in equal shares. She is permitted to stay. It was not my father's wish to turn her out after his passing, and I will respect his wishes.

"However, I hold none of those same reservations for you or the rest of your family. This is my father's wake, and if you'd like to find yourself among those grieving his loss today, I ask now that you leave any further business you have at the door."

"But Remi—" Beline quickly cut to her niece. "What have you to say about this? Does he speak for you?"

"He doesn't speak for me, no, but we are of like mind." Remi gave a slight nod of her chin but did not lower her eyes from Tante Beline's. "I'll honor my late husband's wishes and look after the estate."

Beline drew a hand to her breast and pinched her lips together.

"If I'm not mistaken, Madame Leone is still the lady of the house," Ben added as he pulled the buttered pastry apart. "Would it be wise of you to question her decisions further? Seems disrespectful, given the *unique circumstances* of her position."

From the corner of his eye, he noticed the way Remi perked at the wording he used—the same ones she'd used against him the day before. It pleased him more than he cared to admit.

A tense moment passed before anyone spoke, and to his surprise, Beline was the first.

"I see I have no reason for any further concern," she hissed.

"None at all." Ben agreed with a nod. "She will be well cared for."

Beline waited for a beat as if expecting more. When no one else spoke, she silently dismissed herself. Remi did not follow half as quickly, though he expected she might be giving her aunt a head start. Finally, she stood.

"I should go," she said, rising from the chair.

Ben watched her from the corner of his eye, the other half of his attention on the remainder of his breakfast. It was brief, but when she looked back at him before the doors closed for good, he caught something—the hint of a secret smile gracing her subtly curved lips.

Simple, yet satisfying all the same.

~

REMI

Remi found herself cornered outside the dining room for a second time.

"You'd best watch yourself around him," she warned. "He's a scoundrel, I can tell."

If only she knew, Remi thought. "Of course, I'll be careful."

Ben, like Beline, was easily managed if she avoided him. After their heated battle in the study, Remi surmised he would leave her alone for the day. It was her aunt whose temper was hard to curb, and it wasn't as easily solved as a slap across the cheek.

"You are the lady of this estate," Beline reminded her, though she herself conveniently ignored that fact moments prior. "Don't forget that."

"I could never, Tante Beline," Remi said. "Not when you're gracious enough to remind me."

Her aunt ignored the snide quip.

"The audacity of him! I've never been treated as such or spoken to in my life," Beline went on.

Where is Elise when I need her? Remi thought, suppressing her distress.

Her cousin was nowhere to be seen, not that she could steal a moment to go off in search of her. It was draining enough to sit through the reading, but the longer she spent around anyone else, especially her aunt, the more tired she grew. Remi's eyes felt as heavy as the knot in her chest.

"You look pale, Remi." Beline bluntly stated. "Perhaps you should take some fresh air."

Remi straightened, deciding to grasp the opportunity. She feigned concern. "I couldn't leave you."

"You can, and you will. I would hardly want you to faint in front of all of these people." Beline gestured subtly to the mourners. "What an embarrassment that would be."

Naturally, you're only worried about yourself, Remi thought. Still, fresh air was a welcome change. Excusing herself, she waded through the throng of guests, patient with them as they passed along their condolences. It would be a relief to escape their grievous expressions and her growing nervousness.

Once outside, Remi walked along the side of the manor to the garden's gated entrance. It was alive with greenery, more overgrown by weeds than any actual flower. The wisteria, always vibrant, seemed to sag in respect for the occasion. The weight eased itself from her burdened shoulders as she sat on a low bench. She closed her aching eyes against the cool breeze and drew in a deep breath of fresh air. The ground was soft underfoot, wet from last night's rain, and while the sky appeared as dark and brooding as Ben's expression, it held back for the time being.

Remi unpinned her veil and set the hat down beside her. She loved the smell of flowers after a long rain. It was exactly what she needed.

"Your aunt just told my mother what your stepson said to her this morning," a voice chuckled.

Her momentary peace was lost.

"Hello, Leith."

"My sweet, sweet Remi." A young man with dark gold, feather-like curls sunk beside her on the bench. His honey-brown eyes sparkled. "You look miserable."

"I haven't been sleeping well," she said, suppressing an ill-timed yawn.

Leith took one of her hands and patted it. Though their friendship was unconventional, he was one of her oldest friends, and it felt good to have him there.

"I didn't expect to see you," she said.

"Well, you know me." He winked playfully. "I enjoy a passionate rendezvous in the garden with a beautiful woman as much as the next gentleman."

Remi scoffed and pulled her hand away from his. Leith was never serious about anything. He was an endless flirt, but as much as it vexed her, she still felt special that he continued to shower her with so much attention.

"Yes, but most gentlemen are not as fickle as you."

Leith retracted with a gasp. "Fickle? Me?"

"You are." She leaned toward him. "Admit it."

He shook his golden curls and grinned. "Never with you, my sweet Remi."

There was a sincerity to his voice that left Remi raw. She had missed him since the months following her wedding. Given their history, it never felt appropriate to visit; Leith was a virile creature with a known reputation for being a tomcat. It would look poorly upon her reputation as Madame Leone if they were seen together.

"How are you feeling?" he asked with a frown.

"Not well. I'm exhausted by everything these days."

Leith considered her answer, appraising her tired appearance carefully. Finally, he smiled a wicked smile. "Should I ask my dear Didier to prepare you a tonic? He is quite skilled with his hands." He leaned in closer so that their foreheads were nearly touching. "Or should I sneak into your room this evening and make love to you until you are weary with sleep?"

"Leith," she hissed, flush with embarrassment. "Enough of that."

"It was good before, no?" He wriggled his brows.

Remi covered her reddening face. "We were only children then."

"Who is teasing?" He chuckled low in his throat. "Perhaps I shall have my way with your stepson then, and after, you can join us."

"Please refrain from calling him that!" she exclaimed, turning more serious.

"*Qu'est-ce que c'est?*" He grasped her chin and gently forced her to look at him. "You are too serious, *ma cherie*. I cannot tease you today."

"Unless it has escaped your notice, my husband is dead," she said sternly, pulling her chin from his grasp. "I am in mourning."

"As you may well know," he said, "widows are my specialty. Just last week, I spent a full two nights with a young woman who told me her husband died overseas! And guess what, *cherie?*"

Remi sighed. "What?"

"She was wrong! Her husband came back from the dead and found us together."

"That's awful." Remi frowned.

"Awful? *Non, non, cherie.* It was an excellent night!" Leith grinned devilishly. "He found us together, breathed a great big breath, and dove right into bed with us! Two weeks at sea will do that to a man, you know."

"Leith!" Remi gasped but could not hide her smile. She tucked her reddened face behind both of her hands again and pressed them to her warm skin.

"Too much for my delicate Remi?" He laughed, shaking his head. "I apologize, *ma cherie.* You know me, I'm not a serious man."

"Not at all."

Though his stories were lewd at times, she enjoyed them nevertheless. He was an excellent storyteller, and with his dulcet tone, he could be mesmerizing. After the fiasco in the dining room and the number of people milling around inside, the garden and Leith's company were a welcome distraction.

"I don't mean to be crass. I only meant to brighten you a little, perhaps add a bit of color to your pale cheeks." Leith leaned closer, lending her his warmth and comfort. "I hope you know how deeply sorry I am for your loss."

"I do," Remi said, patting his hand on the bench between them. "Thank you for coming. It means a great deal to me."

"Of course. Anything for you," he breathed.

A long, silent moment passed between them. Remi's peace was somewhat restored.

"I should return," she sighed, reluctant to leave so soon after settling. "I've spent too much time away, and someone will take notice. If it's Beline and she finds me here with you, she'll be cross."

Leith grinned. "Because I'm so charming?"

"No," Remi said as she stood, patting the skirt of her gown. Leith offered her veil, and she took it gingerly. "Because you're so annoying."

"Charming, annoying. What is the difference?" He shrugged.

Remi hid her smile behind black lace as she placed the hat on her head and pinned it in place. "With you? There is no difference."

Taking his arm, Remi guided them through the garden and back into the house, reluctantly leaving serenity behind.

THE NOTE

BEN

"You're like a dog."

"What makes you say that?" Ben asked.

"You haven't stopped watching her," Jacques replied.

Ben narrowed his eyes. "With good reason."

He couldn't help but notice that Remi appeared worse and worse as the day went on. She was gray in pallor, matching the shade of the curtains in the parlor. Even the shine of her hair dulled in color. Madame Leone, for all of her efforts to maintain her appearance, could have been a ghost the way she carried on. Anyone else watching wouldn't have noticed the small slips in her mask—but Ben was keenly aware of her every move throughout the day.

"You could just talk to her. A simple conversation could clear the air between the two of you," Jacques suggested.

"I could."

Jacques groaned. "But you won't."

No, he wouldn't, and it agitated him like an itch he couldn't scratch. He should have written her off after the incident in the study, yet he was drawn to her more than ever.

Ben found himself unsettled when she frowned, tapping his foot, crossing and uncrossing his arms; he could barely hold a conversation without listening or looking for her. Eventually, it reached a peak. He'd kept a close eye on her after she escaped to the garden, joined by another man. Hidden from their view, he'd caught snippets of their conversation and wondered if he was her lover. It would have enraged him, though he wasn't entirely sure why, had he not caught the same fellow advancing on another woman later in the day.

Shameless, but seemingly harmless.

It was another matter entirely when two unfamiliar men stopped him and introduced themselves as Remi's family.

"Arnaud Cuvilyé. My companion here is Hugo Marchand." A man with graying brown hair and a similar disposition to Beline held out his hand to Ben. He waited with an expectant look on his lined face, a forced smile pulling at his thin lips. "I'm Remi's uncle. No doubt you've met my wife."

"Re-acquainted," Ben corrected, "as we are now."

Arnaud retracted his hand when Ben did not take it, though he maintained his calm demeanor. "She said you gave her some trouble earlier."

"Trouble? I simply reminded her of whose home this is."

"Ah. Well, she can be emphatic at times," Remi's uncle mustered.

"Is that at all?" Ben looked between the two men. Hugo, red-headed and red-faced, glared outright. He didn't like the sharp pinch of Marchand's face or the haughty expression that his counterpart wore.

"Well," Arnaud started, "I had hoped to speak with you on my own."

"We," Hugo quickly corrected. "We have some unfinished business with your father. A debt to be settled, if you will."

Arnaud nodded. "In private, perhaps?"

Ben grimaced as the chatter died down around them. Attention shifted as mourners closest to them took notice.

"I can't imagine any business of my father's is important enough to discuss now," Ben sneered, "considering he's dead, lying face up in the parlor."

One of Beline's tea ladies gasped. Ben recognized a feathered hat as it bobbed above the other guests. Behind its plumage, he caught a distinct flash of blue-green. Remi forced herself into the tableau seconds later, grim-faced and gray.

"What's all this then?" she asked politely. "Uncle? Ben?"

The way Hugo's face softened at her arrival shocked Ben. Through less gritted teeth than before, Marchand addressed her gently, "Nothing you need concern yourself with."

"I see," Remi turned her gaze from him to her uncle. "Is there somewhere more private we could move this conversation? Perhaps the study? No need to upset the guests any more than they are."

"Happy to oblige," Ben said flatly.

"Perfect." Remi nodded. "Uncle, Tante Beline was looking for you a moment ago. You might humor her with your presence. I believe she would like to step into the parlor now."

Arnaud's disappointment was clear for Ben to see. He wanted to be part of the conversation as much as Hugo likely wanted to put a hole in the wall.

"Alas, marital duties," Ben said with feigned sympathy and a tight smile.

Arnaud ignored Ben and clapped Hugo on the shoulder. "I trust you to manage this with civility."

Hugo shoved Arnaud's hand away and took off down the hall to the study.

So, he's familiar with the layout, Ben thought. It was hard to argue that his father might not have been in business with anyone. While he was away, there were sure to be things Ben didn't know about.

A moment later, he caught Jacques's shadow move as he followed the redheaded gentleman. It was a lucky thing to have Jacques around. He could move freely and see things that Ben couldn't, and that made it easier for him to focus on everything else.

After Arnaud took his leave, the rest of the guests turned away. There was no doubt that they would be chattering long after they all left the room, but for the time being, they would settle for eaves-dropping.

"Walk with me," Ben said, low enough for Remi alone to hear. She nodded and followed beside him at the same slow, leisurely pace. No one would guess that the pair had been at each other's throats only a couple of hours ago. "Does your aunt faint easily?"

"She and my cousin have similarly weak constitutions," Remi confessed with a sigh. "In fact, Elise nearly fainted a moment ago." She moved closer to Ben and lowered her voice. "I asked Guillaume to take her to the kitchen."

"Then you should go to her," Ben advised, acutely aware of the fabric from her sleeve brushing his arm.

Remi's eyes widened. "I couldn't ask you to sit with Hugo alone."

"I won't be alone. Jacques will be in there," Ben corrected. "And besides, you're not asking me."

They stopped a few steps from the study doors and faced one another. Remi considered him a moment longer. "What does he want? Edgar never said anything to me about his work."

"Apparently, my father was in debt to Hugo and your uncle."

Remi appeared disconcerted. "Debt? He never made that known to me."

"My father was a private man. In any case, I'll learn the truth in a moment." Ben sighed, raking a hand through his hair. "Go and take care of your cousin."

"Are you sure?" she asked. "I would be deeply grateful."

"Consider it done then. I'll summarize it all for you later, assuming there is anything to share."

"Thank you." The softness in her eyes matched the muted lull of her voice. Alone in the hallway, away from the mourners, he felt as though he could see her more clearly. She was sincere, and in the few instances he'd gleaned the nature of her true character, she was resolute. The anger he'd brought with him stood no chance against the woman before him. Incredible to think that she might have smacked some sense into him earlier, after all.

Anything for you, the voice in the back of his head whispered. A wicked part of him hadn't been able to let go of the way her hand had felt on his cheek. He ignored it, flexing his hands at his sides in an effort to fend off the impulse to reach out and touch her.

"Go then," Ben said, his voice steely. "I'll find you later."

Remi nodded and took her leave.

Even if Hugo was a dreadful sort of man, Ben was relieved to escape Remi's gaze as well as the weight of the whispers and melancholy of the mourners.

"Warming up to Madame?" Jacques slinked out from the shadows behind Ben. "I like her. Lamotte said she put you in your place."

Ben narrowed his eyes. "Do you have to hide like that?"

"It's why you keep me around." Jacques shrugged. "I can read the shadows, and I don't like the ones lingering about these halls. They don't have good things to say."

"I can feel it, too." Beneath the tragedy of his father's passing, there was an uneasiness that lurked just beneath the surface.

"This Marchand fellow," Jacques started in a hushed tone, "I don't like him."

"Neither do I." Ben tugged at his waistcoat. "But I can't hear any more stories about my father. They'll put me to sleep."

"Are they boring?"

Ben scoffed. "Boring and utterly sentimental."

Jacques nodded, following Ben into the study as he pushed the doors open. Hugo was waiting, one arm against the mantle, overlooking the fire burning in the hearth. He seemed smaller, surrounded by his father's things, a small man in the jaws of a bigger beast. Ben knew the illusion well enough, and he found relief in the knowledge. He was sure that handling Hugo would be effortless.

"Now then," Ben started, sinking into the seat at his father's desk. Jacques stood guard behind him. "What's this debt you think I owe?"

"Gold," Hugo snapped, crossing the room.

So much for civility. Ben thought, then asked. "Gold? I'm afraid we don't have any of that lying around here."

Hugo's face pulled taut with impatience. "Don't lie! Your father said—"

"My *father* may have said it, but *I* have never heard mention of any gold," Ben said.

There was a whisper of it being somewhere, if his father thought to mention it in his will. Regardless, that wasn't a detail Ben was willing to share. It suddenly made sense why Beline was so upset at being absent during the reading. He was right to make his earlier assumptions, it seemed.

"You will not play me for a fool." Hugo snarled.

Ben narrowed his eyes dangerously. "Monsieur Marchand, I would advise you to lower your voice and maintain some semblance of propriety. I wouldn't want to have you escorted out in front of all the mourners *and* your fiancée's family."

Hugo paused. That struck a chord.

"It would be quite humiliating, don't you think?" Ben pressed.

"Have it your way." He bottled up his anger and held himself rigidly. Through tight lips he said, "Your father promised us gold as payment."

"Payment?" Ben asked, more curious than before. "For what?"

"We made an arrangement." Hugo cleared his throat and straightened himself, though the chip on his shoulder remained. "And signed a contract."

"I see. Do you happen to have said contract?" Ben pressed his lips together, thoughtful as he watched Marchand sweat. There were questions Ben wanted to ask about the business they'd been tangled up in, but there was satisfaction in self-discovery. Ben leaned forward, elbows on the desk, and waited.

"Not presently." Hugo swallowed.

"Interesting." Ben brought his hands to the desk and splayed his fingers over the disorganized papers. "Unfortunately, without proof, I can't help you."

Hugo frowned. "But I—"

"Monsieur Marchand, I returned home to bury my father, whom I have not seen in years," Ben grew serious as he spoke. "I have no knowledge of his work or what debts he owes. I've hardly been home a full day and already the dogs are at my door, barking for their share of a dead man's fortune."

Behind Ben, Jacques grunted.

"That's hardly my problem." Hugo grimaced.

"Correct, Monsieur. It is my problem," Ben said, his words hard and bitter. "As well as Madame Leone's."

Hugo softened again at the mention of Remi. *Perhaps he was fond of her after all*, Ben thought.

"Listen, I don't consider myself an unreasonable man, so I will look into my father's work to find a solution," Ben said. "But it would make things easier if you were amicable, for Madame Leone's sake. Do you find this agreeable?"

Hugo watched him as the gears in his mind turned. "This is important." Hugo struggled to keep his expression neutral, but the mask was slipping.

"You see, I am only appointed half of my father's estate, with the other half belonging to her." Ben watched Hugo's hold finally loosen. "While I would hate to get her involved, I'm afraid I have to bring her into the fold. That said, if you would like to spare her the trouble of looking further, given that her husband has passed, you might grant me more time on my own to do some digging."

"Fine," Hugo snapped. "Fine."

"Worry not. I'll look into this, Monsieur Marchand." Ben would look into it, just not for Hugo. He couldn't care less what debts they felt they were owed. No one would wrest a single cent from his father. "Rest assured that any dealings my father negotiated before his passing will be handled with the utmost care. Whatever I find, I will honor—given the state of its *import*."

Ben locked eyes with Jacques and jerked his chin toward the door. He nodded and sauntered toward the double oaks and pushed one open softly. Hugo watched with narrowed eyes.

"Please convey my thoughts to Monsieur Cuvilyé."

"I will," Hugo said stiffly.

"Good." Ben feigned a smile, feeling somewhat smug as Hugo slumped. "Jacques will show you out."

Without another word, Hugo hurried out of the study and bypassed Jacques entirely. The minute he was gone, Ben let out a deep breath.

"He'll be more trouble for you later on," Jacques said plainly.

Ben frowned, pushing himself up from his father's desk. "Less so if I manage to get my father's affairs in order."

Both men entered the hallway, closing the study door behind them. They walked slowly, voices just above a whisper as they spoke. "Does this warrant a conversation with Madame Leone? Perhaps she knows?"

"No." Ben thought back to her confusion in the study earlier that morning. It seemed to him that his father kept her separate from anything to do with their finances. "She wouldn't know anything."

"Seems strange," Jacques said.

Ben spied Remi bobbing between some of the mourners. She had shed her veil completely, curling tendrils of blonde hair framing her hardened face. She looked one taut string away from losing her grip entirely. He was so focused on her wavering expressions and blue-green eyes that he completely missed what Jacques said to him.

"Did you hear me?" Jacques asked, his brows pulled together in concern.

"My apologies." Ben blinked. "What were you saying?"

"Hugo. What would you like to do?"

"For now..." Ben watched Remi disappear. "For now, we'll keep this between us."

With a nod, Jacques sank back into the shadows and Ben returned reluctantly to the sorrowful mourners and the stories that would inevitably follow, all the while wishing that he could seek out solace in the silence he imagined Remi found in the garden.

OPEN CASKET

REMI

*E*xhausted from the day, Remi wanted nothing more than to turn in for the night. Her feet ached, and her corset pinched uncomfortably. Still, she needed to be sure the manor was clear of any lingering guests before she could find some respite. Suppressing a groan, she stifled her discomfort for a few moments longer.

"You're nearly there," she whispered to herself.

There was no one left in the manor except for those inhabiting its walls. Paul and Martin headed down the drive toward town, and Sylvie was no doubt preparing Remi's room, having already taken care of Elise's accommodations.

With a great sigh, she rounded the corner to the parlor and stopped short of going in. Partly because she'd avoided it all day, but mostly because Ben was there beside his father's casket, his back to her. She could not see his face, but she could hear his voice.

Not wanting to interrupt him, she turned to leave but mistakenly stepped on a floorboard with a notoriously loud creak. It echoed in the hall, calling attention to her presence. In less than a second, Ben was hovering in the door frame with a curious look on his face.

"Why are you out here creeping about?"

Remi blushed and hissed, "I was not *creeping*!"

He seemed unconvinced at first, but finally, the wrinkle between his thick brows smoothed out, and he sighed. "Then what are you doing out here?"

"Nothing scandalous," she said, feeling slightly defensive. "I wanted to be sure that the manor was clear of any guests still loitering about."

"And are we alone?" he asked, his eyes momentarily shifting from her to the open spaces around them.

"Yes, I think so."

He crossed his arms and leaned against the frame. "I overheard your garish aunt mumbling about your cousin. Is she staying?"

"She is." Remi nodded. "She would say it's because I'm in need of comfort. Really, I think this whole situation is an excuse for her to avoid her wedding plans."

Ben smirked. "Fair enough."

"I hope it's alright that she's here. I don't expect my aunt will let her stay for much longer."

"As far as I'm concerned, Madame, you have free reign of this place. It's as much mine as it is yours." He paused. "My father was quite clear about that."

Remi frowned. She wondered if it upset him that his father split the inheritance, little that there was given that the other half might not even exist. It never crossed her mind during their heated exchange earlier that morning to ask him how he felt about the arrangement.

"I'm sorry for earlier," Remi started, feeling breathless as she spoke. "Your cheek, is it sore?"

Ben's eyes widened. "Not necessary. It was well-deserved."

"It was unladylike," Remi insisted.

Ben studied her for a moment longer. "And I am telling you that it was well-deserved."

Remi sucked in a breath, ready to argue, but he smiled, shattering her resolve.

"Besides," his voice dipped lower as he spoke, leaning in toward her face, "I like a woman with a strong right hand. Helps remind us stubborn men of our place."

"Let's not make a habit of it," Remi said.

"Speaking of." Ben's smile remained as he straightened. "How often do you find yourself in the company of Monsieur Marchand?"

"Rarely," she said. "He's not particularly pleasant. Why do you ask?"

"No reason," Ben replied, but it felt like a lie. There was more to his question, he just wouldn't say. "In any case, I am strongly opposed to him ever stepping foot inside this house again. If he so much as crosses that threshold, I will not hesitate to deal with it in the swiftest —perhaps harshest—manner."

"I can only assume that his meeting with you was disagreeable."

"In a manner of speaking." He glared down his nose at her, more serious than ever. "It wasn't anything I couldn't handle. I just don't like him."

"I don't believe anyone does," Remi agreed. "Especially Elise."

"Yes, well." He turned on his heel and tucked his hands behind his back. "I'll be turning in for the night. You should do the same."

Remi nodded and watched him go, an odd ache settling in her breast. For a moment, she felt her composure crack—like a hairline fracture on a porcelain mask. It was difficult to see him go, even if he was a galling ass earlier. For a moment, she imagined reaching for the cuff of his sleeve and pulling him back, if only to delay the inevitable loneliness that would follow his departure.

Tomorrow, there would be no one at their door. Edgar's body would be carried to the family's mausoleum by a black, horse-drawn carriage while Remi, Ben, and the staff would follow to say their final goodbyes.

Edgar would be well and truly gone.

As Remi hesitated in the doorway to the parlor, she could feel eyes watching her.

It's just your nerves, she thought.

"Hello, Edgar," Remi said aloud to the empty room.

The house creaked and groaned in reply. Outside, the storm picked up again. The wind blew against the house, sneaking in through cracks around the window panes. The island's rainy season was just beginning and would last for more than a few months. Rain would be a never-ending backdrop to their mourning.

"I'm sorry I didn't come to see you sooner." She approached his casket reluctantly. His was the first funeral she ever attended, and while they kept him true to life, his likeness was strangely altered. She didn't like the way her skin felt cold, how suddenly the memory of their wedding and vows came to the forefront of her mind.

Until death parts us...

Remi gasped as the words came with an audible ringing in her head. Death pressed itself against her, breathing its low, cold chill down her neck. She pressed her fingers to the bridge of her nose and squeezed, using the edge of his casket to support herself. Panic set in as the ringing in her ears grew louder.

"Remi..."

Her eyes fluttered open. A cry formed in the back of her throat, but no sound escaped her. Two white eyes stared back at her. Edgar's hand shot out from the casket and clamped tightly around her wrist. His mouth widened, his jaw releasing a sickening crack as it opened; a loud, strangled moan that sounded like her name emitted from his throat. A spray of moths flew out of his open mouth, assaulting Remi's face.

She cried out and pushed away from the casket, nearly toppling over one of the side tables in her haste. She pressed the heels of her hands to her eyes and rubbed them raw. When she looked again, the moths were gone and Edgar's face was peaceful.

Remi backed slowly out of the parlor, watching Edgar's casket with every shaky step. She tiptoed around the doors and closed them, hurrying up the stairs. She told herself it was impossible for a corpse to move on its own. It was late, and her mind was playing tricks on her.

Don't look back, her body screamed, sending goose pimples along her arms as a warning.

She did not look back.

Once in her room, Remi sucked in a deep, ragged breath. She dragged her shivering body to the bed, sinking into it without removing her heeled boots or gown. Instead, she curled into herself until she could hear nothing but the sound of her breathing. When she closed her eyes, the moths were there, fluttering their large wings over Edgar's open mouth—crawling from inside him until they took flight.

A sob escaped her.

It wasn't real...

Remi shifted, and something poked her cheek.

She lifted her head and found a crushed envelope with her name written neatly on its front. Picking it up, she turned it in her hand, finding it unsealed. She lit the candle on her bedside table and pulled out a small sheet of torn paper. Her eyes widened at its message:

I've been watching you...and I want you, but I can't have you. Why can't I have you? You don't know how my heart longs for you, how it loves you. Would you love me, if you knew? If only you knew...

Remi read it thrice, each time more afraid than the last. Someone entered her room without her knowing. She looked around, suddenly afraid of the drapes and the dresser and the corners that stared back at her from the darkness. No shadow moved; there was no noise except the wind and rain outside.

Remi sank into the window seat, tucking her knees under her chin. Sleep would not take her now, try as she might. Her eyes trained on the window, she forced herself to count the raindrops sliding down the glass. A flash of lightning illuminated them, making their wet trails sparkle against the darkness. But the light from the flash drew Remi's attention away from the raindrops. There was something below her, a shadow passing in the night. It moved like a person, its shoulders rolled forward, lumbering through the downpour.

She wondered, horrified if it was her mysterious suitor. Lightning struck again and unveiled the figure.

Remi pressed her face to the window, her eyes wide. "Ben?"

RESTLESS

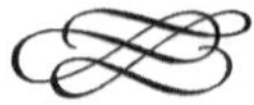

BEN

The knocking at Ben's door seemed to go on endlessly. At first, he ignored it. But it only grew louder, incessant, and violent enough to rouse him from the deepest of dreams. His eyes were bleary as the room came slowly into focus; it was dark, and the fire in his bedroom burned down to glowing embers.

On the other side of the room, his door shook violently against the banging.

"Who is it?" Ben called back. Sleep was still present in his cracked voice. "Jacques? If that's you, I'm going to break your arm."

The noise stopped suddenly. A silent moment passed and Ben drew in a deep breath; the air was cold like ice. He shivered.

"Ben...let me in…" a voice moaned.

He threw the blankets from his legs, irritated by the dramatics. Grasping the handles of the double doors, he threw them wide open. There was no one in the hallway. Confused, he closed the doors.

That was odd.

The moment his hands released the cool brass handles, there was another dry, loud moan on the other side. "Help me...help...me…"

"By hell!" Ben jumped back as the doors again shook with the same banging that had woke him. Fear wound its way into his bones as he pushed them open again, stumbling out into the hall and colliding with a small table. As he righted himself, the voice came again.

"Ben...please, please help me..."

His eyes adjusted to the dark. "Sylvie?"

Light steps echoed in the hall. A white hem as translucent as a newly spun cobweb dragged across the wood floor as if floating. His eyes followed the train, fixating on a female figure that was not Sylvie or Remi. She was a blank, faceless apparition, shimmering in and out like the smoke from a cigar. He brought a shaking hand to his chest, the hairs on his arm standing on end.

The fear in the air was palpable. It held onto Ben with an iron-hard grip, but he forced himself to speak. "Who are you?"

The figure did not answer; instead, she turned and sailed away. She made no noise as she went, and the entire house seemed to silence itself, too. It felt as though the house held its breath as she passed. Ben followed her, despite the rising panic urging him to turn around.

A door on the other end of the hall creaked open, and the apparition disappeared inside. He walked as quietly as he could, stopping at the door as the sound of soft sobbing reached his ears. He peeked inside, jolted by the sight of his sister sitting at her vanity.

"Soleil?"

She did not respond to her name.

"Soleil?" Ben tried again, blinking.

The sobbing grew louder, and then she exploded. Her figure became wisps of smoke; they zipped past him into the hall. He reeled backward, speechless as the split pieces became whole once more.

"Here, Ben...here," she called from the stairs, and he followed.

The phantom kept walking. The front door swung wide open for her as she approached and she walked out into the night, unaffected by the rain. Curiosity filled him, but the suffocating grief inside of him that yearned for answers pushed him forward.

Are you finally going to show me what happened? He wanted to ask.

Because in all of his dreams, in every nightmare he experienced, not once did Soleil unveil her truth.

But there she was, trailing along the garden path, winding her away around the house. Ben followed her to the moors as he tried to keep his breath from catching in his throat. He blinked away the raindrops, squinting to see her through the sheets of rain. It was dark, but the figures were luminescent enough that he could still make them out. Soleil paused at the edge of the cliff that overlooked the beach, but she was no longer alone. A second phantom, taller and broader, towered over her by two heads.

"Is this it?" Ben shouted, bracing himself against the whipping wind and rain."Is this what you want to show me?"

Soleil's voice drifted to him on the wind, shouting broken sentences he could barely make sense of. One phrase did reach him, one sentence repeated over and over in a panic.

"You promised," she cried. "You promised me!"

Promised what?

The other figure did not answer. In the span of a breath, it grasped Soleil's shoulders and threw her over the edge. Soleil's ghost disappeared into the darkness. Her hollow scream echoed as she fell, and the figure, her murderer, watched.

"No!" Ben saw red.

The memory of Soleil's broken, bloodied face in the sand, marred by the expression of surprise and fear broke through the surface. Ben felt the breath leave his body, the anger in him stronger than the helplessness he'd felt as a boy. The figure turned to leave, but Ben, without thinking, rushed forward. He would have met the shadow man head-on, but fate intervened.

He slammed into the wet ground, pummeled by a fierce-looking Remi.

Her voice was as piercing as her wide blue-green eyes. "Benoît Leone!" she yelled. "You absolute idiot!"

～

REMI

"Will you tell me why you were running toward the edge of the cliff?" Remi asked impatiently.

They'd retreated to the study. After the hellish vision, cryptic note, and now Ben's near downward plummet, Remi was barely hanging onto the tatters of her sanity. They were both soaked and caked in mud, sitting in silence for entirely too long.

Even the tea Remi made for them now sat cold in her lap, the cup cradled in her frozen fingers.

"Ben? Did you hear me?"

He nodded vacantly. "Yes."

"Will you talk to me?" Desperation clawed at her chest. "I think I am owed that much, if not more, for saving your life."

Ben straightened a little. "Thank you."

Remi leaned back into the cushion of her chair. Hesitant to broach the subject at all, she tried as gently as she could, "Will you...will you tell me if it was on purpose? Were you intending to end your life tonight?"

Ben's eyes snapped up from the ground, alert and panicked. "No. No, it wasn't."

"That's a relief," she sighed. The coil of tension that had gripped her heart dissolved immediately.

"I didn't mean to worry you," Ben said earnestly. "I'm still trying to understand it all myself. It was like I was walking in my sleep again, somewhere between being lucid and dreaming."

"Does that happen often? The sleepwalking?"

Ben rubbed his face, pushing his dark hair back. A few wet pieces clung to his cheeks. "Not since I was a boy. It stopped a month or two after I started living with my cousins."

"They must have been a great comfort to you if you were able to overcome it so quickly."

Ben scoffed, his jaw tensing. "Not at all. They threatened to leave me at Sainte-Anne if my nightly outings didn't stop. After that, I locked the door to my room and tied myself to the bed with a sheet."

Remi covered her trembling lips and bit back her horror. "That's… that's unthinkable."

"That's family," Ben muttered.

The haunted expression he wore was concerning. His honesty surprised her, especially since he'd accused her of being a money-hungry harlot earlier—in the same room, no less.

"Could it be a coincidence?"

"It could be…"

Remi frowned, "But?"

"My sister," he said. "It was my sister tonight and every night before this one. She's always there, in pain, begging for help. But I wake up somewhere in between, just before she dies again."

"And this time?" Remi asked. She never knew about the night-mares. After Soleil passed, she and Elise were no longer permitted to return. Beline was quite strict about it and kept them on a tight schedule between studies, vocationals, and tea time with the ladies' society. It was one of the hardest days of Remi's life when she learned Ben left without saying goodbye.

"I nearly joined her." He sat back, slouching into the deep cushions of the chair. "It's never happened like that."

"Well, it was quite a spell you were under. I called for you ten times before I finally got through to you," she said.

He sucked in a breath and held it for a long while. Finally, he let it go.

"You know," she started, "you were calling out for her at first. But then I saw you running; you looked angry and afraid. That's why I thought you might have been trying to…to hurt yourself."

"Oh."

"It must have been an awful dream you were having." It was a miracle she'd been able to move him at all in that state, let alone bring his legs out from under him.

Ben considered her in silence. She could see the cogs in his mind working, weighing each unspoken word before he finally said, "It wasn't a dream."

"But you said—"

"I know." He groaned in frustration, leaning forward on his elbows to rest against his knees. He was so large that he was bigger than the chair even when he curled into himself for comfort. "But I don't think it was a dream, per se, more like...more like a memory."

"A memory," Remi repeated.

"But it wasn't *my* memory."

"What?" Remi blinked. "What exactly did you see?"

Ben breathed in deeply. He was still for a moment longer, and then he sprang to his feet. His wet clothes clung to him; through the light of the fire, she could see the outline of his body—the curve of his back, the slight flex in his arms as he crossed them over his chest. She dropped her gaze, trying to fan her desire for him away.

"I saw Soleil fall." He paused as if his plan to tell her might not have been the best idea. But then he said, "Rather, I watched someone push her over the edge of the cliff. She pulled me from my room this evening, and I followed her outside. I watched it all—it was as if she wanted me to see it happen."

"A vision," Remi murmured, frozen as she recalled her own horrifying vision. Edgar's white eyes, her name on his pale, dead lips as he called out to her, just as Ben's sister called to him. It was uncanny that they should both experience a haunting at the same time of the night. The Leones were restless sleepers.

"Yes." He nodded. "A vision. *Her* memory."

Remi swallowed. She didn't believe in ghosts, visions, or phantom apparitions. "Couldn't it just be a nightmare?"

"No." He was adamant. "This was different."

"But Ben—"

He turned, a wild look in his eyes. There was a vulnerability in his expression that she didn't expect to see. It pierced her heart. He was a little boy again, desperate and raw. She waited, her lip quivering as he approached, sinking to his knees in front of her. His eyes, so wide and deep, seemed to plead with her.

"It wasn't my memory, Remi." He spoke her name, low and deep— a mere rumble in his chest. "I know this because I was there when she fell. I was the one who found her body on the beach."

Remi's tea spilled to the side as her hands shook. It soaked into her blanket as the cup tumbled from her fingers and to the floor between them. She pressed her lips together to stave off her quivering.

Ben took her hands, though he was also shaking, and held her gaze. "She was showing me her memories. It can't be just a coincidence."

"What do you mean?" Remi asked, though her voice shook.

Ben pulled away, pushing himself again to his feet. "I would be lying if I said I didn't have an ulterior motive for returning. Outside of my father's passing, I knew I could investigate Soleil's murder. That is the reason why I'm staying and not leaving after tomorrow."

"Murder?" Alarmed, Remi jumped to her feet. "You think she was murdered?"

"I do," he said. "I always have."

Of course, he wouldn't believe the rumors. He'd just said he was there, that he'd seen everything.

Well, almost everything, she thought. "Why didn't you tell anyone?"

Ben scoffed. "As if anyone would listen. I was ten, and Father? Well, you see how well he took the news."

"I know." She frowned. "I don't think I will ever forget." The memory of his leaving brought up the bitterness of her unanswered letter to him. The scent of fresh ink spilling over blank parchment still lingered, as did the words she hoped would reach him. It was a short letter: *You've been gone these too long years and still, my heart has never forgotten you. I yearn for the day that you might turn up on our shores. I need you, please come for me.* Though it was months ago now, the sting of his rejection gripped her heart still.

She knelt to clean up her broken cup, surprised when his hand stopped her from touching the shards.

Gently, he said, "Don't. You'll cut yourself."

"I'm sorry about your sister," she whispered. "And now, your father? I can't imagine how you must be feeling."

Ben squeezed her fingers, and she made the mistake of looking back up at his eyes. The tender expression on his face tore her open. "I'm sorry you're mixed up in our family's misfortune."

The warmth from his fingers distracted her from the broken cup. It felt nice to be touched, to have someone hold her hand again. She licked her lips. "I'm not."

Though he did not fully smile, the tug at the corner of his lips was enough to make her blush. Scooping the broken teacup into one hand, he held out his other and waited.

"You must think me a madman," he said as he pulled her to her feet.

Remi felt dizzy. "I think…nothing is impossible."

For that, she earned a true smile in return. "That's kind of you."

"Is it?" She swallowed, feeling his breath close to her.

He nodded, his next words drowned out by the chiming of the clock behind Edgar's desk. Its timing was a signal to them both.

"It's late," Ben said. "We should return to our rooms."

"Oh." Remi tried not to express her disappointment. "Of course, you're right. I'll just tidy up and take—"

He stopped her as she tried to take from him the broken cup. "Come on then."

Remi grabbed their blankets and bundled them in her arms. She couldn't help but feel somewhat defeated. Their moment, a good one —ruined by the temerity of an old clock. In her head, she cursed it for its timing.

"Goodnight, Remi," Ben said.

"Goodnight," she paused, suddenly too shy to speak his name. "Ben."

She started down the hall alone, shuffling reluctantly. He watched her, lingering in the doorway. Her feet stopped, and her heart fluttered as she turned to face him again. His brows lifted in query.

"I *do* believe you," she said. "I just want you to know that."

She looked at him, waiting for him to say something. His stoicism had returned.

"That's all." She bowed her head. "Goodnight."

The echo of his silent reply followed her up the stairs and back into her room.

Even if he didn't thank her, it was enough for Remi to have said it.

Some part of him, however deeply hidden, must have felt relieved to have been heard.

Once undressed, Remi curled beneath her covers and closed her eyes. She fell asleep to the sound of rain and her heartbeat. When the morning light finally peeked through her window, she realized that sleep came and went without issue. All that was left of the night before was her wet nightgown and a perfectly folded piece of paper on her bedside table.

BURIAL

REMI

APRIL, 1898

$\mathcal{I}$t was only a month before that Edgar first brought Remi to the family mausoleum.

He was at first reluctant, but she had persisted. Though they had just been married, she'd grown too used to the silent halls. The sound of the front door opening had made her jump up from where she sat in the dining room.

"Are you going somewhere?" Remi had asked.

Edgar halted at the threshold, surprised to see her. "I was on my way to the cemetery."

She perked up. "Might I join you?"

He thought for a moment, then smiled. "Your company would be most welcome."

The carriage took them down the hill to a secondary road that led into the Isle's cemetery. It was bumpy and quiet. Remi spent the trip staring out the window, unsure of what to say. They passed headstones of varying age, some new, some weathered by time, and small mausoleums. All the while, she rattled her brain for a topic of common interest, but by the time she found something to talk about, they had stopped.

"Here we are," Edgar said, hurriedly exiting the carriage.

Martin waited to help her to step down.

"Many generations of my family are buried here," Edgar said as she joined him by the stairs.

At a glance, he appeared stoic, but his voice was tight. Like the stone façade of the mausoleum they approached, Edgar was weathered and graying. Remi wondered how often he came to visit and what kind of toll it took on him to outlive so many loved ones.

"How many generations?" Remi asked.

"Four," he said, unlocking the gate.

"This is quite a special spot," Remi said, pointing to the wooded area just beyond the mausoleum. Wildflowers inched along its granite walls. "The flowers are beautiful."

In truth, the greenery seemed out of place. The mausoleum was old, and the flowers were bright and lively as if life had held on despite the flow of time.

"Indeed." Edgar grinned, seemingly delighted by her observation. "Do you recall the specimen encased in my study?"

"I do."

Edgar gestured to the bushes and the trees. "I found it here one spring when I was just a boy."

"It was waiting for you?"

"Goodness no," he chuckled. "The moths led the way, and I followed to find more of their nests behind here, hidden in the woods."

"How wonderful." She smiled. The moth he prized was the only one she'd ever seen. "I can only imagine what you would have looked like in your youth."

Sparked by her comment, his expression changed, and his smile widened. He laughed, "No need to imagine, dear girl. My son, Benoît, looks a great deal like me. We have a similar countenance—though I confess, he is more like his mother."

The mention of Ben made her heart skip.

"I remember him," she said. "How is he?"

Edgar was silent as he turned and fumbled with the gate again.

"He is healthy and well." His voice dropped to just above a whisper as he said, "And *alive.*"

"He must miss being home," she said, but Edgar ignored her as they entered the structure. She chided herself for being forward. Clearly, Ben was a sensitive subject.

With a deep breath, Remi followed him inside. She was surprised by its size; there were two walls with family names and a stone casket in the center. Dying flowers and burned candles were left on its surface, which Edgar collected. She watched him approach each name, mumble something to himself, and move on. He did it for every name. There was a change when he approached his late wife. He lingered, bringing his fingers to his lips, and pressing them to the stone where her name was engraved.

It was a private moment he shared with the departed, a silence that she dared not interrupt. When he spoke again, his heart seemed heavy. "Thank you for your kindness today."

Remi tilted her head. "Have I done something?"

"I have been alone for more than a decade," he said. "It was kind of you to offer me your company."

"There's no need to thank me," she said.

"You are family now," he said, once more pressing a hand to his late wife's name. "And my family holds my treasure."

She smiled. "To hear you say that warms my heart."

He returned her smile in kind. "Shall we return?"

If we must, she thought. "Yes."

Their visit to the mausoleum was brief, but it had been a reprieve from the monotony that had become her days. She knew as soon as they left, they would each return to their respective solace. And she was right. As soon as they walked through the front doors of the manor, they went their separate ways: Remi to the dining room, where Sylvie waited with a lunch tray, and Edgar to his study.

The carriage lurched, pulling Remi from her thoughts.

The pressure of Ben's presence had grown overnight. Remi

couldn't ignore him, especially not after witnessing his state the night before. The only thing that eclipsed him was the sight of the mausoleum.

Near the very back of the cemetery, past the other graves she saw on her first trip, there was the Leone family mausoleum. It was the only granite building of its kind, in both stature and grandiosity. It was almost as large as one of the rooms in the manor, with a set of stairs and a wrought-iron gate fixed against its double doors. Greenery grew flush around its base, bushes and flowers and trees flanking either side. There were no other graves nearby.

"Have you been here before, Madame?" Sylvie asked.

They shared the carriage, as Ben opted to ride with the coach carrying Edgar.

"I have," Remi said as Martin opened the door.

The morning air was thick and chilly, and the ground beneath their feet was soft with wet mud. The damp air clung to Remi's body; she pulled her shawl tighter around her shoulders. Little drops of rain dotted her face, making her shiver.

"Looks like another storm soon, Madame," Martin said, leading them toward the mausoleum.

Ben and his footman, Jacques, helped the undertaker remove the casket. She watched, remembering the vision of Edgar with a shiver. It terrified her to wonder if she would see him there again, standing beside the mausoleum or peering from behind a tree, looking at her with that same dead look in his eyes. A tap on her shoulder drew her back to reality.

"Madame?" Sylvie whispered.

"Are we having trouble?" Ben asked as they approached with the casket. His dark hair fell forward, covering half of his face.

Sylvie tapped Remi's arm again.

"No," she said too quickly, producing the key from her pocket. Her fingers shook as the gate opened. No doubt they were all curious as to why.

"Mind your heads," Remi said as she went ahead.

The coffin was placed atop the stone casket, where it would later be put to rest inside. Unlike the rest of his family, Edgar would not join his family behind the granite walls of the crypt. Instead, he would sit at its heart.

Remi folded herself into the mausoleum as the casket was carried inside. She and the others waited until it was placed atop the stone slab. A collective breath was released the moment it was set down. There was room enough for everyone, but Ben shuffled close to Remi, taking his place beside her. It felt purposeful as if he wanted her to feel every inch of him that towered over her. Remi never considered herself a small woman, but when tucked against Ben's side, she found it hard to be anything *but* small.

"Shall we say a prayer?" Martin asked, his voice heavy with grief.

"Go on." Ben nodded.

Remi closed her eyes and bowed her head, tuning out the sound of the prayer. This would be the final send-off, and then everything would return to normal. Whatever normal would be for her. A shared space again, this time with someone she wasn't sure enjoyed her company at all. The rest of her life, it seemed, would remain as dull and bleak as the weeks following her wedding.

"Madame?"

Remi straightened. "Yes?"

"Would you like to say a few words?" It was Martin who asked, but everyone else's eyes were watching.

"Ah, well—"

Ben touched her arm briefly, and she quieted.

"First, I want to thank you all for your years of service to the family, however long it has been," he said. "While I've been away, it has been a great comfort to see familiar faces upon my return. My father, God rest his soul, was surely grateful for your presence all these years."

"He will be missed." Martin sniffed and wiped at his eyes. His son lingered beside him, almost too small to be seen but just as upset as his father.

Sylvie nodded, her silence her solidarity. They all shared some short story, a meeting, a conversation, or a memory about Edgar. It was special for them, even if the same could not be said for Remi. This was their time to say goodbye. After tears were shed, they all fell back into a comfortable silence.

With Remi's blunder forgotten, the staff shuffled out in their own time, leaving Ben, Remi, and Jacques.

"Shall we return?" Remi asked gently.

"I'll be staying behind a moment longer," Ben said.

"Oh." She felt her shoulders sag. "I'll be sure to have a tray kept warm for each of you."

"Thank you, Madame." Jacques bowed his head. "But I will be returning. My hands are no more helpful here than a pianist's in a tailor's shop."

"It's true." Ben nodded. "I've only kept him near to keep me in line."

"You mean sober," Jacques mumbled under his breath.

Ben waved him off, mildly irritated, but the footman smirked, excusing himself with a bow. From what she had discerned, the two shared a bond like the one she held with Elise. Family, brothers, friends. It was admirable.

"Then I shall see you this afternoon," Remi said, excusing herself.

As she stepped forward, she felt a hand press against the small of her back. Ben was beside her, leading them from the mausoleum. It took a great deal of collectedness on her part to keep the butterflies in her stomach from rioting, for once they started, she knew she would come undone. She was grateful for the fresh air when they stepped outside. They stopped a few paces from the doors, Remi on solid ground and Ben leaning against the doorframe. Tired though he looked, he still cut quite an attractive figure.

"That was lovely," Remi said, releasing a breath. "Thank you for that."

Ben shook his head dismissively. "You seemed distracted. It was the least I could do."

"I admit I wasn't prepared to speak."

Ben glanced over her shoulder, then settled again on her eyes. "Are you well?"

"I am." Her voice was weak with exhaustion. Observant as he was, she could see he was not convinced. The way he held her in his gaze sent a rush of heat to her face. She adjusted her collar and forced a smile. "How are you feeling after last night?"

Ben's brows drew together. "I'm afraid I didn't sleep much after our excursion."

"I must admit that I didn't, either," Remi said, bowing her head.

"Were you worried about me?" Ben said, a teasing note in his voice.

"Partially. Though, if I'm to be honest with you, I had other worries on my mind...a trifling thing really, but all the same concerning."

She didn't want to admit it, but waking up was a difficult task. Groggy and chilled from the night before, she had rediscovered the note on her bedside table. It felt like a dream, reading it again, as if it could not exist outside of her imagination. Yet, it lay heavy in the pocket of her dress.

"Something worse than my own brush with death?"

She watched his expression—measured its sincerity as his brow deepened and the bow of his lips dipped into a frown.

"Perhaps."

"Would you tell me?" he asked. "I feel I owe you that much."

"For saving your life?" She considered him a moment longer. "I believe you owe me a great deal."

"Do I?" His eyes narrowed as he attempted to be serious, but they held a playful gleam.

"Yes. In fact," she said while crossing her arms over her chest, "you may very well owe me a lifetime—an exchange for what remains. Interfering with Death is no easy feat."

Ben smirked. "And yet you managed."

"Yes." She agreed. "I seem to recall that I am quite capable of doing just about anything."

"My own words used against me. Touché." He smirked. "Know that you'll have my time whenever you need it."

The tenderness in his tone was hard to ignore, and she found herself fighting against the blush creeping up her neck and to her ears. *Curse my traitorous body for betraying my heart.*

"Thank you," she whispered.

Just then, a light-footed Martin cleared his throat, drawing their attention to where he stood a few paces behind her.

"*Pardonne*, Madame." He pressed his hands together. "I don't mean to interrupt, but we must return within the hour. The kitchen is expecting a delivery."

"Of course. We'll go now."

"*Merci, merci,*" Martin said as he left.

She turned to Ben. "Do you truly intend to stay behind?"

"Yes," he said. "I offered my assistance to the undertaker. Unfortunately, it will take extra strength to lift this slab."

"I see," she said. "Will you be back soon?"

"Yes, I won't be more than an hour." His gaze lingered on her face, his eyes dropping to her lips as she licked them.

"You'll need this then." Remi produced the key she used to unlock the gate earlier and handed it over. Her fingertips grazed his open palm and she suppressed a shiver, quickly pulling them away.

"I look forward to my return."

"As do I." Remi clutched her fingers to her chest in the hopes that they could somehow hide the fervent beating of her heart. "I'll take my leave."

Ben smiled as she turned. It was the kind of smile that made her cheeks warm, and she decided then that she would not forget it any time soon. She hurried through the cemetery, all the while hoping that the morning air would cool her heated flesh. The carriage waited for her at the far edge of the grass, with Jacques standing by patiently. Remi took the hand he offered and stepped up into the cabin, slipping with ease into the seat beside Sylvie.

"Keep an eye on that one," she said, leaning toward him. "He seems to make trouble wherever he goes."

Jacques grinned. "I am all too familiar, Madame. Trust that I will always return him to you in one piece."

The door to the carriage closed before he could see the blush spread across her cheeks. Ben had not been hers for a very long time. He was completely new to her, even despite her cracking his shell a fraction. There was more to him than anyone could discern by looking, and as much as Remi wanted to sink herself into the layers beneath his shallow surface, she could not yet give in. Though the spark was there, he was still cautious, and that was all she needed to remedy her frivolity. If it wasn't for Sylvie's chattering on the way back, she might have succumbed to the stirring hope that things between her and Ben had changed after their rain-soaked conversation.

"Do you feel a weight has been lifted?" Sylvie asked. "Madame?"

"I'm sorry?"

"A weight, Madame. Do you feel it's been lifted?"

"Oh." Remi exhaled. "In part, I suppose I do."

"That must be such a relief."

Remi only hummed a reply as she leaned against the door of the carriage. It was already starting to rain again, and as the drops raced down the clouded windows, she didn't feel as weightless as they looked. With Edgar laid to rest, there was still the matter of the unsigned letter still folded in her pocket.

DIGGING

BEN

MAY, 1898

*B*en closed the door of the mausoleum firmly behind him and locked it, tucking the key inside his pocket. After placing his father's coffin inside, he'd asked for a moment to say good-bye. Being inside the mausoleum, surrounded by his dead relatives, left a needling pain inside his heart. All of his loved ones were gone, and he was the only one left to mourn them.

"Thank you for waiting," Ben said as he joined the undertaker on the bench of the carriage.

"Say all you needed to?" the man asked, whipping the lead into motion. The carriage started forward.

"I did." Ben spared one last glance back at the mausoleum. "Not sure if he heard any of it, though."

"The dead are always listening." The undertaker tapped his ear. "Make no mistake."

Ben crossed his arms, leaned back against the carriage, and closed his eyes. He wondered if that was true, if they really could hear him. How ashamed would they be, to see how low he'd fallen during his time away? He was not worthy of a parent's praise. Certainly, his mother would have plenty to say about the way he carried on with his life.

It could be different, though. He could be different.

There was an opportunity to change now that he was home. Ben opened his eyes as the carriage rumbled along. He sat forward on the bench and strained to see as the manor came into view. There was another carriage waiting, but no driver to be seen. The front doors were wide open, and two people stumbled out.

"Elise?"

Although she was somewhat obscured by distance, he could make out the color of her hair and the shrill timbre of her voice.

"Please! If you would just let us explain!" she begged. The person beside her, a man, reached for her as Remi came into view.

The carriage rolled to a stop and Ben hopped down to the ground with haste. He sped forward, the gravel crunching beneath his boots, just as Remi was joined by Jacques and another. They seemed to be speaking to her, but she was focused on Elise.

"I don't want to hear it!" She threw her hands out, clearly angry.

"Remi, please!" Elise dissolved into tears. The man beside her became clear—Guillaume. They both looked distraught and guilty.

Jacques waved to Ben as he approached, catching Remi's attention. Her blue-green eyes turned on him then, anger burning in their core. He recognized the wrath, having been at the receiving end of it the morning before. Whatever they'd done, she was incensed.

"What's happened here?" Ben asked.

Guillaume urged Elise along, pushing her toward the other carriage. She turned her pleading eyes to Ben, still full of unshed tears.

"She won't listen to me," Elise cried.

Guillaume held her around the waist as he pulled open the carriage door, ushering her to get inside.

"Forgive me," Guillaume said to Ben, bowing his head in apology.

"What in God's name?" Ben muttered.

Guillaume hurried away, swinging himself up onto the bench. He whipped the lead and took off at an incredible speed, as if willing the horses to soar instead of run. Ben turned back to the door where Remi stood, now joined by a curly-haired young man. He recognized him from the wake, though he could not recall his name.

"Is anyone going to tell me what happened?" Ben repeated.

"Madame caught her cousin dallying with the footman."

Ben's brows shot up his forehead, nearly reaching his hairline. "You mean?"

"They were in the *throes* of passion, as it were." Jacques coughed into his hand as if attempting to hide his amusement.

Remi made a noise akin to irritation and embarrassment. "I couldn't see at first. I only thought someone was hurting Elise."

Next to her, the man took her hand and patted it. "Why don't we move this conversation inside, *ma cherie*?"

Ben sensed a deeper connection between the two. The way she folded into him, and the way he handled her so gently, inspired a glimmer of jealousy. Who was this man and how was it that he came to be in *his* home, with his arms wrapped around Remi? He seemed familiar, though Ben could not quite place how.

Once inside, Ben could see the distress in the way her shoulders tensed at her ears. She was shaking, but from what, he could not say. Humiliation? Anger? Both seemed possible given the circumstances.

"So how long has this been going on?" Ben asked carefully. Part of him wanted to go to her, but the way her companion cradled her, he could hardly find reason to break them apart. His hands twitched with frustration.

"Months, years," said the man beside her.

Remi shook her head. "It hardly matters, Leith. She's *engaged*."

Leith, Ben repeated in his mind. He would commit him to memory and be sure to learn all that he could about him later on.

"Matters of the heart are far more complex, *ma cherie*," Leith said as if he understood Elise's situation better than either of them.

"Yes, well, I hope she can explain it to Tante Beline when she discovers their affair." Remi rubbed at her temples, breaking free of Leith's hold.

"What will you do?" Ben asked.

Remi whirled, ready to turn her anger on him when she suddenly sagged. She looked lost and confused.

"Remi?" Ben asked again.

"I'm going to have a cup of tea," she decided. "And ask Sylvie to clean the sheets."

With that, she turned on her heel and swayed on her feet to the hall that led to the kitchen. Ben made to follow after her, but Leith's hand pressed lightly against his chest.

"I'll keep an eye on her," he said.

There was something about his tone Ben didn't like, but he nodded. "Thank you."

The foyer was quiet after their retreat, with just Ben and Jacques left to inhabit it.

"What an exciting morning," Jacques said, the suggestive tone unmistakable.

Ben tried to hide his annoyance as he watched Remi and her *friend* disappear. "It's not what I would have predicted."

"I might have," Jacques said.

Ben turned to eye him curiously. "What do you mean by that?"

Jacques shrugged. "I might have seen the young lady and the footman running off to the stables at some point during the wake."

Ben sputtered with laughter, grateful for Jacques's presence. "Come on. I need to distract myself."

"With what?"

"My sister's room," Ben said, heading for the stairs.

Jacques tracked behind, falling into step beside him a moment later. "I think now is as good a time as any to start the search."

With Remi distracted, they could take their time to investigate. The night before led him there and he couldn't shake the feeling that there was a reason for it. It could mean nothing, but it felt significant. Why else would her phantom lead him to the one place she spent most of her time? There were secrets there, buried somewhere in a desk drawer. He was sure of it.

"What about lunch?" Jacques inquired.

"It can wait." Though Ben felt his stomach gripe in protest at his remark.

"Fine."

Ben brushed past him. "Come on then. Her room is this way."

They moved down the hall, following the familiar path to Soleil's chambers, Ben following the path where his sister's ghost led. They passed portraits of deceased family members: aunts and uncles, grandfathers and grandmothers, the paint faded and crumbling. There was great-grandmother Mathilde, whose white hair looked like a ferocious street cat had tousled with a puddle of mud in a back alley. Then there was the surly face of an Uncle Bayard and an Aunt Vera, who looked lost and distant with her haunted brown eyes. The largest portrait among them depicted Arthur and his wife, Leyda, the Leones who settled on the Isle and built the manor years ago. They were a serious-looking couple surrounded by three small children.

"Who are they?" Jacques caught him staring.

"More dead family."

Ben used to know them all by name, but now they looked out at him in anonymity. When he was younger, he and Soleil would make a game of it. One stolen scone from the kitchen for every aunt, uncle, or cousin whose name they could guess right. At some point, they could name them all, and the scones were shared. He smiled at the memory. It used to be good fun, but then he was alone, his sister too grown up to play childish games.

Then came the portraits of Ben as a young boy. He ignored them, inching closer to the end of the hall where the gray light of the day hit Soleil's bedroom door. Marked with her name on a faded plaque, its handle was dusty and untouched. He tried to open it, unsurprised to find it locked. It was a silly thing to think that she'd unlocked it for him the night before.

All she really did was show me the way, he thought. *The rest is up to me.*

Beside him, Jacques cleared his throat. "Is that it? Can we eat now?"

Ben scoffed. "We can get in without a key."

Jacques shuffled backward and watched with interest.

Ben held the knob firmly and lifted it slowly, grinning when he felt the familiar shift in the hardware, sliding sideways and away from the lock. The door stuck against the frame, but with a forceful shove, Ben shouldered his way in.

Behind him, Jacques whistled. "How intuitive."

"I was a thief as a boy." Ben chuckled, swinging the door open. He breathed in a cloud of dust as it unsettled from the hardwood floor. His eyes watered, his lungs and throat sore from coughing by the time he caught his breath.

Her room was perfectly preserved. Though her spirit had been bright in life, Soleil's room was full of dark grays, earthy greens, and simple decor. She kept oil paintings and sketches hung in frames on the walls and poetry books stacked in dusty corners. A few dresses lay at the foot of her bed, a sewing kit left beside them, as though she would return at any moment to mend their frayed hems.

A dull twinge pulled at Ben's heart, knowing she never would come back.

"What a rascal you were," Jacques said, bringing Ben back to the present.

"Yes." He smirked. "They did their best to keep me out, but neither my father nor my sister ever knew how I did it. My mother, however, was keenly aware of my antics."

"Why am I not surprised?" Jacques asked, covering his nose and mouth with a handkerchief he pulled from his jacket pocket. He was already scouring the room's surfaces and drawers.

Ben wandered to her writing desk, the same place she had exploded into a cloud of smoke the night before. He went through its drawers quickly, spying only junk and a box halfway hidden beneath ribbons. He picked up a discarded needlepoint project left unfinished from the chair and gave it a quick once over.

A thick sheet of dust covered the surface. He wiped it away, revealing a clump of little purple flowers—ugly smudges of thread all hastily worked into a misshapen form. She was always sewing or writing, anything to keep her hands busy. For as much time as she spent on her hobbies, she never was any good at sewing. She was much better at skipping rocks and hitting bottles with pebbles from thirty feet with Ben's slingshot. He used to tell her as much.

It never failed to bring her joy to hear his praises, no matter how silly they were. Months before their mother died, Soleil would let him in her room to read or play while she practiced her needlepoint or wrote poems. In the weeks leading up to her passing, however, she had closed herself off more and more. It had pained him to see how his sister faded away to little more than skin and bones.

This house has a way of draining away life. He thought then of Remi and how, on the day he returned, she seemed more like a ghost than a person. Her visage resembled that of the peeling wallpaper, worn out and sapped of color. Not unlike his sister.

"I see notes here," Jacques announced loudly as he sifted through papers on her bedside table. "Nothing fully coherent, though; just scratches here and there, some broken sentences."

Ben came to, emotion lodged in his throat.

"Anything you can make out?" Ben sniffed as he set the needlework back down. Suddenly sentimental, he used his clean sleeve to wipe away the dust on the surface of the desk.

"Words, mostly." Jacques's voice filled in the background. "She says 'need more,' 'where else,' and a handful of names. I think."

"What names?" Ben stopped wiping when his sleeve snagged against a rough dip in the wood. He leaned down to observe it, brushing away more of the filth until the lines made sense. Inside a heart, two letters had been sloppily scratched in. He followed the grooves of the first—an 'S'—but could not determine the second. *A...R, or is it an H?*

"Leyda Leone."

Ben straightened. "What?"

"Did you not hear me?"

Ben shot Jacques a confused look. "No. What did you say?"

His friend's shoulders sagged, reflecting the bow of his mouth. "I said 'Arthur, Verity, Helena, Benoît, and Leyda Leone.' Is it family?"

"Yes, but..." Ben ran his fingertips over the letters again. "That's odd."

"What is?"

"Those names. Everyone on that list has been dead for decades," Ben said. "Except me. As far as I'm aware, I'm the only Benoît in the family."

"What could it mean?"

Ben shrugged, instead tapping his fingers to indicate his own findings. "She carved some letters here. There's an 'S' and another, but I can't tell what."

Jacques tucked his notes back into the drawer by Soleil's bed and inspected the little message on the desk. Like Ben, he leaned in until his nose was inches from brushing against the wood. He squinted but could not discern what it was.

"A love letter?" Jacques offered. "Was there anyone courting her at the time?"

"No." Ben shook his head. If his sister had closed herself off to him, there was no doubt in his mind she'd done the same for others. *But the heart and the letters mean something.*

"That you know of," Jacques said. "If I may be so bold, it looks to me like your sister might have been keeping someone a secret."

"But why?" Ben's brows creased.

"Who knows." Jacques shrugged. "Why do any of us keep secrets?"

Ben grimaced. Between Soleil's cryptic notes and carving on the desk, he couldn't be sure what she had been up to. The dream he'd had the night before—the memory—made him wonder about the day she died. If someone had truly pushed her, could it have been the person whose initial she'd embossed into the wood? He thought about the betrayal in her eyes, the way it shone so clearly in her gaze. Was it possible that she trusted someone enough to give him her heart? If she was seeing someone, it made sense that she would search for a way out.

Was that why you wanted the gold? Ben approached the window and looked out toward the moors. How many times before had she done the same? Longing for something, for *someone.* He wondered if she lingered still, her spirit locked up with the dust in a room their home had forgotten. Ben blinked; he swore he could see her there on the moors, standing at the cliff's edge with the wind whipping at her hair. When she looked back, the faceless woman from the night before found him watching from the window.

Ben blinked the vision away, petrified by his own fear and confusion.

Soleil might have shown him a part of the truth, but it did not quiet the scratching at the back of his mind. There was more to her death: he knew it, and the answers were somewhere in her long-forgotten room.

GOLD

REMI

emi returned to her room after her evening bath, the afternoon having sailed by without further disturbance. Truthfully, she'd experienced enough melodrama for one day and was tired of it before supper. Passing on the simple stew Martin had prepared, she retired to her room and found solace in the quiet of the empty washroom. Exhaustion wore on her like one of Tante Beline's drab hand-me-down dresses, thick and uncomfortable as it pinched every part of her body.

Too much of her time was spent worrying over everyone else lately.

"I can feel it in my bones," she said aloud, stretching her arms above her head. The room echoed with the gentle lapping of the bathwater against the tub.

Soon enough, if all went according to Hugo's design, Elise and her affair would be one less concern. Their marriage would end it and lift the weight from Remi's chest. Elise was the closest she had to a sister and the only person who stood between her and Beline. Elise would be well and truly gone after her wedding, and Remi would again be alone.

We'll have to make up, she thought, her heart too heavy to consider the alternative.

Remi abandoned the lukewarm bath water and dried herself off. Once in her nightgown and robe, she padded silently back to her room. Inside, she went to her dressing table and sat for a long moment, staring at the sheet covering the mirror. She didn't remember placing it there, but Tante Beline had been insistent about the tradition. Doubtless she was the culprit. Remi frowned and pulled it away.

The dead be damned, Remi thought, finding her pale reflection in the mirror. She desperately needed a good night's sleep.

Remi turned and pulled open the side drawer to fetch her brush. There was an empty space where she'd last placed the box that held her locket. There was nowhere else it could be. Her blood ran cold.

"My locket." Remi dove into the drawer, forgetting all logic.

Did Sylvie steal it? It was a terrible thought, one that she regretted immediately.

Remi abandoned the vanity and rushed to the bedside table. She pulled open the drawer and rifled through the small trinkets within, her frustration rising with each discarded bauble. The note was there, on the very top, right where she'd left it after lunch. But the locket was nowhere to be found amongst the junk.

"Where did it go?"

"Where did *what* go, Madame?" Sylvie's voice was like a little bell.

Remi straightened and breathed deeply. When had she come in? Why didn't Remi hear a knock? Her ears were ringing from panic.

"My locket is missing."

Sylvie made no reply.

"Don't you remember? It was Edgar's wedding gift to me," Remi said, her eyes falling on the young woman at the door. She had a tray in her hand; it shook slightly in her grip.

"Do you know where it is?" Remi asked.

"No, madame."

A tense beat passed between them, and Remi straightened, leveling her gaze at the maid. She almost looked ill.

"Did you take it, Sylvie?" Remi attempted to keep her voice even.

Her maid's grip on the tray tightened into a white-knuckled grip. "No, of course not, Madame! I would never!"

Remi's building anger wavered.

"I promise." Sylvie's eyes teared up as the china on the tray shook.

It was a harsh and damaging accusation, Remi knew. Maids could be let go for far less. She had no proof to say otherwise, and Sylvie was usually quite honest. With a deep breath, she relaxed her shoulders.

"I don't mean to accuse you of anything, truly." Remi sighed. "Perhaps I misplaced it."

"I will help you look," Sylvie offered quickly.

"Not tonight." Remi took the tray from Sylvie's shaking hands, grateful for the fresh scent of honey and lemon wafting from the cup. Tea would be just what she needed to lull her into some semblance of sleep. "It's far too late to search this place now, and I'm quite tired."

"Of course," Sylvie murmured. "I understand."

"Goodnight, then," Remi said, nodding toward the door. "Thank you for the tea."

Sylvie brightened at her gratitude. "It was no trouble, Madame. Pleasant dreams." She hurried off, shutting the door behind her with a soft click.

Remi sat down on the bed with the tray in her lap. For a moment, she contemplated the locket's disappearance and the note that had been left for her. Could they be connected? Remi stifled a shiver as she picked up the teacup and sipped at the tea. It was still hot enough to warm her cold fingers and cheeks.

Leaving the tray on her vanity, Remi pulled back the duvet and crawled into bed. The moment her head hit the pillow, she should have been asleep, but something sharp and hard connected with the back of her head. She jumped and tore the pillow away.

Beneath it was a square box, the same one that had held her locket. She did not hesitate to reach for it but stopped short of opening the lid. There was no reason why it should be hidden and stranger still to be tucked under a pillow. Remi sucked in a deep breath as she finally opened the lid. Her locket was gone; in its place were a few words scrawled on a ripped piece of parchment.

Let me have it, my love...let me have your heart.

~

BEN

Ben watched the fireplace intently.

After searching his sister's space, he'd departed for the beach to clear his mind. It seemed like a fine idea until he lost too many hours on a washed-up log in deep contemplation. If not for the growing chill and the rumbling in his stomach, he might have been there all night. The fire in his room and a bowl of steaming stew was a welcome sight; he found it hard to leave the room again once he was settled.

"I see you barely ate anything." Jacques's voice startled Ben.

"Gods, man! Do you ever knock?"

His companion peered into the half-eaten bowl. "Too many potatoes?"

Ben rolled his eyes and slumped backward into the chair. "It was fine."

"Well, if you didn't eat, did you at least get anywhere with your daydreaming?" Jacques asked. "Have the mysteries of these bygone halls unveiled themselves to you? I can't imagine there were any answers in the fire."

"I'm not in the mood."

"Clearly," Jacques said, setting the bowl back down. He invited himself to sit in the empty chair opposite Ben's and mimicked a similar posture. "I couldn't find much more after you left."

"I expected as much," Ben sighed, shifting in his chair. There was a persistent pain in his forehead that throbbed when he moved his head.

Jacques must have sensed his frustration, saying, "That doesn't mean there isn't anything to find."

"Naturally, she had secrets," Ben said. "Of course, it would be hard for us, or anyone, to find the truth."

"Do you want to know what I think?" Jacques asked.

"If I'm being honest, no." Ben shot him a weary look. "But you'll tell me anyway."

"I think your father knew something about what your sister was going through, and that initial she carved into her desk means something." Jacques paused, narrowing his eyes. "Those names mean something. There's a silver bullet to be found among the debris she left behind."

"You think my father knew her secret?" Ben's eyes widened. He never even thought to suspect his father, though it would make perfect sense. What better way to keep the questions at bay than to send off the one witness to it all under the pretense of grief? The notion of it boiled Ben's blood.

"All I'm saying is that it's a possibility." Jacques shrugged. "Did you ever read that letter he left you? I'd bet my bum knee that there's a morsel or more of information there."

"No. It's gone missing." *Conveniently.*

Ben ground his teeth together and shoved to his feet. "I need a change of scenery."

"Where are you going?"

"I'll be in my father's study," Ben grabbed his robe again and opened one of the bedroom doors with a flourish. "If you haven't eaten, have Sylvie bring your supper here. Sit, enjoy the fire, and turn in for the night."

Jacques nodded, too tired to argue, and let Ben go without another word.

Ben made quick work of the stairs and closed himself behind the double doors of his father's study. It was anger that brought him there, and it would likely serve to stoke his motivation for the rest of the night. It took a few tries, but Ben relit the neglected fireplace and set the gas lamps ablaze.

He crossed the room to his father's desk and settled into the worn cushion of his chair. Ben eyed the disarray of his father's workspace and huffed a breath.

"How did I fail to notice your mess?" he asked aloud. Being there with Hugo earlier, he barely saw anything except the vein bulging from the other man's forehead.

It would be harder to find anything useful than he thought.

Still, he was there and he was determined. Ben piled every strewn bit of paper together and separated the stack into groups. They were the first papers he'd managed to get his hands on, and of course, none of them seemed unusual at first glance. It was in the third pile that he noticed what he deemed 'out of the ordinary.' There was a short stack of written receipts with the same names scrawled in his father's handwriting: Hugo Marchand and Arnaud Cuvilyé.

Ben skimmed the receipts—a few simple purchases, some older than others, though there were a few that were new. One in particular stood out: a large purchase of wine, but the transaction was incomplete. There was a considerable amount of money lost to the sellers: Marchand and Cuvilyé.

So, Marchand was telling the truth. They really were in business together...

The receipts were damning, and he could hardly blame Hugo for being angry over the loss. Still, it would be impossible to pay either of the men back in full—at least, not for quite a long time. His father should have warned them before negotiating any terms. The Leones were bordering on broke.

His father borrowed money from his cousins from time to time to keep up with the small staff they kept, but never enough to get into bed with any businesses—or partners, for that matter. Ben leaned back in the chair and rubbed his eyes. He wanted to know about Soleil, not about his father's business deals.

Why can't it just be easy? He wondered lamely, catching the look in his mother's painted eyes above the mantelpiece.

She was an inquisitive woman, and the artist had captured that in perfect detail. But the subtle quirk of her lips meant something different to him now, as though her portrait had something to hide, too. He wondered if she knew about her husband, if she was the true keeper of his secrets and not the papers on his untidy desk.

"If only portraits could speak." He yawned, his eyes fluttering shut. Her gaze never left him as he faded into sleep. "You would tell me the truth."

LATE NIGHT ENCOUNTER

REMI

Someone was watching her; she felt a presence as she slept.

Remi's eyes peeled open slowly, adjusting to the darkness. The familiar outline of her bed came into focus, followed by the armoire and the fireplace beside it. Embers shone on the hearth. A chill ran down her spine as the door of her bedroom creaked softly behind her, a breeze washing across her back.

Something loomed in the doorway, unmoving.

Remi trembled, afraid to roll over and look. She pressed her fingers to her eyes as every muscle in her body wound painfully with the fear blooming inside of her.

Go away, she thought. *Please, just go.*

Footsteps sounded on the floor, moving farther and farther away. Remi dropped her hands from her eyes and sat up quickly. No one was there, but the door had been pushed open. She flew to her feet, clutching her hands close together as she crept into the hall.

Not far from where she stood was the outline of a person.

It moved, slipping around the corner. Footsteps echoed on the stairs, one by one and Remi followed slowly behind, careful to avoid any loose floorboards. It waited for her on the landing between floors, moving before she could make out a face. It watched, waiting, just as it had at her bedroom door.

The shadow turned down the hall toward Edgar's study. Her breath caught in her throat as the faint line of a golden light sprawled across the darkness. The curtained window at the end of the hall gave off enough light to lend itself to the silhouette, and Remi's eyes burned with tears of sadness and fear.

"Edgar?" Remi's voice was barely above a whisper.

She inched closer as his white eyes trained on her.

Before, when she had seen him, moths had crawled out of his mouth.

Now he only watched her, unblinking.

What could he want?

Edgar turned back to the doors in front of him and walked through them. His silhouette and his footsteps disappeared as they breached the study's doors. Remi tiptoed after him, closer to the burning golden light. For a brief moment, she felt as if her mind was unraveling. *How could Edgar be there? Was this how Ben felt, chasing after his sister's visage in the rain?* Remi peeked inside the study through a crack.

She swallowed, took the handles, and pushed them down lightly.

They clicked.

Inside there was a fire and lit oil lamps, but Edgar was nowhere to be found. In his place, asleep at his father's desk, was Ben. She thought to turn back and return to her room, but Edgar had led her there for a reason. Quietly, Remi inched inside and approached the desk with as light a foot as she could manage.

Ben snored softly, his expression gentle, unmarred by the lines of his typical scowl. She could have watched him sleep all night, but the door slammed shut behind her. She screamed and jumped backward into the desk, toppling onto Ben's lap and startling him awake.

With a loud thud, they landed on the hardwood floor.

BEN

As a boy, Ben loved to play on the beach below the house. There was a set of old stairs that had been built into the cliff's side a long time ago by his great, great grandfather. His mother warned him to exercise caution and often reprimanded his father for not having them fixed sooner. They had tried to keep him from the beach by blocking off the stairs, but he always found a way down. Ben proved to be too smart and too fiercely determined to be kept away from his special hideaway.

In his opinion, the beach was the best place for thinking. And after his mother's passing, he disappeared there more often, exchanging solemn grieving for long hours of thinking. That suited him just fine.

Soleil would join him in the days before they'd lost their mother. She'd sit on a picnic blanket and read one of her novels. Sometimes Martin, the cook, would surprise them with a packed basket for lunch. Then those days were gone. Ben was ten, and Soleil was seventeen. Her interests changed, and she spent less time with him and more time in her room. It was rare to see her anywhere outside, even at supper. She was a recluse.

Their duet became a solo act, leaving Ben alone.

Thankfully, Martin still packed a basket for lunch, and Ben brought the tattered remains of Soleil's old blanket along with him. Sometimes, he brought a book just to keep his mind sharp. His father's study grew more and more, the once-empty shelves filled with books on everything from insects to botany. Picking out a book was as much time as Ben ever spent with him anymore; their short discussions on his reading habits became somewhat of a comfort.

Still, nothing was ever the same. Each of them grieved in their own ways, yet Ben was the first to surface from it. Then, on one particularly chilly day by the beach, he welcomed an unexpected visitor.

"What are you reading?" a small, soft voice crooned from behind him.

Startled, Ben dropped his snack and book into the wet sand. He grumbled as he picked them up, stopping short when he found himself face to face with a girl he didn't recognize.

"I'm so sorry," the girl said quickly. She stood a few feet away, her hands clutched at her chest, her bright eyes gleaming.

"You shouldn't sneak up on people." Ben felt his face redden, flushed from embarrassment.

"I didn't mean to." She appeared hurt by the accusation. "You just looked lonely, and I thought it would be nice to say hello."

Ben sucked in a breath and sighed deeply. "I suppose it's alright, so long as you don't do it again."

"I promise!" A little grin pulled at her lips and her eyes flashed with excitement. Though there was little sunshine, Ben noted right away their peculiar shade as they blinked between blue and green— much like the ocean around the island. He could have sworn they were little oceans themselves.

I've been reading too much of Soleil's poetry, he thought. "Well then, who are you, and where did you come from?"

"The stairs," she said with a spark of mischief.

He rolled his eyes. "That doesn't answer either of my questions."

"I asked you a question first." She pointed at his now sand-covered book.

Ben glanced down, having entirely forgotten about his ruined snack and book. He wiped the latter on his trousers. "Some entomological journal by an obscure author."

"Entomology?"

"Bugs."

The girl made a face. "I don't like bugs much, but I think butterflies are lovely."

"It's interesting." Ben ran a hand over the cover. "I can identify three different types of beetles now, more than I could before."

Skeptical, she tilted her head. "How many could you identify before?"

"None," Ben said plainly. "Now, who are you, and where are you from? You did not magically appear from nowhere."

"My name is Remi," she said. "I only just arrived on the Isle, and my uncle said there were children near-about, so I went off to explore."

"Alone?"

As if on cue, a pair of voices called out her name. Ben begrudgingly sat his book down and stood. Two more children approached—the Cuvilyé girl who lived at the bottom of the hill and a thin boy.

The girl shrieked, "Remi! I'm going to tell Maman you ran off!"

"Oh no," Remi muttered, turning back to face Ben. "My Tante Beline is dreadful."

If she meant Beline Cuvilyé, then he understood immediately. Elise stomped down the rickety steps, the boy following close behind. Ben watched them as Remi left him to greet them.

"You can't wander off alone!" the dark-haired girl said.

"I'm sorry, Elise," Remi said sheepishly. "I had a magnificent time exploring, though. You see, I walked all this way by following the sound of the water and came to this beach. I stumbled upon this boy, and he told me that he knew every bug on the island just from reading a book! Isn't that fascinating?"

Elise peered over Remi's shoulder. A red blush spread across her cheeks as the boy behind her, a head taller, waved with a quick "Hello."

Ben nodded politely.

"We aren't supposed to be here!" Elise hissed under her breath.

"Really? But why not?" Remi pushed out her bottom lip. "I've just made a friend, Elise. He has a picnic, *and* he reads!"

Ben was startled by her liberal use of the word "friend" but did not correct her. Part of him liked the title. He hadn't had a friend in a long time, perhaps ever.

His closest friend was Soleil—and sometimes Martin.

I don't think adults count, though, he thought.

Remi dragged Elise over to Ben. "This is my friend. He knows about beetles and other bugs."

"Ben," he said without thinking. "My name is Ben."

Unfazed by his informality, Remi grinned. "Lovely to know you, Ben."

"We're going to be in trouble if Maman finds us here," Elise said, ignoring him altogether.

The boy behind her moved past the girls as they chattered and held out a dirty hand. He was mussed and thin, quite the opposite of the polished, put-together Remi and Elise. "I'm Guillaume."

Ben shook his hand.

"Elise, please! I don't want to go just yet," Remi shouted, drawing the boys' attention. Elise was halfway back to the stairs when Ben spoke up.

"You won't be in trouble. The land here is ours," he said. He pointed toward the manor at the top of the cliff, almost smiling when Remi's eyes widened with genuine awe.

There was something easy about her that reminded him of his mother. Her presence was calming, if not absolute in its ability to offer comfort and companionship in the most stagnant silence.

Ben's silence had been edging toward stagnant for the last few months.

"You must be a prince, then." Remi looked down at the abandoned book and cracked another smile. Ben could not help himself and smiled back when she said, "A prince that reads about bugs and eats bread on a beach."

"And knows three types of beetles," he added. "Don't forget that."

Remi scrunched her features humorously at the mention of beetles and shivered. Guillaume and Elise, inched closer, drawn in by Remi's unerring friendliness. Ben supposed that was what made her so easy to be around.

"Remi is my cousin," Elise said. "She's living with my family now."

"Pleasure to meet you all," Ben said, glancing at the other two, but unable to stray for too long from Remi's cheerful grin.

"Then we are all friends!" Remi clapped. "I'm so happy to have friends. We'll have so many adventures."

Ben had believed her, too. For a time, they'd all played together, and the cloud left behind by his mother's loss had moved on, only to be replaced by the great loss of his sister. Then their adventures ceased as he was shipped away to relatives overseas.

He never imagined, after being gone for so long and harboring his anger for so many years, that Remi would once again fall right into his lap—literally. He rubbed the back of his head as he gathered himself up from the floor, wincing at the pain in his stomach where her elbow rammed into him. Twice now, she'd knocked him awake; the only difference was that he wasn't sleepwalking off the edge of the moors in the middle of a storm this time.

"I'm so terribly sorry," she said for the twentieth time. "Did I hurt you?"

"I'm fine," he repeated. "My limbs are all intact."

"I can't apologize to you enough."

Ben groaned. "You can, and you have."

Remi pressed her lips together, the red in her cheeks deepening. Ben lifted himself from the ground and offered his hand. She took it, letting him pull her to her feet.

"You're not in bed," he casually remarked.

"Neither are you."

"I needed a change of scenery." It was the truth. His room felt stuffy, and he was too restless to sit beside a quiet fire all night. "Lost track of time, though, and fell asleep. Why are you awake?"

"I came for a book," she lied.

If only to humor her, Ben gestured to the shelves.

"Do you have any recommendations?" she asked. She hunched forward as she mindlessly ran her slender fingers over the spines lined up neatly on each shelf. Some she pulled out, others she left hanging half-in from their resting places. *Something is troubling her.*

Ben crossed his arms. "Remi."

At the sound of her name, she turned back around. "Hm?"

"Do you really want to read?" Ben moved closer to where she stood.

She tensed. He might have enjoyed her reaction, but the lilac depressions beneath her eyes concerned him.

"Or are you here for something else?"

"What do you mean?"

"I can tell you're lying," he began, vaguely gesturing to the dark oak bookcases. "You're mindlessly tearing books from the shelves without any regard for titles. You're clearly distracted."

The way she frowned pricked at him. She looked confused, and yet —there was some understanding in her expression. She was more than just distracted; she was hiding something.

"Are you trying to find clues?" he pushed without thinking.

"Clues? To what?"

He gritted his teeth. "My father's money. The treasure he left us."

"Ben," she tried, her face pale. "No. That's not—"

"Then why are you in here?" he demanded. "What are you hiding? What is it that you won't say?"

For a moment, her bottom lip trembled, as if her delicate porcelain mask of composure would shatter into a thousand irreparable pieces. But then it was gone; she was changed. Remi straightened her back, dropped her hands from her chest, and held them fisted at her sides.

"Are you quite finished?" she spat in a tone that he hadn't expected. After the slightest pause, as if she were considering whether or not she should speak the words she wanted to, she continued. "Are you quite finished being such...such an insufferable *ass?*"

Ben scowled. "I haven't even started."

Remi's face turned an angry red. A sea of pent-up frustration roared between them. Too many questions unanswered, too many feelings unresolved. The waves crashed against the walls they'd built up against each other.

"I don't understand you!" she finally cried. "One minute, you're angry with me, and the next you're kind, almost sweet. *Why?*"

Her question broke the damn. Ben opened his mouth, and the words rolled off his tongue easily, tasting in equal parts like honey and vinegar. Honey, for the relief they brought; vinegar for the regret that instantly stung. He couldn't take them back.

LOVER'S QUARREL

REMI

"Because you married my father," he snarled, backing her into the shelf, "and I loathe you for it. I loathe myself for being jealous of him."

Remi cringed. The hurt in his voice and the pain in his crumpled expression pierced her heart like a dagger. With fists at her side, she held her ground as Ben unleashed his wrath.

"And then there was your letter," he said, trembling with anger. "Can you imagine for a moment how it felt to receive a formal announcement of your engagement to my *father* weeks after you'd begged me to come home? The first correspondence I'd received in over a decade, and both ripped me apart."

Remi pressed her lips together. She remembered her own words well enough that she could still smell the fresh ink as it soaked into the parchment.

"Do you know what that fucking invitation did to me?" His voice cracked, raw, and almost pleading. "Seeing your name next to his—I thought I'd dreamt it all, but a week went by, and I realized it was true. My father's cousins even sent you gifts! *Gifts!* I burned your letter and the invitation. I couldn't stand another day knowing you'd played me."

"Played you?" she asked tightly.

"Don't pretend, not when I know the truth." He leaned in, his face closer to hers. The lines of his frustration cut deep into his skin. "I almost came for you."

Remi's eyes widened, sparkling with fresh tears. "You did?"

"You have no idea how I yearned to come home." He bared his teeth and hissed at her through them. "And then you married him, and I wanted to die."

"Ben…" Her own voice cracked.

He looked miserable. "When I saw you again, standing on the steps outside *my* home, I knew I had made the wrong choice. I should have come home."

She swallowed. He had wanted to come home. More than that, he almost came for her. Her letter had moved him more than she thought, and with that realization, she was undone. Her heart beat so hard in her chest, she could feel it in her ears.

Their eyes met, trapped in each other's gaze for a few breathless moments. Remi reached up to stroke his cheek; his shoulders sagged as he turned his face into her palm, the warmth of his lips sending a ripple of desire through her body. She sighed as a hand circled her elbow, the other sinking from the wall to hover beside her waist. Ben inched his face along her hand, brushing the tip of his nose along her wrist. A whimper escaped her throat, catching his attention. He looked at her, his dark eyes burning with an unspoken passion.

Remi licked her lips, and Ben surged forward, capturing her mouth with his own. The air left her lungs. His kiss was unlike anything she had ever imagined.

His petal-soft lips moved against hers, teeth nipping at her lips until she parted them enough to feel his tongue. The quietest sigh escaped her, and he moved against her, one hand grabbing the fabric at her waist and bunching it in his fist at her side. His other hand slid to her back, starting a fire across the skin of her shoulders where he tugged at the neckline of her nightdress. At the same time, his leg moved between her knees, the heat at her center building to an unfamiliar ache.

I want more, she thought in ecstasy. *More, more, more.*

Just as Remi pressed her hips into his thigh, Ben stilled, pulling away. The suddenness of his retreat left her spinning, and she drew in a steadying breath.

"I'm sorry," Ben said, out of breath as he dropped his forehead to her shoulder. "I shouldn't have... I should have asked."

Remi felt her heart in her throat. "Don't apologize."

"It wasn't right," he stammered. "You're a widow now."

"I didn't want to marry your father," she said abruptly. "But I did. I thought it was my responsibility to my family, and I didn't want to disappoint them."

Ben raised his head. She couldn't make sense of his expression, but she also couldn't stop herself once the words started forming.

"But I...I also wrote you that letter. That was my choice, too."

"Did you mean any of it?"

Remi grasped his arm. "Yes. Every word."

Ben was silent, a thoughtful look on his face.

"I married your father—out of duty and respect for my family," Remi breathed and lifted her chin a fraction in defiance. "I regret it with every day that goes by, but I won't have you condemn me for my actions, not when I tried so hard to bring you back."

"Duty and respect," he scoffed. "How noble of you."

"Yes," she insisted, hating the way he spoke to her but wishing he would kiss her again. "I owe a debt to my family, and marrying Edgar was part of that reparation."

"And you paid for it with your body."

Remi shoved Ben, though he did not budge. "I paid for it with my *life!*"

"Whores do the same," Ben said.

"Stop it," Remi spat, full of indignation. "No one has ever touched me without my consent, least of all your father."

Ben's lips pressed into a thin line.

"I won't be your villain," she paused. "Not when I want to be your friend."

"And how do you expect to be my friend? You have no idea what it was like for me to be...*exiled*... I'm but a stranger in the home I grew up in."

"We talk. However painful that might be, however, it might hurt us, we talk and we try to understand each other." *And maybe kiss again,* she wanted to add because she desperately wanted to. She wanted that and more.

The wrinkle between Ben's brows deepened. "Is that so?"

She took his hand and held it, palm up. When his fingers finally curled around hers, she spoke. "You've been so honest and I've hurt you. I can see that now."

"I don't like secrets." He sounded exasperated, as if burdened by too many already.

"And I have none." She reached for his chin and held his eyes with her own. "Except this, and that is the reason why I am here. It's why I cannot deny anything asked of me."

He blinked, waiting for what came next.

"I am not my father's daughter."

～

REMI, 1879

On her seventh birthday, Remi's papa bought her a pair of custom silk ballet shoes. They weren't anything like what the ballerinas wore at the opera house, though, for she was too small to dance pointe. Still, they were pink and perfect. Above all other things, Remi considered them her most prized possession. The day she found the box on her bed was the day she condemned her beautiful dolls to a lonesome corner in the playroom, clearing the floor for her to imitate the dances she saw on stage.

"Beautiful." Her father praised her at breakfast. "*Ma petite,* you will put all other ballerinas to shame."

It was the highest compliment he could have paid her.

Her father always doted on her, humored her at the best of times, and spoiled her endlessly. He could never bring himself to say 'no' to her, though he tried.

"The girls will be delighted," her mother announced. They would be visiting the opera house for an early rehearsal, and Remi intended to wear her new ballet shoes.

The other performers, particularly the ballerinas, enjoyed Remi's loveliness and childlike wonder as she 'ooed' and 'ahhed' from the audience. Sometimes, they even taught her the steps, despite how difficult the footwork could be at times. With her new shoes, it would be easier than ever.

"A lark!" They said when they saw her.

"What pretty shoes for a *jolie fille*."

Remi drank up their compliments with great aplomb. The visits to the opera house were the highlights of her youth. She loved to watch the performances and the practices that led up to them. That morning, while her father attended to business and her mother worked on scales and final fittings, Remi was left in the care of the *corps de ballet*.

"Mademoiselle Manon will look after you for me, *ma cherie*," her mother instructed.

Then the director, Monsieur Deschamps, appeared and walked away with her mother. Remi liked him. He'd always been kind to her, spared a smile or two, and favored her mother the way her father did.

Not to mention he often snuck sweets into her waiting hands.

"Come along then!" Manon, the ballerina from the corps, clapped. "Let's break in those new shoes of yours."

For what seemed like hours, Remi danced along with the girls in the wings. They were all graceful dancers, thin and tall, as they swayed elegantly to whatever tune was played on the piano.

"I wish to be like you when I am older." Remi had said to Manon during a break.

"Me, *ma petite*? You could be a star, like your *maman*."

Remi's eyes widened at that. It was impossible. "My papa says that she is one of a kind."

"And so she is." Manon agreed.

The other dancers stirred from their spots on the floor, and Remi's feet ached with the idea of moving again. She pulled at Manon before the music started.

"Could we play a game of hide and seek?" Remi asked.

Manon laughed, sensing Remi's hesitance to continue dancing. *"Absolument!"*

They wandered away from the stage to the space behind the red velvet curtains, which better suited Remi's needs. She liked the extra doors of the dressing rooms and the colorful costumes that hid behind the curtains. There were many places to hide away where one as little as Remi could not be easily found.

"Un, deux, trois, quatre..." Manon counted, turning away from Remi as she fled.

Running backstage, Remi dove deeper and deeper until the sound of Manon's voice could no longer be heard above the racket of the stagehands. She jumped from room to room until one door stood open. Running inside, she hid in the corner behind the skirts of hanging costumes. They were large and billowy enough to cover her. A little space between the dresses gave Remi a perfect hole for peeping.

I am so clever, she thought, covering her mouth to keep from laughing. *Manon will never find me here.*

A beat passed before any footsteps were heard.

Here she comes, Remi thought delightedly.

But it was not Manon. She was surprised to see her mother and the director. The weariness in her mother's figure was evident, and there was a strain on her face that had not been there earlier. Remi would have jumped out but was too afraid that her mother would be furious.

"I'm tired, Claude," her mother said with a sigh.

The director, Monsieur Deschamps, ran a hand over his silver-blonde hair as he closed the door behind him. "Shall I move the date again?"

"No!" her mother said quickly, seizing his hands.

Remi watched, confused.

"I only need a rest. Perhaps a day to gather my wits."

"Do you still plan to leave him?" Claude asked. He pressed a very gentle kiss to her fingers, watching her with an odd softness that Remi only ever saw in her father.

"I want to…"

"But?"

A sob bubbled out of her mother as she crumpled into his arms. He wrapped her in an embrace, hushing her as quietly as he could.

"I am with child again."

A baby sister? Remi felt giddy at the notion. She already had two brothers, one two years younger than her, the other still a baby. They were both with their nurses at home, too young to be brought along. Remi liked them, but they were not little girls, and she so dearly wanted a sister.

"Is it his?" the director asked, his voice pinched.

"You know it is, Claude."

"And the boys?"

Her mother sobbed woefully. "How can I leave them?"

"We bring them with us," the man said, forcing her mother to look at him. The determination in his expression was fierce and intimate. "And the girl, Remi, too."

Her mother was quiet for a moment longer, silent in her contemplation. "She is yours, Claude. The only one that has ever been yours."

"I know, *mon amour.*" A smile spread on his lips, but Remi did not understand. She belonged to her Papa and her Mama, *not* to Monsieur Deschamps. An icky feeling spread throughout her, blooming from her like a bad stomach ache. Remi did not like the way the man held her mother or the way her mother held him. Before she could understand the depths of their betrayal, her mother kissed Monsieur Deschamps.

It was not a chaste kiss.

Maman? Remi thought, tears in her eyes. *What about Papa?*

She could not keep herself from watching as their hands wandered, kisses exchanged in a heat that seven-year-old Remi could not describe. She was utterly petrified, unable to make her feet move or her voice work.

"Remi? *Ma petite*, please come out!"

Manon? Remi's eyes snapped to the door.

"Where are you, Remi? Please come out," the ballerina called again, a tremor of fear in her voice. A knock at the door caused her mother to jump away from Monsieur Deschamps. "I do not mean to disturb, Madame Cuvilyé, but your daughter has disappeared."

"What do you mean? You cannot find her?" Remi's mother pulled open the door. "Where could she have gone?"

The director composed himself quickly. He quieted her mother and led them out into the hall. His voice was reassuring. "We will find her, Madame. She could not have gone far."

When they were gone, Remi pried herself unsteadily from her hiding spot.

She wandered out into the hall, a mess. Her dress was dusty and had snagged on something, and her hair was matted to her cheeks where tears had fallen. She did not feel like herself, and even when her mother found her and scolded her, she did not feel the anger as deeply as she should have. It rolled off of her like a wave against a sturdy rock.

"What is wrong with her?" her father asked.

"She is tired."

Remi would have argued, but she did not know how to say her heart was broken. Later, when they were all home and settled in, Remi's mind wandered back to the dressing room. In bed, she tossed and turned, her body too hot as sweat clung to her skin and nightdress. She felt sick and dizzy. Climbing out of bed, she searched the house for anyone still awake. It was the smell of cigar smoke that brought her to the parlor. Her father was surprised to find her awake at such a late hour.

"*Ma petite?* You should be sleeping."

"Papa? Am I leaving?" Her voice broke as tears sprang from her tired eyes. Alarmed, her father hurried over and tried to calm her. "I don't want to leave you, Papa!"

"No, *ma petite*. Whoever said such a thing?"

"Monsieur Deschamps," she cried, bubbling with more tears. "He told Mama to bring all of us."

The cigar tumbled from her father's lips, his face twisting into a monstrous grimace. He lunged from his chair and grabbed at Remi's shoulders, shaking her. "What? What did you say?"

"Papa, you're hurting me!" she cried.

He let go of her arms but kept a grasp on one of her hands. In a rush of rage, he dragged her up the stairs with him and burst into the bedroom where her mother sat, brushing her hair. A look of sheer horror crossed her mother's face. "Bernard, what are you doing?"

"I knew it!" he shouted. "All this time! You let that little *enfoiré* touch you, you whore!"

Her mother's mouth fell agape, and she tore her gaze from him to Remi. Confusion marred her stricken face.

"Don't look at her!" Remi's father crossed to her mother, cupping her jaw with one hand as he tilted it violently backward. She nearly fell from her stool, uttering a choked cry.

"Tell me the truth. Is she mine?"

"Bernard..." her mother croaked, tears spilling down her face.

Remi trembled at the door, unsure what to do. Her father was a frightening thing to behold as he carried on shouting at her mother.

"Tell me who it is, Alain!" Remi's father shouted. His voice boomed like drums being struck in a concerto. "Is it Deschamps? Is he her father?"

"Please, Bernard." Her mother begged, sparing a pleading glance at Remi. "Not in front of her."

Remi's father twisted, unmoved by the plea. He bared his teeth like an animal. "Perhaps you should have thought about that before you conspired to leave me!"

Her mother's eyes widened. "How could you know that?"

"She was there, Alain! The little bastard girl heard it all," he screamed.

Remi's mother, horrified, found her again. "What have you done?"

Her father gripped her mother's shoulders, and she swiped at him, wriggling to try and escape across the bed. Her father was quick, though, and grasped her ankles. He climbed atop her mother's flailing body and pinned her in place.

A sob ripped through Remi's throat as warmth trickled down her legs. *"Papa, stop!"* she cried. Over and over again, she begged, but her little voice could not abate her father's harsh words.

"You bitch!" he shouted. "You won't leave me! I'll kill him before he can take what's mine, do you understand?"

Her mother said nothing, sobbing.

Eventually, someone came to her rescue. Kind hands found Remi and pulled her from the room as one of the maids closed the door. The sound of their heated voices did not leave her, not even as she bathed and changed out of her soiled nightgown. Her father was loud —louder than she'd ever heard him. His fury rattled Remi to her core. It was a side of him she'd never seen before, and his horrible expression of hate stayed with her throughout the night.

The screaming, the anger—it followed her into a tortured slumber. She knew that nothing would ever be the same.

STARTING OVER

BEN

*B*en's anger abandoned him. Instead, he felt disgusted—not just with her story, but with himself. Her family abandoned her. Left adrift across a channel to live with a family that never truly felt like family.

"My father never treated me the same after that," Remi added meekly. "He couldn't even look at me, so my governess was compensated generously to keep me away from him—*and* my mother. At least until he could arrange to have me sent here."

"What happened to Monsieur Deschamps?" Ben asked.

"He was found dead a week later, floating in the Seine."

Ben cringed as he imagined a bloated corpse with the same color hair as Remi's and, for a moment, saw her dead in the water. It was clear that Bernard Cuvilyé was quite capable of avenging his dignity, even if it meant murder.

"My brothers are grown now, and my mother gave birth to a little girl," Remi said, cutting into his bleak thoughts. "She gave birth to two more girls after that, too. They're both lovely little things. My old governess used to send me their photos, but she stopped when my uncle found out."

"What about your mother?"

Remi deflated at the mention of her mother. "I wrote to her about the wedding. She was happy to hear it, I suppose. She sent me pearls."

He was surprised she'd even heard from her mother. "But nothing from your father?"

She shook her head.

"What a coward," Ben snarled.

"Can you blame him?" Remi asked. "I cannot imagine how it hurt him to learn the truth."

Even so, it did not excuse her father's reaction, Ben thought. "And Arnaud?"

"My uncle? He was welcoming enough. He certainly did not have to take me in." Remi turned from the bookcases and wandered to one of the armchairs close to the fire. Ben followed her, leaning against the mantle as she sat. He could not bring himself to sit yet.

"Then why did he?"

"For the money, I suppose." Remi shrugged, watching the fire. She pulled her knees up to her chest. "My uncle received a stipend each month worth a generous sum for my care. Rather than disown me publicly, he'd been gracious enough to keep it quiet for the family's benefit."

Hush money, Ben thought. It had nothing to do with graciousness and everything to do with the cost of her upkeep. To Ben, it seemed that Arnaud cared little for family and held it over his brother in order to keep the money coming in. It was doubtful Remi ever saw a penny of it; something told him the money wasn't hers to spend.

"I still think your father is a coward."

Remi stilled.

"To simply throw you away," Ben closed his eyes, thinking back to the beach and the day he'd met her. "I cannot fathom it, Remi."

"I do understand fathers to some degree," she said gently. "I wasn't aware that Edgar never wrote to you."

"It's in the past now."

How hard it must have been for her to move elsewhere, to become someone else entirely to people who were not really family. Her worth was a stipend, and no matter what the sum was, her value somehow depreciated because of her parentage, through no fault of her own.

That sounds familiar, doesn't it? A voice in the back of Ben's mind taunted.

"You must believe what I said before to be true," she pleaded. "I did not want to marry your father, but in a way, he gave me freedom. It was a kind gesture."

"An arranged marriage is hardly freedom," Ben said, a bit too harshly.

Remi did not flinch. "I know what my life would look like now if I had fought my uncle. Doubtless I would have become a maid, left to polish Beline's silver."

"Could Elise not have brought you on as her personal maid?" He was reaching, he knew; to even suggest such a thing felt insensitive to her feelings. Immediately, he regretted asking.

"Elise will be leaving the Isle once she's married." Remi paused, suddenly drained of color. "She says New York, perhaps, but I could never be so lucky as to accompany her. My uncle would never allow it, and I shudder to think what might happen to me if the man I called my father ever learned that I left this place."

"I would never let him hurt you," Ben said fiercely, drawing her attention back to him.

She smiled a little at that. "Perhaps not now, but you're only here *because* I didn't fight my uncle. We would be passing strangers in a large crowd if we were still living our lives as they were before all of this." Her head tilted as she spoke, exposing the soft curve where her neck dipped into her shoulder. The ruff of her nightgown hid the secret shape of the collarbone beneath.

Ben squeezed his hands tightly at his sides as he fought the desire to lean in and breathe in the scent of her skin. The need to dispose of her nightdress altogether grew the longer her eyes lingered on his.

"You're right." Finally, Ben sought out a seat and sank into it easily. He tried to focus his mind on places less tempting than the shoulder of her nightdress. "Still, if you wanted to leave, I would not stop you from going."

"And live with a newlywed Elise?" The surprise in her tone was enough to make him second-guess the offer.

"No. I suppose that wouldn't benefit anyone." Ben tried to imagine Remi managing Elise. In his mind, her cousin became Beline, and that was a fate he would not wish on his worst enemy.

"In hindsight," Remi said, "my predicament isn't so awful. Your father was kind, even if our arrangement was a bit unusual."

"Unusual?" Ben asked.

"I never..." Remi's voice trailed off. "....*we* never..."

"Please." A blush crept up Ben's neck and spread across his cheeks. Quickly, he covered his face with his hands, scrubbing at his eyes. "There's no need to explain."

"I don't mind," she said. "He made it clear to me that his heart still belonged to your mother."

"My mother," Ben repeated. He felt the painting's eyes call to him, scolding as they peered down for being so callous. He smiled inwardly at the idea of his mother meeting the current Madame.

"I always thought she was a beautiful lady," Remi mused aloud, drawing his attention back to her. "Edgar once said you looked like him in his youth, but I think you are your mother's son."

Ben liked that she thought he looked like his mother. He didn't hear it enough, at least not as much as he would have liked. He might have had his father's build, the same cut of his jaw and his inscrutable nose, but his mother's distant Romani heritage held strong. He had her dark hair and the same warm complexion.

"My father doted on her when she was alive." Ben slid his gaze from the portrait to Remi, focusing on the curve of her ear and the way she tucked her hair behind it. "I suppose that's one thing we have in common."

"What's that?" Remi chuckled lightly.

Ben smirked, raking a hand through his hair. He held her gaze with purpose as he spoke. "He and I are perilously drawn to beautiful things."

A light blush crept across Remi's pale cheeks.

She shied away, turning her face into her shoulder. "You tease me too much."

"Perhaps I do."

"But I don't hate it," she admitted, her ears red.

"Then prepare yourself." His voice deepened. "I shall find every opportunity to do so more often."

"I won't make it easy."

"I don't expect you will," Ben hummed, pleased by her feisty reply. He enjoyed the thought of teasing her more. It stoked a fire in him that he felt when they kissed. Though he was more than satisfied by the image of her flushed cheeks, he would not mind if his teasing led to more fevered kisses in the middle of the night.

"I wish for us to be friends again." Remi yawned as she curled up in her chair.

Ben snuck a glance at the grandfather clock, suddenly realizing how late it was. He moved to fetch her a blanket from a chest pushed away in a corner.

"Friends," he repeated, draping the blanket across her body.

"Do you think it's possible?" Her eyes were heavy with more than sleep. It undid him in a small way to see her so hopeful, yet sad.

"Would that make you happy?"

"Yes. It would please me greatly." She nodded, her eyes fluttering.

"Then we are friends, Remi." He didn't realize until then how much he missed her friendship. The years lay between them, but he knew it would be easy to pick up where they'd left off.

After a beat, the sound of rain pattering against the windows of the study pulled Ben's attention back to the present. A smile lifted Remi's pink lips just before she dozed off. She was the picture of comfort as she cozied her chin to her chest, sinking into the seat cushion. It was sweet how easily she faded, and he was afraid to wake her.

I guess then, he glanced up at the portrait of his mother, *you and I will be watching over her tonight.*

Ben returned to his father's desk and continued his search among old papers to the rise and fall of her soft breathing until his eyes, too, felt heavy.

BLOATED

BEN

Two hours after he'd collapsed into bed, Ben woke up in terrible pain.

Spending most of the night in his father's study proved to be a terrible decision. His back and buttocks ached; he immediately blamed the stiff chair and its poor stuffing. After Remi dozed off into a peaceful slumber, he followed, woken a short time later by a loud popping from the fire in the hearth. Carrying Remi to bed after that might have made it worse, but she was light and easy to carry, and after her story, he felt the weight of his burdened heart lift.

She was telling the truth; he should have recognized that sooner.

"Knock, knock," Jacques announced loudly, barging into the room with a steaming mug and small plate.

Ben narrowed his eyes as he positioned himself upright.

"You look like shit." Jacques passed the mug to Ben. "You've looked better after binge drinking all night at the bordello. What happened?"

"I went to my father's study," Ben said as he took his first sip of the hot drink, grateful for the energy it might reward him, "and found nothing of value."

"Nothing?"

"There were a few receipts that piqued my interest, but they were small in nature." Ben finished the croissant in one bite and drank the coffee down quickly, unaffected by the heat. "I want to visit the lawyer this morning."

"Shall I accompany you?"

"Yes, I think so."

"I'll bring the carriage around," Jacques said as he left.

Ben tidied himself quickly, exchanging his wrinkled garments for a freshly pressed shirt, and arranged a silk ascot around his neck. After a sharp pull of his hand through tangled hair, he slipped on his boots and grabbed his frock coat before bounding down the stairs to the foyer.

The morning air was frigid from the rain, and Ben could see his breath as he raced toward the waiting carriage.

"What's this about then?" Jacques asked as Ben swung himself up into the seat next to him. He nudged the horses, and they started down the gravel road to the hill. "What did your findings prove?"

"We're nearly penniless," Ben stated, popping his collar to cover his ears. "Land rich, of course, but the money has all but dried up. There is some money from previous arrangements with my cousins, but nothing else. No more than what is necessary to keep up the house. "

"Does Madame know?"

"Doubtful," Ben said. He wondered if she was awake yet. "My father kept her in the dark about everything."

Their finances must have been why he'd been let go from the Institute of Medicine in Paris. It wasn't enough to get in on good terms or from personal relations with a few of the instructors; there needed to be money. His cousins could not afford to further his education without leaving his father destitute. He could have saved any earnings he made, but unfortunately, Ben never kept a dime. Liquor and pretty prostitutes cost a great deal.

He cursed himself for allowing himself to sink so thoroughly into the gutter.

"But you said there was a treasure?" Jacques asked.

"A *lost* treasure," Ben corrected. "I have no idea where it might be; it's a family legend. If my father knew where it was, then I have to find the clue he left behind. He would have left one, I'm sure of it."

"There's a lot of mystery to your family."

"That's not all." Ben shivered. "My father entered into some sort of business and lost someone else's money. It was the reason for my meeting with Marchand at the wake."

"What a reckless thing to do." Jacques bowed his head. "The poor Madame."

Ben grunted his agreement. Remi was in for another shock. He would have to tell her the state of their finances, but before that, he needed to know exactly where they stood on the business end of things. Especially if what Hugo Marchand said was true and his father had already agreed terms. Ben pinched the bridge of his nose, determined to ignore the dull throb that started behind his eyes.

After getting lost and asking for directions, he was relieved when the carriage finally stopped in front of the lawyer's small shack of an office.

"Ben! What a surprise." Lamotte appeared starry-eyed and coated in a fine sheet of sweat when he swung the door open.

"I hope I'm not interrupting."

"Of course not! Come in, come in," He seemed amiable. "You must excuse my appearance. It's been a long morning."

"So it has," Jacques mumbled.

They could smell the alcohol on Lamotte. It was stale but still strong.

"What's your poison, Lamotte?" Ben asked, following the stout man to his desk.

"Red wine." He picked up a dark bottle as he sat and shook it. There was a splash inside, but it was small. "A gift, actually. Not very tasty, more pricey than I'd like, but it has quite a kick."

"Wine, you say?" Ben tried not to think about the connection, but the receipt he'd found last night was damning.

"Mm. A weakness of mine." He yawned, and his breath reached both Ben and Jacques.

Ben tried to mask his disgust. "I apologize for the intrusion."

"Nonsense! Nonsense." Lamotte waved him off jovially. "Your father and I were friends. I hope to honor our friendship through my relationship with you."

"I appreciate that." Ben nodded. "I do have some business with you today, if you could spare me a moment."

"Yes, I have some time. What's on your mind?" Lamotte smiled, eager to change the subject.

Ben leaned forward. "I came across a receipt among my father's papers. It was a large purchase made with no explanation." He paused before he continued. "A gentleman approached me the other day at my father's wake—Hugo Marchand. He claimed to have unfinished business with our family and demanded he be paid. I understand you are aware of our financial situation, *non?*"

Lamotte's eyes never left Ben's face. Despite his intoxication, he appeared sharp and focused. He seemed to grow more sober as Ben went on, nodding as the gears in his mind turned. Finally, he crossed his arms and leaned back in his chair.

"We don't have money, so I fail to see his ability to invest in anything," Ben said.

"That's not exactly true," Lamotte shrugged. "At least, not completely."

Ben stiffened. "What do you mean?"

Lamotte turned wordlessly to a drawer in his desk. He pulled it open and rifled through a few papers before producing a stack bound together in brown paper.

Ben looked between the stack and Lamotte, confused. "What's this?"

"An agreement," Lamotte said with a sigh. "Between Arnaud Cuvilyé, Bernard Cuvilyé, and Edgar Leone. It has to do with Madame Leone."

Ben straightened in his chair. "You mean Remi?"

"*Oui.*"

"May I see it?"

Lamotte ran a hand over the top, hesitant as he licked his wine-stained lips. "This is confidential."

"My father's name is on it," Ben snapped.

"So it is." Lamotte closed his eyes and sighed. "But there are two other names here as well."

Incensed by his reluctance, Ben lurched from his chair until he towered over the lawyer. Through bared teeth, he hissed, "I have inherited my father's estate. I have a right to these documents, Lamotte."

"As does Edgar's widow."

Remi? Of course. "So I must see to it that she is in agreement?"

"A written statement with her signature will do," Lamotte said, nodding. "Then I will release these documents to your care."

Defeated, Ben watched as the stack disappeared into an empty bottom drawer—different from where it was before. Lamotte picked a little key from his pocket and turned the mechanism with a click. When he found Ben watching, he swallowed.

"There is sensitive information contained within," he warned, but a sudden ruckus at the front door called their attention before Ben could respond.

"Monsieur Lamotte! Are you here?" Someone shouted in a panic as the door flew open.

At its threshold was a man about the same age as Lamotte, though he was dressed in workman's clothing and smelled of fish. He appeared shaken, his eyes large and unfocused as they flashed back and forth between the office and the street. Behind him, people hurried along.

Jacques shot Ben a look.

"Oh, hello, George," Lamotte said as he teetered around his desk. He crossed the room with Ben and Jacques close behind him. "What's happened? You look alarmed, my friend."

"There's a body at the dock!"

"Goodness," Lamotte gasped. "Shall I fetch the doctor then?"

"I hoped he was here." George sagged. "Will you find him?"

Intrigued, Ben offered, "I can go in his stead. Until you find him, of course."

Lamotte seemed surprised but did not stop either of them from going.

Ben hurried down the block, following the curiosity of a growing crowd. He quickened his pace as he approached the bodies packed tight into the streets leading to the dock. Forgetting his manners, he pushed and shoved his way through, ignoring snide remarks about his rudeness. Finally, he broke through, greeted by the acrid stench of death mixed with fish. It overwhelmed him, and he covered his nose and mouth with a kerchief.

The end of the cobbled street opened to the docks, where a body lay on the quay. The island wasn't anywhere near the size of Paris, so he wagered a guess that its residents rarely saw a body wash ashore, especially not one so bloated. Careful of his audience, Ben approached the corpse and knelt before anyone could object.

His education, it seemed, would not yet go to waste.

"Are you the doctor's apprentice?" a slight man in tattered clothes asked.

"No, not an apprentice. Just a student," Ben said as he surveyed the body. There was something oddly familiar about the blonde hair, but the swollen face distorted his features. "Were you the one who found him?"

"*Oui*, Monsieur," the man said. "Caught him in my fishing net."

Ben turned the head to the left and to the right, pulling down at the collar of the shirt just a fraction. Just when he decided it was a drowning, he noticed some unusual markings. He ran his hands over them once, studying the ridges and slight punctures.

He didn't drown.

"Oh, it's the doctor! Let him through," someone from the crowd shouted.

Ben reluctantly stood and stepped back from the body.

"Who is it?" the doctor asked no one in particular. Up close, he looked too old to still be in practice. Beside him, his apprentice appeared queasy.

The man who found him in his net hung his head and said with a light shake, "Leith Hersant. The miller's son."

Ben's jaw dropped. It was Remi's friend, the man he'd seen with her earlier.

"I don't think he drowned," Ben spoke up.

"Huh?" the doctor grumbled as if finally noticing him. "Who are you?"

"Benoît Leone, Monsieur."

"Oh, yes. The Leone boy." The doctor considered him. He didn't appear all that impressed; rather, it seemed Ben's presence put him off. "And tell me, what do you think happened?"

The whispers in the crowd shifted from Leith to Leone.

Ben ignored them, kneeling to point at Leith's bruised neck. "He was strangled."

"Interesting." The older man bent down, breathing what smelled like an entire cask of dubonnet in Ben's face. "Are you a doctor?"

"No," Ben said. "A student."

"Then you are no expert." The doctor breathed again, and Ben turned away, disgusted.

The doctor's apprentice brushed Ben aside to kneel beside Leith and shook his head. "Terrible news. They found him floating in the water by some of the boats."

Ben was forgotten as the young man regained the attention of the doctor.

"Ah." The doctor continued to stroke his beard, further irritating Ben. "Well, Leith was quite the lush. He must have been drinking nearby and fell in."

What about you? Ben thought with annoyance.

He opened his mouth to protest and point out what he'd seen, but a cry erupted from the crowd. A woman came barreling forward with tears falling down her face. A burly man followed closely behind her, and then a girl and two younger boys. They saw the body, and their faces full of raw pain. Ben contained himself and waited until the moment passed.

"You see," the doctor said as he shot Ben a hard look. "He drowned."

Ben squared himself in opposition but bit his tongue. A woman had stepped forward and bowed herself over Leith's body. The way she held Leith to her silenced him completely.

His mother. Ben thought.

Unable to offer any other help or explanation, Ben left the docks. It unsettled him to be written off so boldly, but there was nothing more he could do. The doctor might have been drunk, but he was right; Ben was no expert. His credibility on the subject would be questioned by everyone.

"We have a visitor." Jacques sneered when Ben found him waiting near the carriage. "Must have followed you from the docks."

Ben turned in time to catch Hugo a few feet behind. The gentleman looked even more irate than the day before.

"I'd like to have a word with you, Leone," he snarled.

"Afraid I don't have time to spare you." Ben shrugged, crossing his arms.

"What were you doing with Lamotte?"

Ben's brows drew together. "None of your damned business."

"I hope you're not trying to wiggle your way out of our agreement."

"I'm a man of my word." Ben shot him a hard look and sneered. "And once I have what I need from Lamotte, you'll have what's owed to you, *mon ami.*"

Hugo glared.

Ben took the opportunity to leave, joining Jacques again in the driver's seat.

"What a miserable morning," he said, scowling.

"Did I hear you correctly," Jacques asked, "about the body at the docks?"

"Indeed," Ben confirmed with a slight nod. "Besides the manner of death, what was even stranger was the doctor's response. He kept insisting the man had drowned."

Jacques grunted. "They're hiding something."

"Agreed." Ben's jaw ticked. "And it isn't just Lamotte and the doctor. There's obviously something going on here. And it starts with my family."

~

REMI

For the first time in several days, Remi woke feeling well-rested.

Aside from a minor crick in her neck, she felt spritely and rejuvenated. It was the first bout of energy she'd had in a long while, and she finished her breakfast with zeal. Not one crumb left behind, every bite savored. Some part of her felt it had everything to do with the night before. The chance encounter in the study had eased her worries greatly.

Of course, the kiss was just a bonus.

Her heart felt lighter, at peace with a part of herself.

Remi wandered out into the garden at the front of the manor and gathered a fresh bouquet of wisteria. The morning air was sticky with humidity, but a gentle breeze blew by every now and again to chase the discomfort away. Today offered a break in the storms, but no doubt, there would be one later in the evening. She rested on the bench, inhaling the rain-drenched floral scent when Sylvie called out to her.

"Madame? I hope I'm not interrupting."

"Not at all." Remi waved her over, overcome with worry when she noticed her maid's sickly, sweating appearance. "You look unwell, Sylvie. Are you alright?"

"I'm fine, Madame. The weather has been difficult," she said with a weak smile. "Thank you for your concern."

Remi hardly believed her but decided against an argument. "Then what brought you here?"

"A parcel arrived for you just now." Sylvie glanced at the bouquet in Remi's lap and nervously licked her lips. "Shall I put those in water for you?"

"If you don't mind, I'd like to do it myself."

"Of course."

"And the parcel?"

Sylvie blinked. "Inside, Madame. I left it in the parlor."

"Who is it from?" Remi asked as she stood, clutching her bouquet.

"I know not. It is unmarked, save for your name."

Remi followed her to the parlor, where a small parcel wrapped in brown paper waited on the table. It was the size of her palm, with her name written neatly across. Remi turned it around, curious as to its contents.

"Was there a letter?" Remi turned to Sylvie.

The maid appeared confused at first but gasped as she remembered it and quickly reached into her pocket. "I forgot," she admitted sheepishly.

"Thank you," Remi said as she took it, turning away. "Could you have Martin prepare some tea? I'm expecting company."

"Of course."

Alone with the letter, Remi pulled away the unmarked wax seal and withdrew a crisp sheet of paper. The writing was neater than its predecessor—each letter and word written with care. The blood in her veins went cold. She gripped at her chest as she read.

Dearest Remi,
My love...my pearl, my single white rose...you have stolen
my breath, my very heart, and so I have stolen yours.

"My heart?" Remi sucked in a breath, her fingers tightening around the parcel still in her grip. "They mean my locket."

Fear not, for I have sent it back to you as if new. My
Remi, I have bled for you now...all so that a part of me
will always be inside your heart. Keep me close, my dearest
love.

The letter fell from Remi's hands as she tore open the package. She dropped the contents to the floor, startled by a red-stained handkerchief with her initials hastily sewn into it. From the fabric, her locket loosened itself. It lay open on the ground, her own face staring back at her.

FLESH

REMI

Remi turned her nose up at the tea Sylvie brought for her. She couldn't stomach a single thing, and every time she tried, she emptied her stomach again. The bile at the back of her throat burned sour.

"When did this note first arrive?" Ben asked. He'd just returned from a trip into town, and as much as she wanted to ask him about it, she couldn't get him to change subjects.

"The first one? Edgar's wake," she admitted.

They had remained in the parlor, though Remi would have preferred to sit in any other room. It was the last place she had seen Edgar. *With moths crawling out of his mouth.* A trick of her imagination, but terrifying nonetheless.

"And the locket, with the handkerchief, arrived today?" Ben glanced at Sylvie, who shied away at his attention. "Who delivered it, Sylvie?"

"I don't know," she muttered.

"Was it left with you?"

Sylvie shook her head. "No."

Ben let out a sound of frustration, causing both women to flinch. He mumbled an apology and took a deep breath, finally kneeling beside the arm of Remi's chair. Taking her hand, he gave it a squeeze to coax her to look at him.

"What are you thinking?" she asked.

"That these notes are disconcerting," Ben said, frowning. "And that the person who wrote them is deranged. You're sure you have no idea who the author might be?"

"I haven't the slightest idea who might be sending them," Remi said, her stomach turning again at the mild scent of chamomile.

Ben noticed. "No tea, then?"

Remi nodded, her hand on her stomach.

Sylvie took the tray and left without another word, leaving Ben and Remi to their privacy.

"You should rest," he said, his tone soothing.

"I don't think that I could right now." Remi bit back a sob. The safety of her room was violated. Every inch of it felt unfamiliar now, tainted by her unseen admirer. Returning to her room to sleep in her bed would be difficult.

Even the house, once quiet, had come to life in the last few days. Its spirit—or spirits—suddenly restless. Everything wanted her attention, and she felt like her mind was unraveling from the visions and notes.

"You might sleep with me," Ben suggested.

Remi's eyes widened.

Ben, flustered, hurried to correct himself. "I meant you could sleep in my room. I'm happy to sacrifice my bed if it means that you are able to sleep soundly."

"There are other rooms," Remi said.

"There are," he agreed.

"And it would be inappropriate." A blush spread across her cheeks, and she caught him staring.

"You make an excellent point." Ben chuckled with a slight shake of his head, loosing a strand of his black hair from behind his ear.

Remi, without thinking, reached for it and gently tucked it back into place. The tips of her fingers lingered on the soft curve of his ear. Touching him was like sitting under the sun on a summer day after a brisk spring. For too long, she'd felt colorless, another dull penny among the people on their Isle. But not with Ben—not as a child, and certainly not now. The first time she laid eyes on him, she could feel the sunshine rolling off of him.

He was a sunspot in the gloom again.

Remi's fingers brushed along his cheekbone, stirring him. He closed his eyes and turned his lips to her palm. She felt his breath against her skin and shuddered. The notes, the locket—all were momentarily forgotten when his eyes fluttered open again. She found a strangeness to them, an unfamiliar darkness that had swallowed his eyes whole. Remi felt herself lean in closer, smelling wool and salty sea air. She wondered if his lips would also taste like the brackish morning air.

"Did you go into town this morning?" she asked, trying to refocus.

"I did." The curled smile he'd been wearing faded quickly into a frown. "I met briefly with Lamotte."

"How was he?"

"Drunk," Ben stated, suddenly pulling back from Remi. Every inch he put between them felt like a chasm. "I sought him out, but it was a fruitless endeavor."

"I'm afraid Lamotte has never been quite helpful, especially when the mood doesn't suit him." Remi sighed as she leaned against the stiff back of the chair. "I've no idea how he managed anything. It's beyond me."

Ben was silent for a moment as he contemplated. She hoped it was her imagination, but he appeared to grow more distant with the subject.

"Is something the matter?" she finally asked.

Ben crossed and uncrossed his arms, sighing in frustration as he pinched the bridge of his nose. He opened his mouth to speak, but Remi's name echoed throughout the manor. They stared at each other, confused. Footsteps sounded shortly after, pounding hard against the wood floor outside the parlor. The doors opened as the intruder called Remi's name again.

"Elise?"

A bedraggled brunette in a rumpled gown burst in, breathing

heavily as tears rolled down her reddened face.

Remi jumped up from the chair and ran to her cousin, forgetting in the moment what had happened. "Are you unwell? What happened?" Remi took Elise's hand to lead her to the chair she'd been sitting in, but Elise brushed her away.

"Leith," she sobbed. "He's dead!"

All sound left the room, drowned out by a horrid ringing in Remi's ears.

Elise glanced back at Ben, whose face was white; Remi's sunspot suddenly gone. She flicked her eyes to him and saw the conflict still lingering—guilt was written in his expression.

Did he already know? Was that what was bothering him?

"Elise? Did you find her?" Hugo barreled into the room a tick later.

"I don't feel well," Remi mumbled. The floor seemed to spiral underfoot.

Before Ben could move, Hugo had Remi's arm looped around his, and both he and Elise supported her.

"He's dead?" She could hardly believe it. She'd just seen Leith the other day. How could he be gone? The memory of his sweet smile and silly laughter came to her on a wave of sadness. She felt stranded, and though Elise and Hugo held her, she was numb to them.

Ben's eyes...his face...how close he'd been before...

"Shall I escort them upstairs, Monsieur? Madame Leone looks faint." Jacques knocked as he entered the parlor.

"Take her to my room," he said.

"I should think not! She has her own room," Hugo snapped, to Remi's surprise.

"What's all this noise then?"

Remi shot Elise a questioning look as Arnaud slipped past Ben and Jacques. If Beline was close behind, she would surely feel worse than she already did.

"She didn't know yet, Papa," Elise said.

Arnaud's eyes widened slightly. "But I was sure Monsieur Leone would have told you."

Ben scowled. "There were other, more important matters at hand."

Surely he meant to tell me about Leith after addressing the letters? He made no mention of them or the locket, for which she was grateful. They were, for the moment, still a secret. Remi felt Ben's discomfort growing and found strength in her legs. She stepped in between him and Hugo, addressing the latter. "Thank you for coming to my aid."

"Of course." Hugo appeared reluctant but spared her a smile regardless.

"I would like to lie down." Remi felt she could only wear a brave face for so long.

"Madame?" Jacques offered his arm. Remi gave her uncle a quick peck on the cheek and took it.

She looked to Ben. "We'll finish this later, yes?"

He nodded.

"I'll be joining her," Elise said, following not far behind. "I want to be sure that she rests."

"Where to?" Jacques asked in a low voice intended for Remi's ears alone.

"Ben's room, if you please."

Jacques nodded, leading the way. It was a heavy journey to Ben's bedroom. Remi could feel Elise's eyes boring into her. They were silent, but if she listened hard enough, she could hear every thought and question passing through her cousin's mind. They were the same kind of questions Remi would ask if given the chance, and once they were safely deposited, Elise would not hold back.

BEN

Ben left Hugo and Arnaud in the parlor with Sylvie, who brought the tea back in at his request. They could have their drinks and play at the farce of concerned relatives for as long as the tea and shortbread lasted.

His teeth gnashed angrily in his head, making his skull buzz with irritation. He did not like Hugo, and he hardly knew Arnaud. Not even as a child could he recall sparing more than a greeting or two with him. He was a shadow in the background, a lurking creature whose family outshined him in every aspect. To Ben, he was perfectly forgettable. However, given the circumstances, Ben had to keep an eye on him. And Hugo.

Father was up to something, he reminded himself as he intercepted Jacques on the second-floor landing. *And they're involved somehow.*

"This way." Ben jerked his chin upward.

"Monsieur?" Jacques followed him to the other side of the second floor to the door of his sister's room. It was still unlocked, and once inside, he waited until the door was firmly shut.

In a hushed whisper, Ben said, "I want to bring my father's body back here."

Jacques's eyebrows lifted a fraction, but there was no surprise written on his face. "The manor?"

"Yes." Ben rubbed his eyes. "I want to examine him for myself."

"Does this have something to do with Leith's death?"

It had everything to do with his death *and* his sister's. If the same doctor had also examined his father and declared his manner of death, then Ben had the responsibility to set it right. On the dock, the physician had been wrong and his persistence, despite the obvious signs that foul play was involved, convinced Ben of his appalling nescience. The doctor could not be trusted.

"There were markings on Leith's throat," Ben explained, "made before his death. The bruising is consistent with strangulation. I've seen it enough now to know."

Jacques smirked, though his tone was humorless. "I suppose your little escapade as the cemetery intern paid off."

Ben scoffed. "Say what you want, but it was the easiest way to keep my studies relevant."

"Right." Jacques dropped the subject. "And your father? They said he passed from heart failure, but you don't trust that?"

"Not for one second." Ben almost laughed. "I'll have a look at him myself."

It did not sit right with him, and he needed to trust his gut. He could be wrong, but he would rather know for himself than let it go without trying.

"Is it wise to bring him here? You don't live alone."

"She won't be awake," he said. "We can leave late once it's dark, and bring him through the delivery door in the kitchen. There's a latched door in the floor with a set of steps that leads straight to the wine cellar."

Jacques groaned. "It's a big risk."

"That hardly matters." Ben couldn't care less about the danger. He wanted answers, and no one else would give them willingly. "If I know what happened, it will bring me one step closer to solving this damnable puzzle."

"What if you're wrong?" Jacques asked. "What if he was ill and it was the cause of his heart failing?"

Ben bristled. He couldn't be wrong, not when his every instinct screamed that he was onto something. At the door, half-open to the hall, he paused. Jacques waited for him, knowing he wasn't done speculating.

"If my father was sick, if he truly felt that the end was near, he would not have married Remi." Ben felt certain of it. "Not to mention the receipt I found. He started something, Jacques, and my father never started anything that he couldn't finish."

"Are you sure?"

"Yes."

"Then I will take the carriage and retrieve his body tonight."

Ben shook his head. "I'll be going with you, *mon ami*. He is my father, after all."

"Of course."

They left Soleil's room for the second time, leaving it as it was. They did not speak to one another, both worrying about exhuming a corpse in the dead of night. On their way down the main stairs, Sylvie caught them both with a panicked look in her eye. Ben stopped mid-step. "What is it?"

"Men in uniform are asking to speak with you," she said hurriedly, "*and* Madame."

SUSPICIOUS

REMI

Ben's room was vastly different from Remi's. Where hers was soft and feminine, Ben's was plush and luxurious. It was warm, too, and not just because of the fire that crackled in the fireplace. The walls were a fine shade of mulberry, trimmed with birch accents, and the pictures on the walls were landscapes, some grand in scale. There were two wing-backed chairs in front of the fireplace, a tiny table between them. Some books were stacked there, one left open haphazardly over an armrest. Ben must have been reading it and set it aside in haste for something else.

Maybe he reads before bed? She wondered to herself.

Seeing his bed then, she could not blame him for abandoning the book in such a state. His bed was a massive mahogany four-poster, large enough to get lost in, with spired posts and an ornate canopy. Remi approached it with fascination. She ran her fingers along the ridges of carvings along the posts and footboard, admiring the artistry. No doubt it was the most expensive piece in the room. It was dressed with a golden, tawny duvet, with deep red accents and pillows to match. She pictured Ben beneath its sheets, wondering what it would be like to lay beside him.

Shameful, she thought, dousing the flame that grew in her stomach before it could get too hot.

Remi edged to the window and pulled the heavy curtains aside. It was safer to sit on the cushioned seat that overlooked the garden than to daydream herself into a stupor over his bed. Instead of fantasizing, her thoughts drifted to more somber memories. It was only weeks ago that Leith had found her there and comforted her at Edgar's wake. He'd teased her then, too. How shocked he would be if he could see her now, hidden away in Ben's room. Already she could imagine his eyes sparkling with laughter as he prodded her for details.

Tears welled in her eyes knowing that she would never hear him laugh again.

"Remi." Elise's voice was a balm. "I'm so sorry."

Turning to face her cousin, Remi saw in her expression the same sadness. She held out her hands and Elise came to sit beside her on the bench. For a moment, they were quiet.

"This is awful," Elise finally said. Her voice was thick with sorrow. "I cannot be at odds with you anymore, Remi. You are my sister."

Remi untangled herself from Elise and sat back against the frame to address her fully. Any reprimands she had for her cousin about her carelessness were forgotten. The worn, worried look on Elise's face conveyed a sense of culpability, as though she had been punishing herself since Remi's discovery. With a great sigh, Remi relented. "Neither can I."

Elise dissolved into tears. "Thank goodness!"

"You're lucky it was me," Remi said as she pulled Elise into her arms. "If anyone else had discovered you, I don't know what might have happened. You must be more discreet."

Elise sobbed in reply.

"How long has this been going on?" Remi asked.

Elise dabbed at her eyes and straightened. "We have been together since before my engagement," Elise started. "It all happened so fast, so naturally."

As she spoke, Remi noticed that, for the first time in years, Elise's eyes sparkled. She gripped her hands firmly in her lap, listening intently, all the while feeling slightly jealous. *What I would give to have a love so passionate.*

"What about Hugo?" she asked.

"I tried." Elise's eyes welled with tears. "I tried to end it, to give Hugo a chance. I wanted to please Maman, but I could hardly face myself, knowing it was a lie. You know how awful he is!"

"I understand." She might have been the only person Elise knew who understood what it meant to marry someone she didn't want.

"I know you do." Elise reached forward and patted her hands gently.

"So then, where will you go?"

"Guillaume likes the countryside." Elise looked delighted by the idea.

"I'm pleased he wants the splendor of the countryside and not the overcrowded streets of Paris," Remi said, smiling.

"Oh, no. He hates Paris. He visited a few months ago on business with Papa." Elise's face turned red then. "He told me they went to a bordello deep in the city. Guillaume was embarrassed, of course, but could not turn him down."

Remi scrunched her nose. "Uncle? In a bordello?"

"Oui." Elise nodded. "He frequents them on business trips. Guillaume does not approve, but I suppose that doesn't bother Papa. Men do what they want, no?"

"A few months ago? The last I knew, Uncle had been in Paris only once, and that was in September of last year." Remi's stomach churned. One being that her uncle was unfaithful to Beline. She never saw him as anything but a proud, happy husband, despite how ridiculous his wife could be at times.

Elise tilted her head. "I don't understand."

"Don't you remember?" Remi said, suddenly aware of the timing. "When uncle came home, it was only a few days later that he called me into his office to tell me about my engagement."

"Was it really?" Elise's mouth formed a perfect 'o' as realization hit her. "Yes, you're right. I do remember that!"

He said my engagement had been blessed, Remi recalled. *I did not think so then, but perhaps...*

"Do you think he had business with my father?"

Her mother's letter had come quickly in reply as well, and it had only been a day or so before she had received the pearls. The entire arrangement had caught her by surprise.

"I'm afraid I don't know, *ma cherie.*"

It was no surprise if that was the case. How else would she have been able to marry? Her father held all the cards. She knew he was indifferent toward her, but how would her marriage to Edgar benefit him? Then she remembered Edgar's will—it had been revised to include her.

A will that mentioned valuable land, a home, and a fortune.

Did they know about the treasure?

Their conversation was interrupted by two strong knocks at the door.

"Ladies?" Ben peeked in; his countenance was a welcome sight. "An Inspector Marceau would like a word with Remi."

Remi perked. "The inspector?"

Her question was answered when the man from the morning of Edgar's death entered the room. He appraised the space before his blue eyes landed on Remi. He smiled. "Misfortune brings us together again, I'm afraid."

Remi nodded. "It has."

"Might I have a word with you alone?" He glanced at Elise, who pulled away from Remi and stood.

Her cousin spared her a concerned look. "I'll be just outside."

Both Ben and Elise disappeared behind the double doors, but Remi could still feel their presence. It was enough to give her courage when all she wanted to do was collapse.

"How can I be of service?" Remi said.

Marceau bowed his head, offering his respects. "Madame, I must first offer my condolences on this, your second loss."

"Thank you," she replied. "But I'm sure you're here for more than that, *monsieur.*"

"Regrettably, yes." He produced a familiar pad of paper and pen. "I am told you were one of the last people to speak with the deceased. I have already spoken with your staff."

"Leith was a dear friend," she said tenderly as his smile came to mind.

"Could you tell me about your last meeting?"

Remi closed her eyes and recalled their meeting as she attempted to hold back her tears.

"I see." Marceau jotted it down and then asked, "Do you know someone by the name Didier?"

"Yes, I know of him, but I have never met him. Leith mentioned him from time to time. I believe they—" She caught herself. Was Didier a suspicious person? Would knowing him make her one? A lump formed in her throat and in her chest.

"Madame?" Marceau prodded. "You were saying?"

Remi willed herself to continue. "I believe they were together last night. That's what Leith told me before he left, but I have no idea where they might have been."

Marceau skimmed his notes and then put the pad away. With a serious look, he held her attention a moment longer.

"I only have one final question, which I will strike from my records." He hesitated. "Were you involved in a *relationship* with the deceased?"

Remi nearly toppled over, unable to contain her blushing. She covered her cheeks quickly, but the inspector was sharp. He would have surmised as much based on her reaction, and she did not offer any sort of explanation.

"I only ask because—" He cleared his throat. "I do not believe in coincidences. Too much of my life has been spent in the underbelly of society, surrounded by evil men. Please look after yourself."

The lump in her throat bobbed when she swallowed. "I will."

"Thank you for your time." He bowed. "I'll be on my way."

Ben opened the door for him, smiling softly at her from the doorway. Elise was gone, having abandoned her post at the door; perhaps her father or Hugo had called her away. It hardly mattered, though.

All Remi wanted was for Ben to stay with her, but the chance to ask him came and went. He escorted the inspector out in her place, allowing her time to mourn alone.

Remi turned in her seat and watched out the window. There were too many carriages in the drive for her taste. The inspector and a few *gens d'armes* boarded their carriage with a farewell to Ben. He waved them off as they went, unmoving until the carriage was down the hill. When he was free, he searched the windows for Remi and offered her another smile.

She waved as he ducked inside.

Remi closed her eyes and breathed deeply. When she opened them again, she was startled to find another figure watching her from the garden.

Remi choked on a sob at the sight of two milky white eyes staring up at her, unblinking from a pale, blue-lipped face. *Leith.*

BEN'S DISCOVERY

BEN

Remi was standing in the center of the room when Ben and Jacques returned.

"Are you alright?" Ben rushed to her side.

She looked into his face, clearly frightened. "I'm fine. Overwhelmed is all."

Ben waved Jacques out of the room and led her to one of the chairs by the fireplace. It was still dimly lit, orange embers fighting amongst the ash. He stirred some life into it, sitting across from her once there was a flame. Ben pulled the other chair closer to her and reached for her hands.

"Did the inspector say something to rile you?" Ben asked.

"He did." She paused. "And he didn't. This is the second time I've spoken with him, though. I'm sure that doesn't bode well."

Ben encased her fingers. He could feel how cold she was under the heat of his own touch.

"When was the first time you spoke with him?"

Remi croaked a reply. "The morning we found Edgar."

"Will you tell me what happened?" He needed to know what he'd missed.

"He went with me to the study to identify the body…"

Ben was patient as she recounted that day, confident in her memory.

"My uncle was furious, but it was my responsibility as Edgar's wife. Afterward, we spoke, and he asked a few questions. Then he left."

Ben's grip tightened involuntarily, his body tensing at the mention of her uncle. "Why was your uncle furious?"

"He offered to identify Edgar in my place," she said. Confusion marred her face when he pulled away and started digging in his pockets. "What's going on?"

"Take a look at this." He held out the receipt to Remi.

She read through it once, then a second time. Her eyes flicked up, and then down, then back again. He smiled when he noticed her lips moving as she read.

"My uncle was doing business with Edgar?" she asked, reading over the details again.

"Marchand was also in on it." Ben nodded.

Remi's eyes narrowed. "Perhaps I am mistaken...but this is fake, Ben. There is no such person by the seller's name."

"What?" Ben leaned over and peered at the paper over Remi's shoulder. "How did I miss that?"

"Miss what?" Jacques asked as he pushed open the door carrying a full tray.

"The name on the receipt you found," Remi's voice was like a bell again, her earlier fear extinguished. "It's the name of a fictional character."

Jacques set the tray down on the bedside table and joined Ben. Both men looked over the receipt again, mirroring the other's surprise.

"Monsieur Arsene Lupin." Ben nearly laughed outright. "The owner of one 'Gentleman's Adventure Club.'"

Jacques sounded as shocked as Ben felt. "How did you know that, Madame?"

Ben looked up, curious to know her answer as well. She looked between the both of them and shrugged, a cup of tea already in hand.

"Edgar lent me a book. He said it was his favorite collection of stories."

"So, if I am to understand this correctly, my father used the name of a fictional seller to con your uncle and your cousin's fiancé out of money?"

"It appears so," Remi said, sipping her tea.

"I almost can't believe it." Ben shared a look with Jacques, who was rendered speechless.

"Look at the date." Remi returned to her chair opposite Ben. "It was marked a couple of weeks before the wedding."

"Is there some significance to that?" Ben asked.

"There might be," she said, staring into the cup balanced on her lap. "I learned something interesting today. My uncle was in Paris last September; my engagement was announced after he returned home."

"Strange."

"I suspect he met with my father."

Ben's eyes widened. "Are you certain?"

"It's mostly speculation on my part, and that's only because Elise told me he'd made the trip." Remi grimaced. "She said that Guillaume accompanied him and they went to a bordello somewhere deep in the city. I suppose he didn't want anyone to know who they were—and if he was meeting my father, they would need to find someplace far away from anyone who might notice him."

"A bordello?" Ben looked shocked.

"There's only one place I can think of," Jacques said as he took up a spot beside the mantle. "It has a reputation for dealing with shady folks. They take money to keep big secrets."

Ben knew exactly which bordello; he'd only ever gone there one time. "I know the place. The Madame that runs the business is a ruthless money-hound."

Remi eyed Ben curiously.

"Worry not," he said quickly. "I went once, and they robbed me blind. I never went back."

"I'm sure you learned an invaluable lesson."

By the fire, Jacques coughed to cover his laughter.

Ben wished she was right; unfortunately, he'd learned only to avoid the place. He found better establishments that were worthwhile with women who didn't look at him like a meal. But the bordellos were in Paris, and he was on an island with Remi again. He was content to quit his habit. In the past, those women had brought him the comfort and companionship he so badly longed for. Remi's presence in his life softened that ache.

"It's been a long day." Ben leaned forward in his chair and covered his face. "I could use a bath."

"I'll find Sylvie," Jacques said, already moving toward the door.

"I'm sorry for your burdens." Remi reached a hand out to touch his arm.

"They were yours first." He smiled meekly, moving his hands to his chin. "That was brilliant of you, though. I never would have known otherwise."

"Thank you." Remi's cheeks sparked bright pink. "Part of me wonders if he gave me the book on purpose."

"Perhaps," Ben stretched and then stood. "To think that he would do something as risky as forging a sale for that large a sum."

"There must be a reason for it."

"Yes, but why?" Ben grasped the back of his neck, massaging the tender muscles. "And where did the money go?"

"There are more questions than answers, aren't there?"

Ben met Remi's green-blue eyes. She was tangled up in more than she realized, and it was all thanks to her uncle. "You asked earlier if I saw Lamotte, but I did not tell you why."

She arched a brow, waiting for him to continue.

"He has a private ledger." Ben remembered how thick it was, and it made him all the more anxious to get his hands on it. "A large file full of papers and possibly documents about this sham of a sale he set up. I'm certain there's more to it, but he would not release it to me without you."

"And you think we need it."

He nodded. "Without it, we are left to the wolves."

"I trust your judgment."

A moment later, Sylvie knocked and announced that Ben's bath was drawn. She collected the untouched tray and Remi's cup before excusing herself. She appeared ragged and seemed to be growing worse every day. Ben and Remi shared a sympathetic look as Sylvie left them.

He ran a hand along Remi's cheek lightly, watching her eyes as they darted across his face. *What is she looking for?* He wondered. *Or rather, what does she see in me?*

"Stay here," he said gently. "Rest as much as you can."

Before his hand fell away, she grabbed it and pulled it close to her chest.

"What is it?"

"Do you think," she gasped, sucking in a sharp breath, "that the letters have something to do with Leith?"

Ben hadn't considered it, but it was not entirely out of the question. He meant to tell her his suspicions regarding Leith's death but hadn't had the chance. Unsure of what to do and worried he would upset her further, Ben had decided against sharing. Better to ease her into it once he was sure of his own father's death. Without proof, he had nothing but layers of speculation.

"Whoever sent those letters..." Remi's voice strained, and her brows furrowed. "They might have seen him as—"

Her sadness pierced his heart, and he drew her into his arms without a moment's hesitation. She folded into him, shaking from tears or fear. He could not blame her for either, and he did not deny her the relief that grieving brought. His bath would be cold, but he couldn't bring himself to care. He would stay until every last one of her tears had dried itself against the fabric on his chest.

EXHUMATION

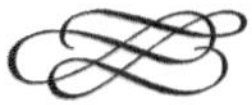

BEN

*P*lacing his father's casket inside the mausoleum's stone coffin days ago was difficult with three sets of hands. Removing it with one less man was nearly impossible. More than that, he was glad that he happened to wear the same jacket he'd worn the day they deposited him. Without the key to get in, their trip would have been for nothing.

"Lucky that." Ben had said to himself when he found it there, cool against his fingers.

"This is damned difficult." Jacques heaved against the stone after they made it in.

Ben and Jacques used as much force as they could muster to budge the stone lid. When strength alone could not move it, they went in search of a sturdy, fallen branch. With added leverage to fully support the stone, they managed to hoist it. Inch by painful inch, they moved the lid just enough to retrieve his father.

"Remind me why we aren't doing this during daylight hours?" Jacques grunted.

"Because that would draw too much suspicion."

Jacques wheezed as he lifted one end of the casket. "Whose suspicion?"

"Remi's," Ben said, hoisting the other end of the polished wood. "Martin's. Everyone's. It isn't safe."

"It isn't safe now," Jacques hissed.

With careful precision, they lifted the casket from inside the stone sarcophagus. It sat on the ground between them as they pushed the slab back into place. Once shut, they stopped to catch their breath.

"That was miserable," Ben groaned.

"It was your idea," Jacques said.

Ben let the snide remark pass. He looked down at the floor where his father's body waited, snug inside the casket, his chest aching with guilt and grief.

Am I doing the right thing? He wondered. More than once on their short journey to the cemetery, Ben caught himself second-guessing his motives. If they were discovered, there would be serious consequences. Disturbing a grave was unforgivable. Yet, it was the only way he could get the answers he needed.

Much more desperate men have done worse, he assured himself.

"Let's get moving."

On a three-count, they hoisted the casket upward. They waded through the darkness with no light to show them where they were going or what they might bump into.

"How much farther?" Jacques complained.

An answer came in the form of the carriage colliding with Ben's shoulder. He winced at the sharp pain, nearly dropping his father from the force.

"You drop it," Jacques snapped in a hushed voice, "and you're carrying him into the cellar by yourself."

Ben believed him.

With great effort, they managed to maneuver the casket into the carriage. Part of it hung from the side, the door unable to close. Ben climbed inside and held it in place as Jacques led the carriage back to the manor.

"I think you would be ashamed of me," he whispered in the dark.

His shame would have to wait, as would the many years of anger and disappointment he'd endured. This would all be worth it in the end if he was right about his father's death.

"It's been sixteen years," Ben breathed, wishing his father could hear him, "and after all that time has passed, this is how I'm welcomed home. Is that what you wanted? To leave before I could say my piece?"

There was nothing but the rumbling gravel underfoot.

"If you had called me home sooner, I would have forgiven everything. For Soleil, for sending me away, for marrying Remi...I would have forgiven it all. But here we are. One Leone left alive, and the other a stiff corpse wrapped up in an old sheet."

His father did not respond.

The carriage came to a stop.

"Let's get him inside," Jacques said as he hoisted one end of the coffin.

Carrying the casket into the wine cellar was an easier feat than carrying it in the cemetery. Once concealed behind the wine racks, they opened the casket. Both of them turned their noses up at the smell, hardly able to contain their disgust. But they persevered, carefully lifting the body onto an empty table.

Ben tried not to stare at what had once been his father's face. It was easier to imagine he was another of the cadavers he'd worked on in school. Nothing he couldn't stomach.

Jacques, however, looked ill. "I'm going to put the horse away. Then I'll be turning in for the rest of the night."

"Thank you," Ben said.

Jacques didn't reply. He carried on to the next task, as was his nature.

Ben, on the other hand, was in no rush to begin his examination. Instead, he found a bottle of wine from his mother's collection and downed it in a few long gulps. It was dry and tart, just the way he liked it. After one bottle, and halfway through the next, he stopped to laugh at himself; the key to the mausoleum was still tucked in his pocket.

"I forgot to lock up."

He fell into a fit of silent laughter, beside himself with the notion that no one would bother robbing a grave that was already empty.

~

REMI

When Remi finally woke, the morning had come.

She groaned and rolled to her side, her body heavy with the after-effects of the sedative she'd taken. At first, she thought it was a trick of the light, but then she saw a solid outline. Someone was in the bed with her. The duvet covered their head, and they did not appear to be breathing. For one panicked moment, she thought it was the person leaving her the notes.

The person beside her twitched.

Remi bit her lip to suppress a scream and, without thinking of the consequences, snapped her hand out to grab the duvet, revealing a mop of curly golden hair. Remi stilled, her body tethered to the spot.

No, no...

The body itself shifted slowly, the bones in its neck snapping as it twisted around to face her.

"Leith," she gasped.

Remi had seen him in the garden—a phantom, a hallucination. But he was there again, closer than ever. She felt her blood run cold.

"Oh, Leith..."

His blue lips fell open, swinging downward on an unhinged jaw.

"No, no...no..."

Milky white eyes held her gaze, unblinking. His hands shot out and clamped around her throat, squeezing until black spots floated across her vision. Remi kicked and scratched, trying to pull herself from Leith's unrelenting grasp. His mouth yawned wide, the ocean spilling from his throat. A guttural cry followed, like that of a dying animal. Remi pushed against the pain and struggled until his hold loosened.

Finally, she broke away, kicking at the sheets in her rush to escape.

Leith's inhuman groan chased her from the room and down the hallway. She nearly slipped and toppled down the stairs, catching herself against the railing as she collided with Ben's chest.

"Remi! What the hell—"

"Leith!" she screamed. "Leith! I saw him—he was there…in the bed."

Ben snapped to. "What? How?"

"I don't know," she sobbed. "I don't know!"

"I believe you," he said, steadying her to stand on her own feet. "Are you alright?"

She nodded, wiping at her cheeks.

"Now then," he stepped in front of her, offering his hand, "let's go back and see if he's still there."

Feeling like a child, she let him lead her to his room. The bed was empty where Leith had been, the bedsheets were strewn across the mattress from her hasty escape.

"You put up quite a fight." He chuckled.

"I could feel him," she said, touching her neck. The phantom touch of his fingers lingered, leaving behind goose pimples. "It was as if…as if he was trying to strangle me."

Ben's eyes widened. He turned Remi to face him and moved her hair away from her shoulder. He was eerily quiet as his fingers traced her tender flesh.

"I don't want to alarm you," he murmured, "but there are red marks the size of fingerprints on your skin."

"What?" The hair on her arms stood on end.

"They're faint." He moved her hair back over her shoulder. "But they are there."

Remi cupped her neck, walking backward until the back of her knees caught the bed. She collapsed, tears streaming down her face again. She bit back a sob, too afraid to admit it was real, too afraid to question why.

"Remi?" Ben's voice was muffled. "I'm going to have Sylvie draw you a bath, and then I'm going to send Paul to fetch your cousin." He was a blur as he knelt in front of her. "I need to leave you, but only for a moment. Will you be alright?"

No, she thought, but she nodded anyway.

He wasn't gone for long, returning with Sylvie close behind him.

"I'm going to leave you with Sylvie now," he said, his voice soothing, "but will you give me your hands first?"

No, no, no, she thought, but she gave them over anyway.

She stood. Her legs were taken out from underneath her as Ben swept her into his arms. He carried her to the washroom and waited until the bath was full, whispering: *You're safe*. It was what she needed to hear, and eventually, it was enough to convince her there were no longer hands wrapped around her throat.

"Monsieur." Sylvie's voice trembled. "I can take her from here."

Ben set her down wordlessly and offered Remi an encouraging nod before he ducked out of the room. Sylvie closed the door and helped her undress.

The water was hot, but Remi barely felt it against her skin. If it wasn't for the quiet string of Sylvie's apologies and sniffles, Remi might have forgotten she was there.

After a long bath, Remi put on a simple black dress. Sylvie plaited her hair, then dutifully led her to the foyer. At the bottom of the stairs, Elise and Ben chatted quietly, stopping altogether when Remi made her appearance. Sylvie excused herself, keeping her eyes downcast.

"You're pale." Elise frowned.

"I had a fright."

Elise eyed Ben, who had stepped beside Remi. "So I've heard."

"Your cousin has offered to take you out for the day," Ben said.

Remi turned on him. "But I can't. I'm not allowed."

His expression hinted at his concern. "I think we can forgo tradition this once."

"If you think it's best." She was hesitant to go, but it was a far better option than hiding herself away in another room. Or clinging needlessly to Ben at all hours.

"It is," Elise exclaimed, looping her arm through Remi's. "You won't even need to leave the carriage. We'll simply take a long ride around the island. Guillaume has kindly offered to be our escort."

Poor Guillaume, Remi thought. *She must have begged him.*

"No one will see you," Ben confirmed, sensing her hesitation.

Remi did not argue further. She let Elise whisk her away and stuff her inside the coach. They huddled together and, with one last look, Remi waved to Ben. He was worried, pretending not to be for her benefit. Still, she was grateful to leave, to have a moment outside of the manor to breathe.

Once they were down the hill and the manor was out of sight, Elise unleashed question after question.

"What happened?"

Remi touched the collar of her dress and swallowed. "A nightmare."

"About Leith?"

"Yes." Remi nodded and bit her lip. "But it isn't the first one. I've been having a lot of nightmares recently."

"That's awful." Elise frowned.

"And it's not just that." Remi took a deep breath. "Someone has been sending me...letters."

Elise scrunched her nose. "What kind of letters?"

"Crooked love letters," she said plainly. "The first one was waiting in my room after the wake. My locket, a wedding gift from Edgar, went missing then, too."

Elise covered her mouth. "A stranger was in your room?"

"I don't know how, but yes." Remi nodded. "Multiple times."

"Why would anyone do such a thing?"

"I asked myself the same question, and I think the truth is much darker than you or I want to believe." Remi wished she'd brought the letters with her. "The second letter came with a parcel, and inside was my locket—wrapped in a bloody kerchief. Whoever this is...they're not an admirer."

Elise turned pale white. "Whose blood?"

"I don't know." Remi shivered. "I don't want to know."

While Elise ruminated, Remi banged on the roof of the carriage. "Take us into town," she called.

Guillaume called back, "Where?"

"To the miller!"

Elise pulled at her skirt and yanked Remi back down. She hissed, "What are you thinking?"

"I'm thinking," she said, recalling Leith's face and empty white eyes, "that I would like to visit the miller and his wife."

There might never be another chance to visit or offer her condolences. It was the least she could do when they had been kind enough to visit during Edgar's wake. But part of Remi wanted to reassure herself, in some small way, that Leith would never hurt her. That the phantom she saw meant no ill will, that in death, he did not blame her for his end.

When the carriage finally stopped, they were on the outskirts of town, having passed through the market and its many faces. Remi exited the carriage with Elise close behind. Nothing, not even fear, could keep her from knocking on the door.

Leith's mother, Manette, answered just as quickly as the first tap.

"Remi?"

If Manette had not started crying, Remi would have been the first. She embraced the petite woman for as long as the other held on. Another familiar face finally broke them apart.

"Madame Leone?"

"Monsieur Lamotte?" Remi pulled away, surprised. Another friendly face would have been nice any other time, but Lamotte's presence was suspicious. "What are you doing here?"

Manette stepped inside and pulled Remi along. Elise followed behind her. "He came to pay his respects and share tea with a grieving mother," Manette explained.

"I brought biscuits," he added awkwardly. Lamotte was never short on words.

"You must join us," Manette insisted as she pulled Remi toward a table.

It was the first time Remi had seen the inside of their home. It was small; without Leith's other siblings running around, it was quiet and calm.

"Have a seat, please," Manette said. "I'll put together a cup of tea for you both."

Elise, ever the humble guest, took her seat first. "I take sugar with mine."

"Two for me," Remi said, sitting beside Elise.

Lamotte opted for the chair on the opposite side and busied himself with a biscuit.

"My Leith knew just about everyone in town." The cups clinked as Manette spoke. "There isn't a soul who hasn't come to see me yet."

"My condolences to you and your family," Elise offered. "He was so kind."

"He was one of my closest friends," Remi said, sharing a pointed look with Lamotte. He nibbled at his biscuit, unshakable. Manette set their tea down and joined them at the table. She was beside herself with grief, as anyone would be.

Remi's heart broke for her.

"I just can't believe he drowned," Manette choked, gathering her apron in two shaking hands. "He was a good boy. Never drank too much, and there wasn't a single body of water he couldn't conquer. We made sure of that."

Every child on the Isle was a strong swimmer, even Remi, who had been taught much later on. It was part of the island life; the water could turn at any point. Learning early on spared mothers the worry of their children drowning while they played. Leith would have been no stranger to an ornery undercurrent. He was, to Remi's observance, a strong swimmer. They'd spent enough time together in her youth to know he could brave the most treacherous tides.

Manette turned to Remi and touched her arm. "Do you think Monsieur Leone might be right?"

"Pardon?" Remi asked.

"About Leith." Her dark eyes pleaded.

Remi looked to Elise, who was just as confused, then to Lamotte, whose alarm was tangible. *What does he know?*

"My dear lady," Lamotte said as he tried to coax her away from Remi, "I think it is wise to trust in our doctor."

Manette turned to him, bordering on mania. "But Monsieur Leone was there, too! And he didn't agree with the doctor. We all heard him!"

"What do you mean?"

"Manette, please," Lamotte pleaded. "He *drowned*."

"But I—"

"Monsieur Lamotte," Remi snapped harder than she meant to. "May I speak with you outside?"

He hesitated. He seemed out of place in Manette's small kitchen. His face drenched in sweat, he wiped at his brow with a kerchief from his pocket. "I'll take my leave then."

"So soon?" Manette asked.

But he was already walking away with Remi steps behind him. Elise stole the conversation, her voice a song as she recounted some of Remi's stories about Leith.

Outside, Lamotte patted his face again and wiped at his mustache. "I'm sorry you had to hear that."

"What's this about?" Remi demanded. "What did she mean?"

"There is a rumor making its way around the Isle that Leith was murdered." His joviality turned dour. "Ben inspected his body at the docks and, despite what the doctor said, some believe it to be true."

Remi's body went cold. "Ben...did what?"

"He inspected the body." Lamotte frowned. "He was there moments after they pulled Leith from the water."

"He said nothing to me."

"Ah." Lamotte smacked his lips together. "Well, it is best that he kept it to himself. The last thing anyone on the island needs to worry about is murder."

"Do you disagree with him?" Remi asked, her stomach sick with worry and confusion.

"I am a lawyer," he said with great aplomb, "*not* a doctor. My business is in books, not bodies."

He doesn't agree, she thought.

"I'm off then," he said but stopped halfway. "Oh, would you please remind Ben about the documents he asked about? I assume he mentioned that, at least."

"Yes." Remi didn't like his tone. "He mentioned something of the sort."

"Very well then. If you are in agreement, he can come to get them at his leisure. I'll send along some paperwork with a courier this evening." He added, "You'll need to sign them, Madame."

"Of course." Remi nodded.

"Then I'll be off."

Remi watched him go, tottering off into town as though nothing had happened. As if he hadn't floored her, shaken her world again with suspicions and rumors that Leith might have been murdered. And Ben *knew*. He'd seen the body and inspected it for himself. There were so many complicated feelings taking up space inside of her, and she wanted them gone.

"How could he have known?" she asked herself quietly, her voice barely a whisper.

"Psst."

Remi's ear twitched.

"Psst."

She spun on her heel, jolted by the interruption. A young man with brown curls and hazel eyes peered around the corner from the alley of Manette's home. He beckoned her closer, wary eyes trained on everything. He shifted slightly, making room for Remi in the small space.

"Who are you?"

"Don't trust the lawyer," he said. "It's true; Leith was murdered."

Remi's heart skipped. "What? How do you know that?"

"I was there," the young man said. His eyes were red and puffy, a telltale sign that he had been crying. "He was with me, but I'd hidden myself away before we were caught. Leith wasn't fast enough."

"Didier?" She recognized him from Leith's description. "How—do you know who it was?"

He shook his head, shaking his curls. "No. It was too dark, but we heard voices and men approaching. He told me to hide, to run if things went badly."

Remi covered her mouth. She pressed her back to the wall and held herself up as best she could, even though her knees felt weak and she wanted to fall.

"I saw it," he said again. "I saw it happen."

Who would murder Leith? And for what? Remi wondered.

"I have to go now before someone sees me."

Remi only heard him, unwilling to stop Didier from running off. Her arms felt numb, grief weighing heavily on her chest. Too many things were taking up space inside her mind, and Lamotte's words followed by Didier's admission of the truth he'd witnessed had tipped her over the edge. She lost herself in the alley, crumbling while the fragile pieces of her sanity spiraled downward.

<h1 style="text-align:center">SEVERED</h1>

<h2 style="text-align:center">BEN</h2>

*A*fter Remi left for her drive around town with Elise, Ben spent most of his morning in the wine cellar. He grappled with his distress, bouncing back and forth between cutting his father open and taking him back in broad daylight. Jacques would wring his neck if he chose the latter.

The late night in the cemetery had done both of them in.

"We have to get on with it." Jacques's voice cut in from the stairs. He'd left to take stock of the staff and keep an eye out for Remi.

"I know," Ben clipped, his jaw ticking with irritation.

"Need I also remind you that we're working on borrowed time." To emphasize his point, he looked back up the cellar stairs. "Madame won't be gone for much longer."

Ben forced himself to his feet. Jacques was right. Remi would be back soon, and he didn't want to think about her finding him bent over her husband's dead body. With a careful hand, Ben undid the tie and the buttons of his father's shirt. He stripped away the collar and pulled the fabric apart to expose his throat and chest.

"Fils de pute!" Ben's hands flew to the sides of the table, gripping them with all of his strength.

Jacques hurried to his side, noiseless as he observed.

Deep bruises stretched the length of Edgar's torso, with pockets of stitched flesh sewn haphazardly together. There were fingerprint-sized marks at the base of his throat, similar to the ones he'd seen on Remi. Ben's eyes burned with fury at the sight.

"By God," Jacques said. "You were right."

"I didn't want to be right." Ben choked on his words.

"But you are. You might even be right about all of it. Your sister included."

"I wanted to be *wrong!*" Ben snapped, pushing away from the table.

Jacques took Ben's place to get a closer look. He scrutinized the wounds, his face turning up as he moved part of the shirt further back. There were several visible lines from chest to waistline that they could see.

"These are stab wounds," he said.

Ben scrubbed at his face and sucked in a deep breath. Fighting his anger, he joined Jacques. His friend was right. His father had been injured multiple times. Whoever attacked him intended to kill.

"Your father is as big as you," Jacques said quietly. "He would have put up a fight."

Ben turned to his father's hands, lifting one from the table to inspect it. The knuckles weren't bruised, and his nail beds were clean. His father might have been as tall as him, but he was no fighter. He may have struggled, perhaps, but his attacker must have caught him off guard.

"Do you think the stitches were to save him?" Jacques asked.

With a breath, Ben covered his father with the sheet again and backed away. The collar of his shirt was high enough to cover the marks on his neck, no doubt chosen to ensure no one would see the damage. "No, not to save him," Ben said. "To hide their handiwork."

"Where did they find his body?" Jacques asked.

"Remi said that they discovered him in the study." Ben flexed his fingers.

"Wouldn't there have been blood?"

Ben felt cold all over again. Not once during his time in the study did he see anything hinting at a struggle.

"Someone was clearly very thorough," Ben said.

Quiet settled over them, leaving only the sound of their breathing to occupy the space. Ben wanted to cry, to fill the hurt in his chest with something tangible and raw. He scraped his knuckles against his legs, digging into the fabric of his trousers until the pain filtered through his mind. He couldn't believe what he'd seen, that his father had been handled with such carelessness.

"You mentioned the doctor at the docks. Do you think he's involved?" Jacques asked.

"It's likely that he is." Ben could still smell the stale alcohol on the doctor's breath. "But he was a lousy drunk. Anything he has to say isn't worth listening to."

"It's important we keep this quiet."

"For now," Ben agreed. "Until I've ruled out Lamotte, Marchand, and Remi's uncle."

"Maybe they knew the sale was falsified. That would be reason enough."

"It would be."

"But we need proof?"

Ben nodded. "We need the papers that Lamotte has in his desk."

"What are you thinking?" Jacques asked.

"Leith...he was strangled," Ben said, gauging Jacques's reaction. He only frowned.

"They'll turn him to ash before I can prove he was murdered, too."

"Then I'll bring his body here." Another body would spell certain disaster if they were caught, but they'd already exhumed one for the sake of exposing a crime. If it meant justice for both by the end, then it made the most sense to bring Leith's body.

"Then do it." Ben gestured towards the stairs. He needed to rest for a few hours and clean his hands.

"I'll leave this evening," Jacques said as they parted ways.

Ben retreated to his room and filled the washbowl. He splashed his face and scrubbed his hands twice, yet he could not erase the feeling of his father's skin. His father's bruised flesh flashed in and out of his mind, the image searing itself into the back of his eyelids.

He'd never forget it.

"Ben!" someone shouted.

Angry footsteps pounded up the stairs.

"Ben!" It was Remi's voice that drifted down the hall. "Ben! Where are you?"

"Here," he called back.

Whatever exhaustion was left behind in his tired bones left him the second he felt the intensity of her anger. She flew through the door, the brass handle slamming into the wall, as she forced her way into the room. Shocked, he held up his hands to stop her from falling over as she narrowly avoided tripping over her hem.

"You knew," she hissed, her face reddening as she went on. "You knew, and you didn't tell me!"

Ben spoke softly. "What do you mean?"

Panic seeped its way into his veins, pumping a fresh dose of fear into his beating heart. Did she know about the body in the cellar? Had she overheard him and Jacques somehow? He waited anxiously for her to catch her breath.

"Leith! They say he was murdered." She shook with anger, her eyes watering with fresh tears. "Lamotte says you inspected his body, and you didn't tell me."

"I did see his body, you're right." Ben weighed his words carefully. "But how did you know that? Where did you go?"

She whirled on him. "I went to visit Leith's mother! I needed to after this morning. I just couldn't bear the thought of seeing him again...not like that."

She must have meant her dream. Nightmares were something he could sympathize with, given Soleil's penchant for haunting his dreams. It seemed her trip around the Isle became an altogether different excursion, not that he could blame her. She'd gone out seeking closure and instead found herself with new information. Information he should have shared with her the minute he learned the truth.

"You should have told me." Her tears fell down her smooth cheeks.

"I'm sorry," he offered weakly. "You must know that."

"Why didn't you tell me?" Her voice cracked. With her arms pressed tight to her chest, she was the picture of grief. One word away from crumbling.

"I wanted to be sure," he admitted. Though he was confident in his deduction, he still wanted a second chance to examine Leith closely without additional eyes bearing down on him. "That is my only reason for holding back. Forgive me."

Remi didn't move for a long while. She just stood, lost in sorrow.

Ben squeezed his fists at his sides, willing himself to wait. He desperately wanted to offer her comfort.

"I'm tired, Ben." She sounded small as she said it. "Edgar is dead, and now Leith is gone. These notes...so many notes. I can't...I can't go on like this."

Ben approached her carefully, reminding himself to be gentle with her. "Remi?"

She looked up at him.

"I'm sorry about Leith," he whispered. "About my father. About me."

"Everyone is leaving me," she choked. "Elise will be gone soon, too. There will be no one left..."

His heart ached. "I won't leave. Not again."

"Prove it." Her lips shook as she grasped the front of his shirt, pulling him closer. Her voice was weak, yet her hold on him was strong. "Prove that you won't leave me, too."

His hands wrapped over hers, and he bent his head lower. "Tell me how, and I will. Whatever you want from me, I will give it to you."

Her voice did not waver. "Kiss me."

At her command, Ben felt the scorching heat of his needs and desires crash together, two demons of their own design that battled often in his mind. Ever at odds, it seemed, they were suddenly unified, singular in their desires. "Certainly," he hummed deeply.

If she was keen to give him the lead, he would not waste a second longer lingering on the fantasy; he would make it real.

～

REMI

Ben's fingers tangled in her hair, pulling at the roots just enough that there was pleasure in the pain. His other arm wrapped around her, pulling their bodies together as his mouth closed over hers. It was a heady kiss, thoughtful even. His teeth grazed her lower lip, nipping at her flesh, the sting soothed immediately with a gentle stroke of his wet tongue. She missed the feeling the moment his mouth left hers, traveling to nip her ear.

"Have I proven myself?" His voice was deep as he spoke. "Or is there more you want from me?"

Her mind still spun from the kiss. *What more could she want?*

Ben groaned, pressing into her. "Say it, and I will give it to you."

She blushed, turning her face into his. "I want...*everything*."

"Do you want me to touch you?" he asked, pressing his forehead to hers. His eyes probed hers, and she felt as if she'd explode into flames. "Is that how I'm meant to prove myself to you?"

Remi held her breath as she searched for the right words to say. "I want you to undo me," she whispered finally, "and put me back together after it's been done."

Ben's smile was tender as he nodded. "That I can promise."

He kissed her again, softer. He lingered, pulling on her lips with his own. She was beside herself with the sweetness of it, the way it made her center warm. She felt his fingers on her chest, undoing the buttons of her blouse. The fabric brushed against her breasts as it fell away, making her gasp.

Ben moved on to her skirt, careful in his ministrations. Standing before him in her stockings and a chemise, she felt for the first time the chill in the room.

"Cold?" His eyes dropped to her chest.

Remi glanced down and bit her lip. Her nipples were peaked, pressing against the thin fabric of her chemise.

He turned on his heel and dragged the duvet and pillows to a spot by the fire. He surprised her, lifting her up into his arms and carrying her to the nest he'd made by the fire. Lowering them both, he kept her firmly on his lap.

"Swing your leg around here," he murmured, kissing her shoulder gently.

Remi moved until she straddled his middle, her center pressed against the hardest part of his body. He nearly growled when she moved against him, gripping her thighs above the stockings when she finally settled.

"Better?" she asked.

"Much." He slid a finger down the skin between her breasts with a teasing smirk. "But your chemise is in the way."

"Then take it off," she said, her voice tight with longing.

Ben didn't hesitate. He grasped the hem and lifted it above her head, discarding it to the side. Dipping his head toward her chest, he closed his lips over the tip of her breast.

Remi jumped at the sensation, earning another groan as she rubbed against him. He rewarded her with a pinch to her other nipple, kneading the bud between his fingers as he continued his attention to the other. The pleasure was overwhelming but fleeting, for he moved away within a breath, leaving her wanting.

Ben watched her face as he eased back. "I want to taste more of you."

Remi blushed. "Whatever do you mean?"

His hand splayed against the space between her shoulders, and his legs shifted as he moved her to lay on her back. She waited, breathless, as his fingers moved to the band of her underclothes. Her breath caught in her chest with every inch they moved down her skin. She throbbed between her legs as he stripped the final barrier between them away.

Ben bunched the fabric in one fist and brought it to his face.

"Ben!" Remi hissed.

"Gods," he breathed, "you smell as sweet as you look. Now, come here so that I can taste you."

She yelped as he lifted her hips and swung her legs over his shoulders. His face, propped squarely between her thighs, focused on her center. His warm breath met the damp skin, sending a shiver through her body, followed by another when lips and tongue enfolded her.

Remi gripped the blankets beneath her, twisting the sheet in her hands as he sucked and licked. Her thighs clamped against the sides of his head, encouraging him as he pushed her to her peak. She shook with her climax, sighing as the aftershocks of pleasure overtook her. Ben didn't stop until she relaxed again, humming in his throat as he licked her one last time. When he pulled his face away, she could see herself on his lips. He grinned, the evidence of her pleasure coating his face.

"I can only imagine what it would feel like to have you quiver so desperately around me," he growled, setting her down. "Would you like that?"

Remi swallowed and nodded weakly. "Yes."

Without another word, he undid the button of his breeches. They fell past his hips, revealing his erection. Remi sucked in a breath as he leaned over her, capturing her lips in another kiss. Ben lowered himself between her legs, brushing against her already sensitive skin. Her mouth went dry.

"Please," she moaned.

It was all that she needed to say.

Ben moved slowly, gentle as he pushed inside her. He set a slow pace at first, as though testing himself, but Remi arched up into him, meeting each thrust and he lost himself. He panted, moving his hips in tandem with her own, gripping her thighs as they moved together. She gave herself over to him completely. Flames of passion flared between them. Remi's body shook with release once more, and she cried out his name as she shook from her toes to her fingertips. Ben moved faster, his own climax nearing; he pulled out of her, the warmth of his orgasm covering her womanhood and belly.

Everything was a blur as Ben disappeared, reappearing with a wet cloth. He took his time wiping her clean, his eyes warm and dark as he watched her. When he was done, he lay beside her, pulling her into his embrace. She felt his heart racing and lay against him, listening as his breathing slowed.

Finally, he spoke. "Have I done it, then? Have I proven myself to you?"

Remi lifted her eyes to meet his. "I could not doubt you now."

He smiled genuinely and then brought his lips to hers. He kissed her deeply, cupping her face with one hand as he pulled her closer with the other. She lost herself in the kiss, in him, in the moment.

The last few days of pain receded, along with the embers of their discord, fading like the fire in the hearth. It was as if the notes, the hallucinations, and the loneliness that had been taking up space inside her since she'd married Edgar were scrubbed away. She felt cleansed by his touch. She didn't need love to want what they'd done, though she was certain her heart was already there.

THE LEONES

REMI

Remi stretched her arms above her head, wriggling against the cool satin of Ben's sheets. Her muscles thanked her for the stretch, aching in places that she hadn't known existed. For the last few hours, she and Ben had been tangled up in one another. From the floor by the fire, where he'd been rough, to the bed where he'd stripped her down to nothing and taken his time, each experience was as different as it was pleasurable.

She curled her toes at the fresh memories.

"Ben?" she started, feeling bold as she rolled over to face him. The space where he'd been beside her was empty.

The room was dark, save for the glow of waning candles. Remi was stunned by the hour; it was later than she had realized. Without anything to cover herself, she wrapped the blanket around her body and tiptoed to the door. She pressed her ear to it first, picking up the sound of faint mumbling on the other side. Peeking out into the hallway, she spied Ben in just his trousers, holding a silver tray and speaking with Jacques. She could only see Jacques's back, but Ben seemed focused, his lips moving quickly. There was an air of business about him.

I wonder what they're discussing.

Whatever it was, it was a brief encounter. Ben and Jacques parted ways, and Remi stepped back to let him through.

"Awake already?" he asked, eyeing her bed sheet-wrapped frame as he shut the door. "A shame. I had planned to wake you myself."

"Really?"

"Yes." He breezed by to the table next to the bed and set it down. "Creatively, of course."

She followed with her eyes, spying a simple plate with an assortment of cheese, bread, and fruit. In his other hand, he lifted a pitcher of water and poured them each a glass.

"Should I pretend to sleep, then?" Remi asked, taking the glass he offered.

He chuckled, slipping his legs under the duvet as he settled back into bed. "We have all night and morning to be creative. For now, I'm famished."

Remi snuggled in closer to his side, clinging to the warmth of his body and relishing the comfort it brought.

Ben downed his water in three gulps and reached for the platter, placing it between them. He offered some to her before hungrily attacking the spread.

Remi chewed her slice of concorde gratefully. "Did something happen?" she asked.

"What do you mean?"

"You were speaking with Jacques," she said, inclining her head toward the door. "Was it important?"

"He reminded me that I have other responsibilities today," Ben said, weighing his words carefully.

"Did he?"

"Yes." Ben looked sheepish. "He knows that I have a certain proclivity for…staying in bed when there's a woman with me."

Remi blushed.

"And I would prefer to stay in bed with you today," he said, brushing a thumb over her red cheek. It sent a pleasant chill down her spine. "There is so much more I'd like to do."

"You're a scoundrel," she teased.

With a light chuckle, Ben leaned back against the headboard and stretched his long legs out in front of him. There was a deviousness about him as he watched her with hooded eyes. Remi felt his gaze everywhere. "Why don't we play a game?"

"I don't know," she said cautiously. "I sense you're leading me into something I might regret."

"A simple game of questions and answers." He shrugged. "But first, you should take that off."

He lifted a hand and gave the sheet she wore a small tug.

"I might," she said, clutching it closer to her breast, "if you give me a straight answer for once."

Ben laughed. "Fine, fine."

"What sort of questions am I allowed?"

"They must be direct questions," he said, "and you must give direct answers. Always tell the truth."

The truth? Remi squirmed. "How many am I allowed?"

"Five questions." He held up a hand. "Are you ready?"

Remi mirrored his gesture and nodded.

"Then my first question," Ben started. "Was I your first?"

A blush crept across her cheeks and warmed her chest. She drew the bedsheet closer and sucked in a breath. His brows shot up, wide-eyed when she said, "No."

"I want details." He breathed in deeply, his nostrils flared.

"Not without asking a question," she reminded him.

He held her gaze, his stubbornness draining as she held fast. Finally, he relented, and Remi went next.

"Since you asked such a personal question of me, then I must know, how many women have you shared a bed with?"

"Excluding *present* company..." He smirked, drawling each syllable suggestively. "More than I can count on two hands. Had you asked me about my first, I would have told you what an experience that was."

"A good one, I hope."

Ben shook his head and grinned. "For neither of us, I'm afraid. She was a good sport about it all, though."

Remi hid her face, embarrassed by his brazen reply.

He laughed again.

Remi realized this was the most she'd heard him laugh in a long time. He so rarely smiled either, but that seemed to have passed, replaced by good humor and lifted spirits. Her toes curled at the thought that she might have contributed to his change in mood.

She wasn't sure if she would survive his game if his questions were going to be so revealing. "Your turn," she mumbled.

"Who were you with?"

Sorrowfully, she answered, "Leith."

Ben's expression sunk. "I apologize. That was unfair of me."

"It's the truth. I've no need to hide it any longer." But she avoided his gaze, instead staring into the bottom of her cup; empty though it was, it felt heavy in her hands. "Did you ever love any of the women you were with?"

"Love?" He leaned back, crossing his arms at his chest. His dark hair fell over his face. "No...not that I can remember. I enjoyed their company, and they enjoyed my money, but there was never love."

"I loved Leith," she said, but quickly added, "Not in the way that you might think. He was one of my dearest friends."

"After I was gone," Ben said. It was not a question.

Remi snuggled up closer to him, brushing her fingers along the roots of his hair. "Would it comfort you to know that the boy who used to live here, in this manor, was my first love? I kissed him once in a dusty attic."

"It would." He sounded pained, though, as if thinking about what could have been hurt too much.

"Ben?"

"I blame my father for what's happened."

Remi tilted her head. "What do you mean by that?"

"If he hadn't sent me away...if only I had been here." Ben stopped himself and paused, collecting his thoughts. "My family has a talent for making rash decisions."

"What do you mean?"

"Just that," he said absently, looking distantly off into some unseen space. "The man who built this house, Arthur, nearly lost everything. He went mad because of it."

"How?" she asked.

"There was a fire," he said, "and half of the original house burned down. No one died, thankfully, but he went on and on about the family curse. How it had almost claimed him and his family's life. He was so paranoid that during reconstruction, he installed secret passages throughout the manor."

"We found some of those," Remi confirmed with a slight nod. When they were children, they'd found plenty of hiding places all over. It made the game of hide-and-seek much more challenging.

"We did..." Ben's brows furrowed. "But we never found the tunnels."

"Tunnels?"

"Apparently, they're all over the Isle."

"Sounds like a children's bedtime story." She was skeptical, unsure that she could believe a series of channels existed below them. "I almost don't believe it."

"I do," he said with a smile. "So did Soleil."

Her eyes widened.

"Arthur almost lost his whole family the night of that fire." Ben paused and rubbed his eyes, "He made an escape route in case anything happened and he couldn't save them. I can't say I blame him for his choices."

"Your family has quite an interesting history," she sighed.

"Only certain parts." Ben nodded. "There's no ending in any of my family's stories where someone doesn't die. The same is true for Arthur and Leyda."

"What happened to Arthur?" Remi asked.

"Naturally, as is tradition in our family," Ben started as he lifted his head and eyed her with a great deal of attention, focusing intently on the way her hair covered her chest. He licked his lips. "Arthur was shot down in the street. One day before his birthday, according to his death records. He was murdered by a man named Pattrin Gilliam. No one had ever heard of him, but it was rumored that he'd been looking for Arthur for over a decade—seeking vengeance of some kind."

Remi gasped. "What for?"

"Money, maybe." Ben shrugged. "But we'll never know. Pattrin was hanged shortly after."

"That's terrible," Remi said. "About Arthur, I mean."

"He was rumored to be a scoundrel, too," Ben winked. "Runs in our blood."

"What about the rest of your family?" Remi asked, wrapping her arms around herself.

"Misfortune followed them throughout the years." He shifted and rested his head back again. "They all passed away in some brutal event or another. My own grandfather died at sea shortly after my father was born."

Remi was quiet for a moment.

"I do know one thing about Arthur that was never mentioned in any of the official family registers," Ben said conspiratorially.

Remi sat up a little straighter, leaning into him until she was practically on top of him. He peered at her from under his lashes and smirked.

"What is it?" she asked.

"Arthur was a thief," he whispered just loud enough for Remi to hear. "He amassed a fortune. That's how he started the family home, and what he didn't use, he saved. That's the treasure, but it's been well-hidden to this day. No one in my family has ever discovered its whereabouts."

"Except perhaps your father," Remi said quickly, but added, "but if it really was lost, why would he make a point to mention it in his will?"

Ben shook his head. "I don't know."

"Would he have done that if he didn't know where it was?" She looked into his dark eyes, holding his gaze with her own.

"He was clever, there's no doubt about that." Ben ran a hand through his hair and grasped it at the back of his neck. "If we intend to find anything, we'll need to be *more* clever."

"But?"

He groaned. "That leaves us in a bit of a predicament, doesn't it?"

"Perhaps he's left us clues somewhere?" she offered. "Only, we haven't found them yet."

"Clues would be useful, yes." He bobbed his head and paused, thinking before he spoke again. "But you must understand. Even my sister, who was twice the man my father was, couldn't find it."

"That is, *if* it exists?" Remi asked, echoing his previous skepticism. She knew there were few things he believed in, save for the string of tragedies that followed him and his family.

He chuckled. "Yes, *if* it exists."

"I'll help you find it." Remi stood, taking the bedsheet with her.

"Of course you will." His eyes roamed over her body as he stood to put his hands around her waist. He guided her gently to sit in his lap and folded her to his chest. "But we can worry about that later. There are more important things I want to attend to first."

Remi gasped when he flipped her to her back, caging her between his arms and broad chest. She ran her hands up his arms to his neck, prompting him to bend lower. Their lips met with a feverish need for each other. As she deepened the kiss, Ben wrapped her up in his embrace, trapping her beneath him. Soon enough, they were tangled in the sheets and duvet, breathless.

FIRE

BEN

*B*en had taken to watching a sliver of Remi's hair flutter as she breathed, still sound asleep. The hypnotic push and pull had convinced him to stay longer, to see it gently touch the tip of her nose and dance away—over and over again. Eventually, he smoothed it back behind her ear and forced himself to leave the bed before he fell asleep again. Jacques had caught him in the hall earlier to let him know he'd successfully delivered Leith's body to the cellar.

Ben extracted himself from Remi as gently as he could, hoping not to disturb her.

He located his trousers near the foot of the bed and dressed himself, sneaking from the room and closing the door. Jacques waited patiently near the steps, wearing a disapproving look that already tried Ben's patience.

He wasn't sure how to say it aloud, but Remi would not be like the others.

"Sleep well?" Jacques raised a thin brow.

"I did." Ben grinned. "And so did she."

"Madame has earned a lifetime of rest, in my opinion."

"I couldn't agree more," Ben said, stopping at the base of the last step. Jacques unlocked the cellar, and the two descended into the dim lantern light. Leith's body had replaced his father's, which had been moved to another corner on a smaller table. They would have to find time to return both bodies once he had completed his study.

"It was difficult to bring him here."

"I can imagine."

"Can you?" Jacques grumbled. "Had to wrap him in a sheet and pull him from the cart into the cellar like a child with a wagon."

"That's crude."

Jacques blinked slowly. "It's the truth."

"Let's just get on with it." Ben approached the head of the table, all the while reminding himself that it isn't a violation if it's for the right reason. It wasn't as though he delighted in the act of exhumation; he liked it even less when it was a person he knew. Leith was a victim like his father and if his death was in fact murder like his father's, then he needed to be certain of the cause.

I'm sorry for this. Truly.

Ben unbuttoned the collar of Leith's shirt. The marks on his neck and wrists that Ben had seen at the dock were still evident. Ben ran his fingers along the bruises to feel the impressions.

"Write down what I observe," he bid Jacques, and the other man reached for one of Ben's notebooks. Without waiting, Ben explained in detail the size of the markings and the distinctive impressions.

"A rope no thicker than nine millimeters in diameter," he hypothesized. "The blue color of his lips suggests strangulation, which could be mistaken for drowning. The tips of his fingers are raw, and the debris beneath his fingernails includes flecks of dried blood."

Ben reached for his scalpel, prepared for Leith's chest to be as botched as his father's, and sighed at how poorly stitched up it was. It almost felt wrong to conduct an autopsy on a man Remi had grown up with, especially one she'd been intimate with. He couldn't help thinking that if he'd stayed on the island, then he would have been with Remi, not Leith. The possible scenarios of their life together had played over in his mind on a perpetual, torturous loop.

Certainly, he would have courted her properly and then proposed to her with her family's blessing. In the moments they shared leading up to their wedding, they would have stolen kisses and held hands when no one was looking. He would have married her in September when the leaves were turning, once the stormy season had finally broken into peaceful weather.

Remi in a wedding gown.

And the wedding night...

He shivered. Had he stayed, he could have been her first—and last—everything. He looked down at the Leith then, suddenly feeling as cold as the other man's corpse. Ben gave his head a quick shake, banishing the thought. Remi's friend was beneath his scalpel and he was busy thinking about her body in wicked ways. "Forgive me," Ben muttered quietly under his breath. He owed the man his respect in death, at least.

Thoughts cleansed of Remi, Ben opened Leith's ribs with his tools and a forceful pull, wincing when they cracked. He was jealous of a man who'd been murdered. He felt awful for even thinking such trivial things. Remi had been lucky. She'd had someone other than Elise to lean on.

A noticeable silence surrounded them until Jacques coughed, bringing Ben back to the present.

"What are you searching for?" he asked.

"Lesions in the lung tissue." Ben removed both organs and transferred them to an empty surface to examine them. "Even if the original report said they'd found water in his lungs, there would be markings on the tissue. Thankfully, the body hasn't decayed enough that I won't be able to see them."

Jacques nodded, waiting patiently as Ben worked.

"I was right. They're clean," he finally announced.

"So he didn't drown," Jacques stated plainly.

"No he didn't," Ben said, stepping back from the body. Leith's body was handled just as poorly, and purposefully, as his father's. It couldn't be a coincidence. "The doctor lied about it entirely."

Jacques clicked his tongue. "Paid off, I think."

"By who?" Ben's shoulders sank. "Lamotte? Marchand? Remi's uncle?"

"Could be all of them."

It was merely conjecture. Ben couldn't do anything yet, even with his notes and observations. Even if the doctor was a negligent fool, he wasn't wrong about Ben's standing. He had no certification outside of hearsay and he couldn't exactly admit that he'd conducted a posthumous examination on the body.

He needed to come up with a solution, and fast.

REMI

Remi licked her lips. She could taste…*fire*.

She inhaled and smoke burned her lungs. She coughed, terror seizing her as she jolted back to consciousness. She didn't recognize the room, but in the roaring fire, everything was indiscernible. She only felt the sensation of being trapped, like a moth caught in the flame.

Where is the door?

She tried to spin around, but her feet would not move.

A window! What about a window?

The flames grew hotter, licking up her feet to her waist, racing along her arms. She was melting into the floor, losing herself to the uncontrolled fury of the fire. Remi's eyes flashed back and forth until a face surfaced from the blaze, reaching a hand out for her to take. She grasped it with her own and pulled with as much strength as she could muster, but found that she could not be moved.

"Save yourself."

The visage in the firestorm stepped forward, crowned in flames from head to toe. Pink skin bubbled and charred before her eyes as Lamotte's smile faltered. His eyes bled from the empty holes in his head, his skin melting away from bone.

"Save yourself," he said again, his arm burning up in her hand.

She screamed, losing her grip on him as she fell backward. The inferno swallowed her, and just as the heat reached its peak, Remi's eyes burst open.

Sweat dripped down her brow. Her body was covered in a thin sheen of it, her blanket soaked and her hair sticky. She sat up, chest heaving with each panicked breath. Another nightmare, another phantom disrupting her peace. Lamotte had certainly caused a great deal of anguish in town. Remi held him accountable for the nightmare.

"Madame?" A voice called to her from the other side of the door. "We have a problem."

Is that Jacques? Whatever could he want? Remi wondered as she shifted herself to sit. "Come in."

Two bodies tumbled through into her room, one of them being Sylvie, followed by Jacques. Her maid was in tears and Ben's footman wore a grim expression.

"Sylvie?" Remi asked, startled as the young woman fell to her knees. She bowed her head, shaking with unsuppressed sobs. "What's going on?"

Jacques crossed his arms. "She's a thief, Madame. I caught her rifling through Monsieur's desk in his study."

Remi's eyes widened. "What? Sylvie, is that true?"

The young woman broke into tears, sobbing louder with each breath she took. It was an awful, agonizing sound. Her pain, her frustration—Remi could feel it all. Pulling the blankets aside, she went to Sylvie's side to comfort her, but Sylvie pushed her away. Jacques moved to intercept her, but Remi held up a hand to stop him.

"Sylvie, I can't help you if you won't talk to me." Remi tried.

"I'm so sorry, Madame," Sylvie sobbed, wiping at her face with her sleeves. "I'm so sorry for what I've done."

Remi stilled, sharing a quick look with Jacques. He appeared just as confused as she felt.

"I don't understand. What have you done?"

Sylvie looked at her through swollen eyes. "Too much, I've done too much! But they told me I had to do it. They told me if I didn't—if I told you, they would do much worse things. I shouldn't have believed them, Madame. I shouldn't have."

"Who?" Remi felt a chill and crossed her arms tightly against her chest. "Who told you to do what?"

"Stealing, Madame! Delivering those awful letters." Sylvie sobbed. "I didn't want to, but they threatened to hurt me, or you, if I didn't!"

Remi tensed. "*You* delivered those letters?"

"What have you stolen?" Jacques asked, his jaw ticking with anger.

Remi wondered the same, though she assumed it was her belongings, like the locket.

Sylvie looked like a wounded foal, her large, wet eyes bouncing between them. "I'm so sorry for what I've done."

"Sylvie, listen," Remi started, cautious as she spoke. "If you tell us who threatened you, we can fetch the *gens d'armes* and send word to your family. We can help you."

Her eyes grew impossibly wide, lips quivering. "I can't, Madame. I can't!"

Both Jacques and Remi reached for her, hoping to calm her, but Sylvie screamed, "I can't!"

Small and sleight, the young woman slipped past Jacques with incredible speed. She raced through the hall and down the stairs. Remi hurried after her but wasn't nearly fast enough. The doors burst open with a simple push and she was gone. She was already halfway down the gravel drive when Remi reached the doorway, breathless as she watched Sylvie's retreating figure from the threshold.

"Remi?"

She spared a glance over her shoulder, catching movement from the hall that led to the study. Ben emerged from the shadows with concern clear in his expression. He came straight to her and wrapped an arm around her shaking shoulders.

"What's going on?" he asked, herding her away from the door after shutting it. "Why are you crying?"

"Crying?" She wiped at her cheeks. Traitorous tears had been falling unknowingly from her eyes the whole time. "I didn't realize..."

Jacques cleared his throat. "It was Sylvie. I caught her rifling around in your room. She had some papers in hand, trying to tuck them away when I found her. Madame and I confronted her moments ago."

Ben turned Remi in his arms. "Is it true?"

"Sylvie was leaving the letters," Remi nodded stiffly. "She said that someone coerced her into doing it."

"Did she say who it was?" Ben asked, looking between her and Jacques. Neither of them had the answer he wanted to hear.

"No." Remi rubbed at her temples. "She ran off before we could learn anything more."

Ben swore under his breath.

Jacques asked him a question, and Ben replied so softly that she couldn't hear. Her head began to pound. It felt as if someone was hammering nails into the back of her skull; if not for Ben holding her steady, she might have collapsed where she stood.

"Ben?" Remi swayed, gripping his arm to steady herself. "We have to help her."

He lifted her, cradling her against a warm, broad chest. Ben's voice vibrated against her body as he addressed Jacques. "Get the horses and bring them around front."

Jacques went wordlessly.

Ben carried Remi into the parlor and set her down on one of the armchairs. She was grateful for the seat but missed the warmth of his solid frame almost instantly. He knelt down in front of her and reached one hand out to touch her chin, keeping her gaze focused on his face. The intensity in his dark eyes made her heart flutter.

"I'm going to find her," he declared. "And when I do, I will bring her back here so that we can get to the bottom of this."

"I'm worried about her, Ben." She grasped his wrists with both hands.

"Sylvie seems resourceful," he said with a half-hearted smile. "After all, she's been cunning enough to escape suspicion up until this point."

Remi relaxed. "This is true."

Carefully, he wove their fingers together and brought her knuckles to his lips. "I will find her," he promised.

"You'll find her," Remi echoed.

Ben searched her face, his own set with determination. She hoped he could see how much she trusted him, how deeply she needed him. Then, just as he reached for her, she leaned in and met his eager lips. His hands flew to her head, cradling it as he stroked her cheeks with his thumbs. She would have melted into him, let him take her there in the parlor, but the spell between them broke as he pulled away.

"Wait for me." With a short nod, Ben took off. Remi watched him go, hopeful that he would manage to bring Sylvie home.

THE SEARCH

BEN

Sylvie might have had a head start, but Ben hadn't anticipated her complete disappearance. She couldn't have gone far—her legs could only take her to so many places in such a short amount of time. The hour had grown late, and there were only so many places a young woman could run without drawing attention to herself.

"Shall we split up?" Jacques suggested. "We can cover more ground that way."

Ben nodded. "I'll meet you in an hour."

The town of Flottante was large, but its streets were narrow. He dismounted, guiding the horse with him through the quiet cobbled roads. There weren't many people out at this hour; the docks were empty, the seamen asleep in their boats. He stopped to inquire at the inn, but everyone he spoke with eyed him warily. Ben was beginning to lose hope when Jacques suddenly appeared around the bend.

"Lamotte!" he yelled.

"What about him?"

Jacques brought the horse to a stop, clearly out of breath. "She's gone to see Lamotte," Jacques sucked in a deep breath and grasped at his chest.

"Are you certain?" Ben furrowed his brow.

"I heard it at a bar down the way." Jacques shook his head. "The owner is her uncle."

Ben sighed deeply.

"Lamotte lives on the other side of town," Jacques shouted above the whipping wind. "Easy to find, but if we intend to catch her, we need to go now!"

Ben nodded and kicked his heels. They took off down the hill, squinting in the meager lantern light. Part of Ben wished that they were in Paris. At least there the streets were alive with electricity. The island had yet to see them, outside of the few homes they'd passed.

"Nearly there!" Jacques shouted.

Ben wished he could move his horse at the same speed his mind was racing. Of all the places for Sylvie to go, Lamotte's was the last place he expected her to go.

Jacques's horse came to an immediate halt, startling Ben and his own horse. He careened to the side to avoid colliding but found it hard to tear his eyes away from the obstacle in their path.

"No," he rasped.

Jacques mirrored Ben's horror.

Lamotte's home, the only house on this side of town, burned against the night sky. With the force of the wind, it had spread rapidly, tearing through the house like it had been constructed of paper. Ben watched it with a dark expression. He could feel the fire dancing under his eyelids when he blinked, sinking its heat deep into his skin until it had burned its way into his blood.

"We must go." Jacques hissed suddenly, turning himself and the horse around. "The crowd."

He jerked his head and indicated the amassing number of spectators as they cried out and screamed for help. Little black figures darted around the house, throwing shimmering buckets of water onto its charring figure in a fruitless attempt at stopping the spread. There was no doubt in Ben's mind that Lamotte had been inside. The fire, he felt in his gut, had been started by someone who wanted him to stay quiet.

What of Sylvie?

"This way." Ben heard Jacques's command.

"No!" he shouted from behind, cutting him off. "Follow me."

Ben led his horse down a narrow road until it came out on the other end. He followed it to the docks, back toward Lamotte's office. It was a few buildings away from where they'd pulled Leith from the water, and with everyone else preoccupied with the fire, he would be able to break in unseen. If Lamotte was well and truly dead, then he needed the papers stashed inside the bottom drawer of his desk.

"Someone was here before us," Jacques said as they pulled up beside the small building.

Its door stood wide open, the glass windows shattered.

"Apparently." Ben's stomach dropped. He wanted to ignore it, but there was an answer to the mystery already. He thought about the letters again as he wandered into the darkness of Lamotte's office. A little light shone through from outside, enough for him to see how ruined it was. Chairs overturned, broken pieces of shattered glass, books on the floor with strewn pages; and his desk with its clear surface. Some drawers had been pulled out, but the one on the bottom was left undisturbed.

I need to get in there.

He was surprised that it had been left untouched, but then, it blended into the desk and it was dark. Whoever had stormed in had made quick work of the place, tearing it apart without the knowledge of what it was hiding. Still locked, Ben surveyed the floor around his feet, dropping to his knees to dig through the debris. He patted around until a flash of silver caught his eye. He reached for it—a heavy silver letter opener.

"Let us hope this is sturdy enough," Ben muttered. The desk was heavy and old, a work of art. He bit his lip as he wedged the silver tip of the opener into the thin crevice of the drawer. Once its lip had opened a fraction, he reached for the heaviest book on Lamotte's floor and brought it down with great force—over and over again—until it popped the lock and the drawer came free.

"I hear voices—hurry!" Jacques hissed from the door.

Ben pulled the drawer open and retrieved the thick file that

Lamotte had shown him days ago. Tucking it safely under his arm, he hurried to his feet and breezed through the door. Mounting their horses again, they made haste for the manor.

REMI

Voices roused Remi from sleep. She'd heard them outside the window but had rolled to her side instead of searching for the source. Her eyes had been heavy at the time, but a moth had perched itself beside her on the tuft of her pillow. Its wings batted softly, the familiar array of colors and shapes demanding her attention.

"I know you," she whispered, and it moved.

The moth fluttered away and Remi sat up, shocked by the number of moths covering every surface in her bedroom. Some took flight when the bedroom door creaked open. Remi found herself gaping at the silhouette standing halfway in the darkness. Moths clung to his shirt and hair, another covering one of his white eyes.

"Edgar," she breathed. "Why are you here?"

His mouth stretched to a yawn, releasing a strangled cry like the creak of the door from his translucent chest. It was loud enough to disturb the creatures that had woken her, sending them into a frenzy. Remi held her arms up to cover her face, hoping it would not wake Elise, who slept beside her.

"I don't know what you want," she hissed under her breath, fear gripping her.

When the moths settled, she looked back at the door. Edgar was gone, and they were chasing after him. Remi had followed him once before and had stumbled upon Ben. He didn't seem to want to harm her, only to get her attention. She pushed the covers back and climbed from the bed without waking her cousin. Tiptoeing across the floor, she followed Edgar and his moths.

He was nearly a blur between them and the darkness, but she could make out his figure all the same. She felt in her gut that he was leading her to the study, but she doubted she would find Ben there again. The manor was quiet, the only light piercing the shadows was a fire burning in the parlor. She saw Martin lounged in a chair, a small book open on his chest and his eyes closed; lost in some dream outside of reality.

Where is Ben? she wondered.

A moth fluttered by, brushing against a wisp of her hair—as if tugging her along, like a child beckoning its mother.

"I'm coming," she said, swatting at it gently. It fell into line behind the others.

At the end of the hall, Edgar waited by the door.

The study. But why?

Twice Edgar had brought her there, and when he disappeared inside again, the moths dispersed into dust. Remi opened the doors, swallowed by the dark within. At its center, beside the display, he waited. Watching her with unblinking eyes. Without his mouth ever moving, she felt his voice echo inside her head from a memory from weeks ago.

*The moths led the way…*he'd said about the petrified specimen in its display. *My family holds my treasure…*

"What are you trying to tell me?"

Remi crossed to the center of the room, beside the display. Edgar did not withdraw or vanish into thin air. His figure moved like smoke —in and out of form, he blurred between a solid body and an ethereal being without form. He watched her, expressionless.

"I wish you had left clues," Remi said to him, frustration rising in her. "What could you have meant? What are you trying to tell me?"

His mouth opened as if to speak, but his head whipped around— drawing Remi's attention as the fireplace suddenly came to life. A rush of fire burst from the burned wood and ashes inside its hearth. Edgar was gone before she could learn anything else, and the fire had not stopped growing. As if it had grown arms and hands, it reached out to her, screaming.

Remi felt its heat too close to her face and turned to escape before it could consume her. But the doors slammed shut, stopping her halfway. Blocking her from the only exit was a new figure—a phantom born from the fire. It wore flames like a second skin, and though its true figure was charred and ruined, she could see its face for what it had been.

"Lamotte?" she gasped.

He bellowed from the door like the fire in the hearth. His painful cry reverberated in her ears and head. Remi screamed and backed away from him, but her foot caught against the rug and she fell back onto the floor with a hard thud. Something else moved beneath her as the rug curled under her legs, caught between her body and the floor. Remi did not stop screaming until a face appeared above her.

It was Elise.

"What happened?" her cousin asked as she helped her stand.

Remi shook violently, barely able to speak. "W-why are you here?"

"Shh, let's get you to bed," Elise murmured. "Maman and Papa are here too, and we don't want to alarm them."

Elise tried to press her again, but Remi wordlessly curled into a ball under the covers. Silence had sewn her lips together, and Lamotte's flare scorched a terrifying image behind her eyes.

CAUGHT

BEN

The moon peeked over the top of the manor as Ben and Jacques approached.

"I'll take care of the horses," Jacques said as they dismounted. Ben nodded, heading to the front door when it surprised him by opening.

He recognized Arnaud, Remi's uncle, immediately. "Welcome back."

"What are you doing here at such a late hour?"

"Do my family and I need a reason to visit my niece?"

Ben tried not to scowl. The last thing he needed was more things to worry about. "Come inside," he tried. "Make yourself at home."

"Oh, we have," Arnaud said jovially.

We?

Ben said nothing else to him as they entered the foyer together. He knew, even before he heard the voices in the parlor, that "we" meant the entire Cuvilyé family. Beline and Hugo were present and accounted for.

"Good morning," Ben greeted them with a forced smile.

"It took you long enough," Beline sniffed. "Remi had a terrible fright this evening."

Ben's heart leaped in alarm.

"Did she?"

"Elise found her screaming in the study," Beline said. "I think she had a nightmare."

Ben moved to go to Remi when Armand stopped him. "You should let her rest," he said. "Madame Cuvilyé and I also wish to retire."

"Please feel free to make yourselves comfortable in the guest rooms," Ben grumbled.

The Cuvilyé family headed upstairs.

Ben had planned to spend the night in the study, but he made haste for the second floor and found himself in front of his own room. Breaking the news about Lamotte's home would have to wait until morning, especially if it meant that the lawyer was dead and Sylvie was still missing.

Carefully, he opened the door. Ben knew it was improper to walk in on them while they slept, but knowing that Remi had experienced something earlier only encouraged him to check on her. Under the current circumstances, seeing her asleep on her side, breathing softly as her cousin slept beside her was a comfort. After the night he'd had, already sore from the time spent on his horse, kneeling next to her wasn't nearly as bad.

"Sss cold," she mumbled.

Ben cracked a smile. Her lashes moved with her eyes; blue-green peeking at him from half-open lids. "Did I wake you?"

"No," she whispered. "I'm still asleep."

"Then I am a dream," he said.

"A beautiful dream," she hummed. His heart felt soft in his chest, and had Elise not been there, he would have kicked off his boots and crawled into bed with Remi.

"Beline said you had a fright."

"Mm," she breathed. "I saw your father...and the fireplace...flames."

"My father." His stomach dropped. "Fireplace and flames?"

She couldn't have known about Lamotte, not yet. But then, she was half-asleep and he wasn't sure what she meant.

"Bed," she hummed softly. "Morning...I'll tell you."

Ben waited a moment longer until he was sure Remi was asleep again. She said nothing more as her body rose and fell with slow, steady breathing. He leaned forward despite himself and pressed a light kiss to the top of her head. She did not stir again, so he made for the door. To be near, he stayed in the room across from his own and started a fire for himself. When it burned steadily, he sat on the floor and spread out the papers. He spent a few moments straining to read them before he heard Jacques' footsteps approaching. The other man knocked and invited himself in.

"Horses are put away," he said plainly. "They'll be tired tomorrow. We'll have to delay our search for Sylvie until they're fully rested."

"I thought as much." Ben sighed, setting the papers down. He ran his hands through his hair, exhausted. "I need something strong."

"Coffee?"

Ben nodded. "And a dash of *creme*."

"I'll return with it shortly."

He picked up the papers he'd set down and skimmed through them. There were correspondences passed between the lawyer and his father, and a few left between him and Arnaud Cuvilyé. Each suggested a deal that had been brokered between his father and a man in Paris—someone who intended to make a large purchase. Ben guessed it was the same as the receipt he'd found in the study under the piles of paper on the desk.

"What's this?" he asked aloud when Remi's name was mentioned.

The passage of funds...hereby sign over the final amount of allowance for the proposed dowry between Edgar Leone II and Arnaud Cuvilyé to broker the marriage between the aforementioned and one Remi Cuvilyé.

Signed at the bottom were four names: Ben's father, his lawyer, Remi's uncle, and a man by the name 'Bernard Cuvilyé.' He guessed that was her father, who had agreed to sign over his daughter with an allowance, which spoke of her worth to him. It had been a meager sum, but the funds would be used as a payment to Edgar, upfront, for his hand in the sale of expensive wine to a wealthy friend connected to him—a friend that did not exist.

"She was sold," he said to himself.

His father had bought her outright.

"Learn anything?" Jacques asked when he finally came back, a coffee in hand. He brought a tray along with the *cafetière* and *creme.* Ben gestured to a side table as he brought himself to stand.

"Too much, unfortunately." He picked up the saucer and cup and took a drink, feeling it burn down the back of his throat. He missed coffee. It had a flavor, unlike tea or liquor. "I have an inkling about these recent deaths and the papers only corroborate my suspicions."

"What are they?" Jacques asked.

"That we might have been right to cast Hugo as our villain," Ben took another drink, and while it warmed him, it did nothing to chase away his growing distress. He remembered again the carved letters on his sister's desk and her desperate need for money. If it was an 'H' she'd drawn beside her own initial, then it was Hugo who had pushed her—and it explained his new obsession. "Remi asked me one night if I thought the letters were tied to Leith."

"And?"

Ben grimaced. "I didn't give her an answer."

"But now?" Jacques scratched at his chin.

"I'm still not sure," he said.

"Sleep on it then."

"I'll be awake for hours now," Ben said, indicating the coffee. "You go on. No need for both of us to be deprived of a few hours' rest."

Jacques dipped his chin. "Goodnight, then."

Alone, Ben stoked the fire and rejoined his papers. He read them again, word for word, right down to the minute details. His eyes felt heavier, sleep impending as it weighed on him. The last thing he read before sleep took him was a letter to his father from Bernard. Inside the envelope was the wedding announcement, the same one that he'd received, and a handwritten note:

Dear Sir,

My family and I will not be in attendance. As this is merely a means to tie some unusual knots between your family and mine, I do not see the benefit in watching you marry the creature I have disposed of. That being said, you will receive the agreed upon sum one week prior to this engagement.

Signed,
Bernard Cuvilyé

It was a cruel note, and the last thing that he'd been conscious enough to read. When the darkness came for him, it was cold like the words in the letter. Without joy, without meaning, without love—a reminder that Remi had been passed from one member of her family to another, only to be bought by a man that Ben had once thought of as an immaculate scholar.

"I wanted to save her," a voice in the darkness said. "To give her a home."

"They paid you," he mumbled, pushing through sleep to finally open his bleary eyes. The air was damp; the bed he found himself on was a table in the cellar. Ben sat up and looked about. Sheet-covered corpses covered every surface in the room. He clambered off the table and peeled back the sheet from the closest body. Beneath it was Lamotte, half-burned.

The voice spoke again. "She was alone."

"So was I," Ben replied, moving to the next table. Leith lay beneath the sheet, a rope fastened around his thin neck.

"I married her."

"She was even more alone then!" Ben felt his frustration reaching a peak, but at the next table, it snuffed itself out.

"Forgive your father, *mon coeur.*" His mother's dry lips moved, her decaying flesh peeling away from bone. She wasn't anything like the portrait hanging above the mantelpiece, not anymore. Time had eaten away at her, though he knew she was ashes in their mausoleum.

A white sheet moved beside his mother and Soleil peeled it back to reveal herself—twisted and broken from her fall, covered in a thin layer of sand and slick from the water. She sang, "Yes. Papa meant well."

Fear gripped him. "He was wrong! He made a mistake."

A hand slid over his shoulder, a gentle squeeze. He turned to face his father—a moth like the display in his study clinging to his chest. There was blood caked around his ears and neck.

"Forgive me, Ben," he rasped between blue lips. "I should have brought you home."

Ben choked on a sob.

"I should have brought you home," his father repeated, his hand tightening on his shoulder. "I should have brought you home."

Red tears rolled from the corners of his white eyes and blood dribbled down his chin from where it spilled over his bottom lip. He sputtered, "Come home, Ben. Come home."

He blinked, forced to the ground with his father on top of him. He fought, but he could not escape. His father's weight pressed down on him, his blood raining on Ben's face. Two more bodies crawled on top and held him down from either side—his mother and Soleil. They smiled. "Come home, Ben. Come home."

The ground at his back shifted, suddenly sinking as it enveloped them. He gasped amid their chanting.

"Ben," a distant voice shouted, "*wake up*."

REMI

"The *gens d'armes* are here," Remi said. Ben was covered in sweat and tangled on the floor among papers she'd only glanced at. He was shaking and hard to wake, which she prescribed to the tray of coffee on the side table nearby.

"The what?" he groaned.

"*Les gens d'armes*," she hissed. "Inspector Marceau is here, asking for you."

That got his attention. He woke with eyes as wide as she'd ever seen them, and the concern she felt worsened. "Where's Jacques?"

"I don't know."

Ben scrambled to his knees, collecting the papers and stacking them neatly. "I'll be down in a moment."

"Is everything alright?" Feeling uneasy, she gripped her skirt.

Ben glanced up, and seeing how she white-knuckled her dress, he sat the papers to one side and stood. He brought her hands to his lips. "Would you believe me if I said yes?"

She narrowed her eyes. "I struggle to believe you, especially when I almost tripped over you. Why were you sleeping on the floor?"

"Later," he said, kissing her fingers again. "I'll explain later. First I need to change."

"He's in the parlor," Elise said from the doorway. "I offered him tea."

Ben nodded and took off for his bedroom, a flash of dark hair and wrinkled clothes.

Remi chanced a look at the papers he'd forgotten but decided to leave them behind. Her nerves had been too tightly wound since they'd been woken by the raucous pounding at the door. She and Elise had had precious little time to ready themselves before being shocked by the sight of *gens d'armes* at the door.

"Ben is upstairs changing," Remi told the inspector as she entered the parlor. "He'll be down in a moment." She took the seat across from him. "Might I ask what this is about?"

"Well, you see," he started, putting away his teacup, "there was a fire last night."

A fire? Remi's memory flashed with the image of the raging fireplace from last night. *Could it be?*

"There was a casualty," he continued. "I believe you know the victim in question."

The burning specter had shared his countenance, but it couldn't have been him. *Please, not Lamotte.*

"I'm here." Ben appeared in the doorway before the inspector could finish.

Remi noticed his grim expression, and made to ask after him, but noticed her *tante* and *oncle* following close behind.

"Get rid of them, Arnaud. It's much too early for this." Remi heard her *tante* hiss to her *oncle*. Arnaud was watching the inspector, though, uninterested in what Beline had to say.

Marceau's eyes followed Ben as he rounded Remi's chair, stopping beside her. "Monsieur Benoît Leone."

From the corner of her eye, Remi saw the *gens d'armes* enter the room one at a time. They blended into the wall, their expressions unreadable. The atmosphere in the room shifted drastically. Between the space in which they stood, packed with her onlooking family and the austere *gens d'armes*, Remi almost felt sick. Her stomach turned as the ominous silence dragged on.

"Welcome," Marceau said, not a note about him having changed. He remained calm. "We were just discussing the fire."

Ben paled.

"So it has been made known to you?" Marceau asked.

"I saw it last night."

Remi's throat compressed and she grasped at her collar.

"What's this about?" Ben asked.

"The home belonged to Lamotte, your father's lawyer." Marceau waved his hand and the *gens d'armes* against the wall marched to Ben's side. "I was told that you had been spotted in the area before the fire. A witness puts you at the scene."

"What?" Ben and Remi said in unison.

Elise shot her a look of warning.

"Yes," Marceau paused, producing a small notebook from his breast pocket. He flipped through it and stopped on a few pages. "Leading up to this event, people in town described you as hysterical and unhinged. You were searching for a young woman named Sylvie. Did you know she was going to see your father's lawyer last night?"

Ben looked conflicted, but he said, "Yes, I knew."

"Well, it seems that whoever was after her set the house on fire." Marceau leaned back in his chair. "They ended up killing an unintended target. Monsieur Lamotte is dead, and the young woman in question is still missing."

Remi gasped and covered her mouth with both hands. The specter she'd seen, what thing she'd seen in the study—it *had* been real. The fire had been Lamotte the whole time, and he'd appeared to her the same way that Leith and Edgar had.

"That is unfortunate news," Ben said.

"Yes, it is." Marceau tucked the booklet away and narrowed his light eyes at Ben. "Was Lamotte an intended target then? Or was it just the maid?"

"Excuse me?" Ben licked his lips. "What are you implying, Inspector?"

"As I said, you have been placed at the scene before the fire, and we later learned that Lamotte's office had been broken into with items missing—the same witness places you there as well."

Remi thought of the papers again in the bedroom. Lamotte had mentioned important documents to her the last time they'd crossed paths. Had Ben taken them?

"Say it plainly, sir." Ben pulled back his lips like a snarl. "Are you accusing me of something?"

A moment of tense silence passed before footsteps outside hurried in a thrush of motion against the hardwood. The other two *gens d'armes* that had come with the inspector had Jacques with them. He appeared beaten and bruised, as if he'd tried to run and they'd stopped him in time. Remi rose from her seat.

"Did you find them?" the inspector asked.

"*Oui.* The bodies are in the cellar," one of them said.

"Bodies?" Remi felt as if someone had pummeled into her chest with their bare fists. Her breathing came out sharp and haggard. She would have spiraled had it not been for the very sharp scream that came from Tante Beline as she fainted.

"Madame, I will require your assistance." The inspector's voice was muffled against the thrashing of her heart. "I'll need you to identify them for me."

Remi shot a glance at Ben, whose face had lost an immeasurable amount of color. Confusion and fear gripped her. "What bodies?"

Ben pressed his lips into a tight line, refusing to answer her.

"This way, Madame," Marceau said gently, guiding her through the darkness toward a back room.

"What is this?" It had never crossed her mind to go below the manor's first floor. Its secrets had been undiscovered until the moment the backroom door opened; the pungent odor of death and decay made her eyes water.

Two bodies covered in white sheets lay on the floor among shelves that had been meant for wine and other storage. It appeared as though the cellar's contents had long since been emptied, the space unused for its intended purpose.

"The young man who drowned. His body was reported missing," Marceau snapped his fingers, and one of the men near Remi knelt beside a body and lifted back the sheet. "When we spoke, you said the two of you were close. Is this him, Madame?"

Remi shriveled against the wall behind her, startling the inspector.

"Leith," she choked. Pain clamped down on her heart, and she found it harder and harder to breathe. "Why is—why is he here?"

"Madame?" The inspector's concern was genuine as he held out his hand for her. She did not take it, too fixated on Leith's body. He'd been there the entire time, and she hadn't known. "Madame Leone, I'm terribly sorry, but I need your eyes. Just one more, please."

Remi tried to stand on her own and peered around the inspector as he lifted the sheet from the second body. She breathed gasps of air between words. "Edgar. My late husband."

The inspector gave his men a subtle nod. "Thank you."

Remi hurried back through the cellar on weak legs, falling to her knees with a hard thump at the top of the stairs. Her mind felt miles away from her body. The tingling in her limbs ceded to numbness as if she'd been dipped into a frozen lake and left out to dry in a snowstorm.

"Madame..." Marceau's voice was warm, but what he said was

harsh. "We have reason to believe that your late husband's son is guilty of the charges presented before him."

Elise drifted into view with a pinched face resembling her mother's. "What bodies did my cousin need to identify?"

"Edgar's," Remi mumbled. "Edgar's and Leith's."

Elise held back her own shock.

"It is unfortunate but true. I wish it wasn't." Marceau hung his head, aggrieved by the admittance. "We'll need to take him for further questioning."

Remi's eyes snapped open wide as Ben emerged from the parlor, a doleful expression worn heavily upon his brow like a crown made of sorrow and guilt. The *gens d'armes* beside him were like two vices and, for all of his height, Ben appeared small between them. Her feet moved beneath her, nearly tripping on the skirt of her gown, and closed the space that lay between them.

"I know it wasn't you," she said, reaching for his face with shaking hands. "Someone… Someone else must have brought them here to frame you. To make you look guilty."

Ben's dark eyes crinkled around the edges. Behind him, Jacques lingered in the doorway, the other two guards that had escorted Remi and the inspector to the cellar flanking him. Both of them were prisoners.

"No." Ben swallowed. "I—we—did it."

Remi's throat tightened.

"I thought I… I thought I could remedy the situation." He looked as though he wanted to say more, but his eyes flicked to the inspector. "It was an error in judgment."

"But Leith…" Her voice was a whisper.

"I know."

A raw, guttural cry like a wounded animal tore from her breast. *"Why?"*

Ben did not flinch.

"Madame"—the inspector tapped her shoulder—"I apologize, but we must be on our way. My men will return for the bodies once we have secured these two."

Ben wrapped his fingers around Remi's wrists and pulled them gently away from his face. There were shadows under his eyes where there had been none before. It was as if he'd aged considerably since she'd found him asleep on the floor in the bedroom. The moments they'd shared felt distant now; the further out the door he walked, the more blurred the edges of her memory became. He disappeared inside a carriage.

"Remi, you're shaking," Elise said.

And she was. Remi trembled with rage and sorrow. She wrapped her arms around herself, digging her blunt nails into the fabric of her dress until she could feel the bite of them against her flesh. Questions taunted her, bereft of the answers that would ease her mind. All she could do to keep from spiraling was speculate on the unknown with every scenario in her arsenal.

NOT GUILTY

BEN

Ben tortured himself the entire way to the carriage.

Hands bound and body aching, he played through every moment since he'd come home. He agonized over his pig-headedness. Had he just let Sylvie flee, he might not be in a carriage with the inspector. *No. I should have left their bodies alone.*

"For the record, I don't believe you to be guilty." Inspector Marceau cleared his throat. "But the evidence is heavily against you."

"Overwhelmingly." Ben scoffed.

Jacques had been separated from him and escorted to a second carriage. A parade through town to the *gaol* on its outskirts would be a welcome sight to the island's residents after the events of the day before. Their villain was caught, and they were no doubt relieved.

"Perhaps too much, don't you agree?"

Ben glanced at the inspector. "Then why take me in at all?"

"Due to the aforementioned."

"Yes, the evidence." Ben sat up straighter. "Might I know your sources?"

Inspector Marceau shook his head.

"What will you do with me then?" Ben asked.

"Bring you to the *gaol*," he replied, "deliver you to your cell, perhaps ask a few more questions, and then write a report based on my findings."

"Do you intend to find the real murderer?"

"I shall do my best."

Ben felt helpless. The inspector might have been sincere, but there was an absence of confidence in his tone. He knew he could explain why he had the bodies in the cellar, but without a license to practice, his explanations would not matter.

As if reading his mind, the inspector said, "Exhumation is a serious crime."

"There was a reason."

"What good reason is there to disturb the dead?" Marceau crossed his arms. "You caused a great deal of pain to the boy's family."

"I understand that."

"Then why?"

He heard the echo of Remi's pain. *Why?*

"Leith, the young man, was murdered. He did not drown." Ben said.

The inspector raised his silver brows. "No?"

"I was at the docks the morning they discovered him." Ben gestured to his own neck and wrists, indicating the lacerations he'd found. "He'd been bound and strangled. If he'd drowned, there would have been water in his lungs."

"But the doctor reported—"

"If you think the doctor is a reputable source, you are sadly mistaken."

Marceau's mustache twitched with the hint of a smirk. "He said you might disagree."

"And I do!" Ben snapped. "He's a drunk."

"But he practices within the law, whereas you do not," Marceau said. It was an observation, not an insult, but Ben still felt its sting. "You have a great deal of knowledge on the subject, however, so I might be inclined to hear your side."

"And what would you do with that information?" Ben asked.

"Delay your sentence."

A flicker of hope found its way to Ben. "How?"

"Truthfully, I'm not from the Isle." Marceau glanced out the window. "I was dispatched from the mainland and asked to look into current matters. As I said, I do not think you are guilty, but I will need the entire story if I am to aid you."

Ben considered the inspector thoughtfully. "What do you want in return?"

Marceau shrugged. "Above all else, I want the truth."

"That's very honorable of you."

Ben pressed his lips together and sucked in a breath as the door opened. He was not yet ready to leave the safety of the carriage or its meager comfort. But Marceau did not wait, and *les gens d'armes* were there to guide him out. Jacques waited on the cobbled path, and people had started to gather. Ben ignored them as he stepped out of the carriage and into their scrutiny.

"Do we have a deal?" Marceau leaned in a fraction to be heard above the growing noise.

"If you send for Remi," Ben paused, catching movement in the crowd. A red tuft of hair bobbed above the other heads, and Hugo's inscrutable countenance made itself known among the others. There was a darkness about him that left him blackened, even when the rest of the world was bathed in light. "If you send for Remi—let her speak with me—then we have a deal."

"I will do as you ask." Marceau nodded. His eyes sparkled with understanding. "It has been quite a long time since I last heard a love story."

"Thank you."

The inspector left him in the care of *les gens d'armes*. As they led him to one side of the *gaol*, he watched Jacques dragged to another. He felt the alarm rising in his chest, and when they brought him to a cell with iron bars, he gawked. The island was more behind on modern progress than he had originally thought.

"The inspector requested that we bring you to an uncrowded cell," one of the men said, shouldering Ben inside the cage. His height made it impossible for him to find a comfortable position in the cramped space, but he said nothing.

When the men eventually left him, locked up and alone, he collapsed on the cot and sat on its edge with his head pressed between his palms. Hours passed in silence before the inspector returned for him; by then, it was evening, and Ben had been wading in misery. He approached the bars as Marceau sat in a chair he'd brought along with him.

"Did you speak with Remi?" he asked. "Will she come?"

With a notepad in hand, he frowned. "No, she refused."

Ben's heart sank.

"I will try again tomorrow," the inspector assured him. "Give her time."

Ben did not speak. His hands stiffened on the cold bars as he held back the nausea roiling in his gut. She would not come to him, would not see him. He couldn't blame her, and yet, he still felt himself breaking.

I might have lost her forever.

A moment of shared sympathy passed between the men before the inspector cleared his throat and tapped the notepad's blank face with his pen.

"Now then, let's start from the beginning."

REMI

Remi could not eat and barely slept.

Losing sleep meant nothing to her, but eating had been hard. Everything that touched her tongue tasted like ash. Elise called for the doctor on the second day, but he'd been drunk and dismissive.

"She's hysterical," he'd said simply. "I'll prescribe her laudanum for sleep, but I cannot help any further than that. Widows in mourning often need sunshine."

Elise sent him off immediately, the same way she'd sent her mother and father away. Their presence had proven unhelpful in pulling Remi from her wretched state.

Remi had asked Elise to leave, too. Her cousin's constant hovering agitated her in the worst way and, though she meant well, Remi could not find it in her to be cheery. She had locked herself in Ben's room, sequestered to the bed and sometimes the bath. Elise had tried her best to comfort her, to pull her free from the chaos, but it was always there to pull her back down.

"I want to be alone," Remi had said. "Please. Go home."

When Elise had finally gone, reluctant as she was to leave, Remi fell apart all over again. She thought too much, saw too much. Between Edgar's body and Leith's, she wondered if the specters she had been seeing were trying to warn her all along. Maybe they had come to her, begging her to follow them to the cellar where she might discover their bodies—restless spirits whose peace had been disturbed.

I failed them.

On the third day, Remi refused everything but tea.

She finally accepted the laudanum and slept for hours, waking on the fourth day feeling worse. Her head throbbed, and her eyes burned, dry, and swollen from too many tears. She bathed and dressed with little regard for her appearance and would have missed the subtle knock at the door if she hadn't been descending the stairs at that moment. Loathe to answer, she forced herself to open the door.

Inspector Marceau's shock was evident. "Madame Leone. How wonderful to see you."

"Hello," she muttered half-heartedly.

"I did not expect to see you," he said, glancing over her shoulder.

Remi knew he was looking for Elise. She had taken to answering the door after the events that had transpired.

"She's not here," Remi stated plainly. "I sent her home."

"I see." Marceau gestured to the door. "Might I come in?"

Remi moved aside. "Of course."

"I'm here on behalf of Benoît," he started. "He's asked that I implore you to see him. One last time, but as I told him, your cousin made it quite clear that—"

"My cousin?" She floundered. "Elise told me he didn't want to see *me*."

Marceau straightened. "Not at all, Madame. He has been eager to speak with you."

Remi covered her mouth, suppressing a sob. She'd hidden herself away, hideous with the thought that Ben had refused to see her the last three days. She'd wanted to go to him, to ask her questions. He had the answers she needed, and if there was a way she could clear his name, then she wanted to do it. But when Elise had told her that Ben refused, she'd fallen into a pit of despair she hadn't bothered to try and climb out from.

"I believe your cousin might have misled you." He frowned.

"With the best intentions, I'm sure," Remi replied, though the words felt empty.

"He would do well to see your face. His spirits have been quite low these days, and I'm afraid conversation has been difficult." Marceau scratched at his chin absently, concern written in his expression. "I know both you and I believe him to be innocent."

Remi's heart leaped. "I do!"

Elise had spent some time comforting Remi but had also tried to make her see how Ben would be guilty. She had even tried to convince her that Ben had written the letters to keep her occupied and away from his own business. But despite Elise's colorful efforts, Remi had not changed her opinion about Ben's innocence.

The inspector's eyes widened. "Then you will come and see him?"

"Yes, of course I will!"

"I shall ride ahead and alert *les gens d'armes* of your arrival." The inspector tipped his hat and hurried out the door.

Remi ran to the kitchen and found Martin at the stove. He was preparing tea with a side of bread and jam for her. He jumped at her sudden entry, nearly knocking the tray to the ground.

"I apologize, Martin, but I need you to fetch the carriage."

He frowned. "I'm sorry, Madame, but one of the wheels is being fixed."

"A horse then," she said in reply. "Bring me a horse, please."

"Of course. I'll have Paul bring one around for you," he said unquestioningly.

Remi thanked him and offered him the tea in her stead. While she was away, he could have the morning off.

Hurrying up the stairs, Remi found stray pins on the bedside table in Ben's room. She twisted her hair up, pinning it in place. It had been a long time since she'd been on a horse, and with the weather as unsteady as it was, she might get caught in another storm. She ran down the stairs in a simple wool coat, her boots clattering on the hardwood, and hoped that she would make it to Ben before the rain caught her.

Remi burst through the front doors, the horse already waiting. But before she could reach it, a figure stepped out from the garden and blocked her path.

"Where are you going?" Hugo asked.

Startled, she took a step back. "Hugo, my goodness. Where did you come from?"

He squared on her, his mouth bowing into a hard line. He asked again, more forceful than before, "Where are you going?"

Remi tensed.

"Do you plan to see him?" Hugo asked, nostrils flaring. He did not seem like himself at all, and the harder she looked, the more maniacal he seemed—as if some vital piece was missing. He took a step toward her, cracking his neck in a volatile fashion, and sighed. "You shouldn't do that."

"It's none of your concern, Hugo," Remi said, backing up another step.

"You're a good girl, Remi." He licked his lips. "*My* good girl."

The stone wall of the manor collided with her back, and Hugo pressed himself closer. A loose strand of hair had come free from her pins, and he snapped it up in his fingers. He leaned forward and brought it to his lips, whispering, "Always good, so well-behaved."

Remi froze. "Hugo…"

"Soft, sweet…" He hummed lowly in his chest. "Nothing like Elise. You would listen to me, obey me, like a proper wife."

"You're out of line," she said, trying to stave off the fear she knew could be heard in her voice. "Let me go."

"Invite me inside," he snarled, pulling at the hair in his hand.

"No," she yelped, pushing her hands to his chest and shoving him.

He stumbled back and caught himself before falling. "What's gotten into you?"

Where she expected to find rage, Remi saw only hurt. He held out his arms for her, an awaiting embrace. "Don't you know? Haven't you read my letters?"

The hair on the back of Remi's neck stood on end. A sickly chill coiled around her body with a serpentine grip. "I hope you jest."

"I love you, Remi," he professed. If it wasn't for the soulless look in his eyes, she would have believed him.

The violation she'd felt in finding the letters among her things grew; he'd seen a part of her that no one else had without her permission. She shook at the thought. When she didn't answer right away, his frustration grew crazed, breaking past the serenity of his false calm.

"I said I love you," he snarled. "I have confessed!"

"I do not owe you a reply." Remi summoned all of her strength and willed herself away from the wall, forcing her feet to move as she walked past him. "I suggest you find a place to hide away, *Monsieur.*"

He followed her, hot against her heels. The force of his strength fastened around her right wrist and stopped her dead in her tracks. Through bared teeth, he growled, "Is that a threat?"

Remi whipped her head around and mirrored his scowl. He was a brute. *No wonder Sylvie could not tell him no.* He would have done much worse to her if she had not done as he instructed.

"Yes," she hissed. "Make no mistake that my family will hear about this, and you will lose everything you might have ever had with my cousin. Now, *release me, sir.*"

He reluctantly released her.

Remi spared him nothing else. She instructed Martin's son to run straight inside and tell his father what happened, then climbed atop her horse and made haste down the hill to the *gaol* where Ben waited.

BARRED

BEN

"I spoke with Madame Leone," Inspector Marceau had announced upon his return to Ben's cell. "She'll be here presently."

It was the first good news he'd received in days.

The days had felt like months, with the silence dragging on. He swore he heard whispers at night, even though he'd only seen rats scurrying from hidden corners in the walls. His conversations with the inspector had been conducted at certain hours of the day, but little strategy had been devised. The person he truly needed was Remi— and more than that, he missed every second he couldn't see her.

On the first day, he felt desolate.

By the third day, he'd dizzied himself with enraged pacing.

But the news Marceau had delivered some twenty minutes ago had lifted a weight from his chest that had settled there overnight. He paced the cell like a madman, jumping when he heard voices or footsteps. Doubt that she would not show snuffed itself out when her blue-green eyes and wind-blown red cheeks appeared in the hallway. He collapsed against the bars, pressing himself as close to her as he could through the iron barrier.

"You came," he breathed.

"Elise said…" Remi gasped, curling her fists into his dirtied shirt. "…it doesn't matter. I'm here now."

Between the bars, Ben kissed every inch of Remi's face, until he reached her lips. He never thought he would know desperation so intimately as he did when he clung to her warmth through the bars of his cell. The echo of a strangled cry left his chest, and he would have reduced himself to tears if she had not been crying herself. He pulled away and lifted her face up, cradling it in his palms.

"Forgive me," he pleaded. "Forgive me for what I've done to you—to your friend. I made a grievous mistake."

"Tell me why you did it."

"To right a wrong, to get answers I couldn't find in paperwork." Ben swallowed. "Does it matter? I hurt you."

"It matters," she whispered. "It matters…if Leith was well and truly murdere—"

"He was," Ben said without a hint of doubt. "Trust me, please."

"And your father?" she asked, fear and realization mingled in her expression.

He gave her a solemn nod. The anguish in her was written across her face, and the grief he imagined she felt at the truth was tangible. Remi sank to her knees, and he went with her, the joy at their reunion replaced by inconsolable sorrow.

Finally, she managed to say, "It's Hugo."

"What about Hugo?"

"The letters," she paused. "He wrote the letters. It's no wonder Sylvie was so distressed. I can't imagine what he said or did to her."

He'd been right to suspect her uncle's associate then. "How do you know?"

"He tried to stop me from seeing you." She bit her lip. "And then he admitted to it…just before he confessed his love for me."

"Did he hurt you?" Ben's anger slammed into him like a forgotten door in a long passage. "What about Soleil? Did he mention my sister?"

"No," she said. "He made no mention of Soleil. Do you think perhaps it was him who pushed her?"

"It could very well be," Ben said, no happier about being proven right than he would have been if his assumptions had been wrong. "He could have wanted her for money—he's the type to kill for it."

"Oh, Ben." Her eyes were wide like saucers as she rubbed absently at her wrist. "If it's true—if it was him—I'm sorry."

"He'll get what's owed to him. Rest assured," Ben said as he reached for her hand and brought it to his lips through the bars. He muttered against her knuckles, "I saw him as well. He was there the day they brought me, watching from the crowd."

She looked incredulous. "But why?"

"Jacques and I..." Ben hesitated, unsure of his suspicions. Both of them had wondered if Hugo was the true culprit, and if the letters were his, then it aligned. If it hadn't been about money, then it had to be about Remi. "We thought it might be him. He's been sneaking around and poking his head into everything."

Quickly, he added, "Of course, the letters he'd been sending to you were a piece of the puzzle that didn't fit...until now."

"Then...you think he killed Leith?" Remi asked. Ben remembered her question outside of the study some nights ago. She'd only speculated at Leith's untimely passing, but it seemed possible now that jealousy had driven Hugo to the brink. Greed had done his sister in, of that he was sure.

"Possibly."

"And that's why the bodies were...in the cellar?" She hesitated, afraid to bring it up.

"Yes."

Remi bit her bottom lip. "Edgar as well?"

"Strangled. He'd been beaten and stabbed," Ben said, not withholding the gruesome truth. "When we looked, the wounds had been stitched up with a sloppy hand. Someone was trying to cover their tracks."

"That's horrible."

"It is." Ben's tone dropped to a warning and whispered to Remi softly through the bars. "Now listen—Inspector Marceau believes me to be innocent. He's heard my side and wants to help, but we need proof. We need to provide him with something solid."

"The papers from Lamotte's office?" Remi asked, remembering the stack in the guest room.

Ben shook his head. "Perhaps, but those don't incriminate him. They paint a colorful picture, but otherwise, they prove nothing."

Remi's face scrunched in thought as she postulated the situation further. Finally, a light went off in her head, he could see it in the way her eyes brightened. "Didier!"

"Who is Didier?"

"Leith's lover," Remi stated. "He stopped me on my visit with Leith's mother. He said that he saw someone, that Leith had been attacked. I didn't want to believe him, but perhaps he can help."

"Yes!" Pride swelled in Ben's chest. "But why didn't you tell me this sooner?"

Remi blushed. "We were...preoccupied."

"Ah."

They were silent for a moment, Ben lost in the memory and Remi seemingly embarrassed at how easily she had forgotten something so important. Finally, she broke their individual reverie. "I'll find Didier, but what should I do about Hugo? He may return for me. There's no saying what will happen then..."

"One step at a time, love," he said softly. "Find Didier, and when you do, ask him to speak with the inspector. No one else."

Remi nodded.

"Go home, lock the doors," Ben instructed carefully. "Find the papers and come back with them tomorrow. Deliver them *only* to the inspector."

"I don't want to leave you," Remi said quietly, eyeing the cell and its bars.

He knew what she was thinking, and he couldn't have agreed more. It was a medieval relic, a step back in time. It reminded him of a night once spent in a dark and odious alleyway after a long night of drinking.

"Remi, you are my salvation," Ben said, drawing her attention back to him. He reached for her cold hands and held them tightly against his chest. "From the moment we met as children, you saved me. You cannot know how you revived me after all these years, how you have set my soul aflame with your unwavering spirit and caring heart. I cannot undo the last few months, but I will devote myself to you from this moment until the end of my life, if you will have me."

Her eyes widened, wet with tears. "You have so much faith in me."

"I do." He smiled, bringing her hands to his lips and nuzzling her fingers. She smelled like rain and soap, with a distinct undertone that was all Remi. "You *can* do this."

REMI

Remi dressed herself early the following morning, sorely missing Sylvie's aid. She'd chosen a gown with buttons up the front for ease of access, though it was much too heavy for the spring. She pinned her hair up as best as she could and hurried to collect the papers from the guest room. They'd been left in a messy pile on one of the armchairs, and when she reached to pick them up, a few fell from the bottom.

Half-asleep, Remi knelt to pick them up.

A weathered slip of parchment opened in her hand as she grabbed it by its folded corner. An image of the manor had been sketched onto its yellowing face, complete with a layout of each floor. Remi hesitated before putting it back, her eyes focusing on an extra room that had been placed below the study.

"Could that be the cellar?" she asked aloud.

But the cellar had been drawn in separately, labeled alongside the wine vault. Remi put the papers down again and brought the sketch closer to the window to examine it. Her eyes widened.

Ben's voice echoed in her memory. *After that, he went a bit mad and installed secret passages throughout the manor.*

"These are blueprints," she said to herself, "and they are different from the original floor plan."

The story of Arthur and Leyda and the fire that had nearly killed them and their child returned to the forefront of Remi's mind. The passages were marked on the blueprints, and suddenly, the paper seemed much older than it first appeared. It was an updated version of the home after it had been rebuilt sometime in the 1600s, after the fire.

Remi covered her mouth to suppress her surprise.

"Tunnels," she mouthed against her palm. "He'd mentioned tunnels."

One was marked clearly on the newer blueprints.

Remi gathered her skirts and stumbled toward the door. She hurried down the hall, her boots hammering against the hardwood as rapidly as her heart beat inside her chest. A wave of dizziness struck her when she finally breached the study and dropped to her knees in front of the wrinkled rug. She took a deep breath. The floors groaned underneath her weight as it shifted.

"It was here," she murmured. "This entire time."

The moths led the way.

"Is that what you were trying to show me?" she asked aloud. Remi moved the rug until its lip curled up and over, revealing a hidden trapdoor built into the floorboards.

She stood and removed Edgar's prized moth display, pushing it away from the center of the room.

Remi shifted the furniture until she could roll the rug away completely. Sweat dripped down her back in the warm velvet gown, and she pulled at the collar to breathe. The rug was heavier than she expected it would be; by the time she had the shallow handle in her fingers, she was almost out of breath.

"This is it," she said.

The door creaked open as she pulled it up. It took every last bit of her strength to raise the hidden door. Like the rug, it was much heavier than it appeared. Once its weight shifted, she let it fall open with a loud thud and fell to her knees. She took a few steadying breaths while the numbness in her fingers wore off, then examined her newfound mystery.

A black hole extended into the ground; its yawning emergence ignited a combination of fear and excitement in Remi. Edgar had known about it the entire time, she was certain. There was no telling how many times he must have disappeared into the tunnel to explore; if the stories were true, the treasure that had once been lost had been found again in its sprawling darkness.

Remi dangled her feet over the hole, finding footing against a thin ladder that had been built into its side.

"There's a way down!" she exclaimed, unable to contain herself.

She hesitated, an alarm going off inside of her.

Ben was waiting for her. She had responsibilities and too little time to accomplish everything in a matter of hours. "It can wait."

Though she felt its beckoning—a mystery to be solved, laid bare at her feet.

"Can't it?"

The resounding echo of knocking at the front door pulled her from her conflict.

Who could that be?

Remi gathered her skirts and tore herself from the tunnel's entrance. Hastily, she drew the doors to the study shut. No one ever went into Edgar's study anymore, but she wished she had the key so she could secure the lock.

The knocking at the door grew more impatient until it finally stopped. In the foyer, she spied a single envelope as it was pushed through the mail slot. She waited before approaching, afraid of who might be waiting on the other side. After a moment, Remi tiptoed as lightly as she could toward the door. Her name peered up at her from the white face of the envelope, the handwriting familiar.

Remi's stomach plummeted as she picked it up, tearing it open on the spot. The message did not immediately register, for shock had numbed her thoughts. Disbelief warred against the reality of the words on the page.

Dearest Remi,

I see there is not enough room in your heart for me. Yet. But I will carve a space, my love. Once he and she are gone, I will be all that's left in the world for you.

He and she, Remi thought over and over again. Both turned in her mind, their meanings taking different faces. If *he* meant Ben, who sat in a cell with the weight of false charges against him, then who could he have meant by *she?*

"Elise."

Her cousin, his bride-to-be—the woman who stood between him and Remi. But he wouldn't hurt her, would he? She thought of Leith and his relationship with her. Hugo had been at the wake; if he had spied them together, he might have suspected something. Anyone would have. And there was Edgar, who'd died one month after marrying her. Remi gripped the letter, shaking from head to toe.

"I was wrong," she said, thinking of her cousin's face. "I should have told her, I should have warned her."

Of course, Hugo wouldn't hurt Elise. He wanted Remi.

But love—in any of its many faces—could drive people mad.

THE TRUTH

BEN

Remi's visit had been too short, leaving him longing.

In the hours that had passed, Ben had thought of countless things he'd wanted to say, all of them involving how sorry he was. He wanted to tell her why he kept the bodies a secret, why he'd chosen to keep her in the dark—why he sabotaged what little good he did have within him. He'd become his father, keeping secrets from the people he loved most. Seeing her anguish over the last few days had broken something inside of him, shifting fundamental knowledge in his mind so that it could be rebuilt.

He wanted to be better, somehow.

And if she managed to save him, his life was hers. He meant it, too. She could have it all, every jagged part of him for her to reshape and remake to fit alongside her.

I only have to live, he thought to himself miserably.

"Apparently, you've had a visitor."

Ben's eyes dried. He hadn't heard anyone approaching, let alone realized the hall outside his cell wasn't as empty as he'd thought.

"Have I interrupted you?"

Arnaud Cuvilyé curled a hand around the cool bar of the damp cell. He was the last person Ben expected to see and one of the few visitors he could have done without.

"Why are you here?" Ben sneered.

"To make sure you are blamed for all of this."

Ben blinked, unsure he was hearing correctly. Then it dawned on him. "You're covering for Hugo."

"Hugo?" Arnaud's eyes widened. "Do you have proof?"

"He's been sending Remi cryptic love letters."

Arnaud threw back his head and laughed.

Stunned by his reaction, Ben recoiled at the sound. It was wild, belligerent, and full.

"Hugo has been an unexpected complication, but none of this is his doing," Arnaud said. "He's too blinded by his obsession with my niece to be of any help."

Ben felt the air leave his lungs as if he'd been punched in the gut. "It's you."

"All of the pieces have fallen into place and I'll make sure they stay that way," Arnaud continued as if Ben hadn't even spoken. "After the hand I've been dealt, and after so much miserable luck—I'm finally winning."

Ben bared his teeth. "Were you the one who murdered my father?"

"Of course."

Rage shot through Ben's veins, boiling under the surface of his skin, chasing away the cell's chill. "And Lamotte? That was you, too?"

Arnaud smiled. "Will you ask about Sylvie next?"

Ben shot his hands through the bars.

Arnaud stepped out of reach, unaffected. "Don't worry. She's alive for the moment. I've incapacitated her."

"Do you plan to kill her as well?"

"Of course." Arnaud did not hesitate. "She's just another loose end. One I should have snipped clean weeks ago."

Grief and rage overwhelmed Ben. He felt helpless, trapped in his cell. He couldn't be of any help to Remi, and not a single soul was around to hear Arnaud's confession. They'd been wrong earlier. Hugo might have been sending letters, deranged as he was, but he wasn't the source of their troubles—Remi's uncle was.

"Leith was an unfortunate loss," Arnaud added with an air of relief. "Wrong place, wrong time, I'm afraid. I don't know how much of our conversation he heard, but it was more than enough to make him a liability. A shame, too. My wife was fond of him."

"It broke Remi's heart."

"You'll hang for my crimes." Arnaud leaned casually against the bars again. "If it eases your mind any, I have something delicious planned for my niece. If all goes accordingly, that is."

"Why are you doing this?" Ben tensed his fists at his sides.

"Because I want what's owed to me." Arnaud leveled his gaze with Ben's. Without an ounce of feeling, he spoke. "Because your sister made promises, and your father was a fool for robbing me. Your family is indebted to me, and I plan to take everything I am owed."

"My sister?" Ben felt his body go cold, paralyzed by the mere mention of Soleil.

"Yes," Arnaud grinned. "You didn't know? You'll be my third Leone."

A sick feeling overcame Ben then, his stomach churning with disgust as the realization sank in. "Soleil..."

"Yes." Arnaud grinned, his expression wicked and taunting. "Soleil was a delightful thing."

A, not H, Ben thought, unable to speak.

"I enjoyed her company well enough, but she failed to provide any real value to me."

"So you pushed her?" Ben asked through gritted teeth. "Why?"

"She threatened to tell my wife if I didn't break off my marriage." The man scoffed and shook his head as though the idea of leaving his wife was an inconceivable notion. "Really, I only wanted the money she had been saving. I needed an easy ticket. Raising a family with a wife as materialistic as mine added extra strain to my coin purse, as it were."

Ben white-knuckled the bars. "Murderer."

"You should know that it wasn't my intention to hurt her. I was only going to take the money," Arnaud shrugged as if it was a minor matter that he killed Soleil. "In the end, she left me no choice."

"There is no money." Ben snapped. "Surely you must know that by now."

"Unfortunately, I learned that much too late." Arnaud scowled. "However, that is easily remedied. With you and my niece gone, I can take the land and sell it for what it's truly worth."

Again, he reached for Arnaud's throat—but the man stayed just out of reach.

Ben swallowed his rage and waited until Arnaud calmed. *He's completely mad.*

Sniffing, the other man composed himself and smoothed a wrinkle from his jacket. He pulled a watch from his pocket and clicked open its bright face. Licking his lips, he ran a hand over his hair and smoothed it back. "In any case, I must be off. I'm working within a sensitive time frame, and I would hate to make my niece wait."

"Mark me," Ben called after Arnaud. "I will make you regret every move you've made since Soleil's death!"

His footsteps grew farther and farther away.

Ben slumped into the cell and grasped his head, squeezing his temples. It helped with the shaking that had now wracked his body, undermining his nerves as everything inside of him fell apart. He'd been wrong about Hugo, despite how certain he'd been at first.

Arnaud, not Hugo, he thought, closing his eyes. But then they flashed and widened, realization oozing from every cracked surface of his mind.

"Remi!"

~

REMI

Remi's feet kicked up rocks and mud behind her.

She'd gone from the foyer down the hill to the manors along the sea. The way was easy, the house she'd grown up in was still the same as it ever was. The first time she'd seen its large bay windows and traditional French doors, she'd been eight and heartbroken. Many times, she would find herself staring out longingly toward the ocean, wishing on every star in the night sky that she could go home again. But time had passed, and her aunt and uncle's home had become hers; precious memories lingered there, ingrained into its walls and floors.

She would not let Hugo defile them.

Remi burst through the servant's entrance in the back and raced past the cook in the kitchen. She weaved around the obstacles she'd memorized from her youth: the table in the dining room with its bum leg, the buffet she'd bumped her head on during hide-and-seek, and the rickety balustrade that gave way under too much pressure. As she ran, she could hear the memory of their laughter and feet pattering as they chased each other down the halls and into dimly lit rooms.

Elise will be alright, she tried to tell herself. *Hugo will not harm her. It's me he wants, not her.*

But there was a pit in her stomach, and doubt swarmed her thoughts.

"Remi!" Tante Beline's voice was as loud as thunder. "What are you doing?"

Beline didn't know. She couldn't know.

Remi did not stop herself from propelling up the stairs. Her feet moved faster than they ever had, the urgency in her nerves forcing more momentum behind each purposeful step. Others joined her, their cries at her back, but she did not stop. She could not stop.

Elise is in danger, she wanted to shout. But she could hardly breathe, and at the top of the landing on the second floor, she saw Elise's open door. In the span of a breath, Remi fell through it and collapsed to her knees

"No," her voice cracked, "no, no, no."

There was a bloodcurdling scream.

"Elise!" Beline's voice was pained, and it tore at Remi's heart as if breaking open her chest and ripping it out.

Her cousin—the closest thing to a sister she'd ever had—lay pale and still on the floor of her bedroom. She was dead; Remi had been too late. Elise's hair and freshly powdered face were caked with blood and vomit, soaking into her new gown. There would be ladies from the tea society arriving soon for the little party her mother had been planning to celebrate her marriage to the man who had killed her.

Beline shoved Remi aside, caging her daughter between her arms like a fierce lioness.

"Guillaume! Guillaume!" Beline sobbed, shaking as she cradled her daughter. "Find Arnaud—find him! Where is Hugo?"

Remi felt a chill embrace her.

Nothing but the vague ringing of a little bell could be heard inside her head. Muffled voices shuffled in and around her, and then two hands locked beneath Remi's arms and pulled her up. She swayed on her feet, unsteady as she was moved away from Elise.

Remi recognized her uncle as he ushered her into her old room. The passive look of indifference on his face gave her pause.

"You should rest."

He dropped her to the floor in the bedroom and, using the weight of his body, pressed down on her chest with his knee. Remi tried to fight him off, kicking and bucking beneath him, but she was too weak. Her muscles tingled and buzzed as if she were drunk.

"Sleep now," her uncle said, producing a bottle from inside his jacket. He uncapped it and tipped it into a handkerchief. He pressed the wet cloth to her face; she breathed it in despite herself.

The lines of her vision blurred as her body slackened and everything went black.

FREEDOM

BEN

*B*en paced his cell like a rat trapped in a maze. He felt wild, out of his mind with worry.

Remi had not returned, and with her uncle's alarming visit, he grew more and more frantic. *He's going to kill her. He's going to kill Remi, and I can't stop him!*

His thoughts spiraled into darkness, tearing the fragile corners that frayed in his mind. Arnaud's confession had been biting, and it still stung. First his sister, then his father. Soon, it would be Ben's turn, too. His whole family snuffed out.

He banged on the bars of his cell and shouted for what seemed like hours. Finally, an officer of the *gens d'armes* came to inspect the ruckus.

"What's all this?"

"Where is the inspector?"

The man frowned. "He's busy."

"I need to talk to him," Ben said. His urgency grew wilder by the second. *"Now."*

The officer gave him a once over and banged on the bars with his baton. It shook Ben's sore hands, but he held on. "He doesn't have time for the likes of you."

"Tell him to make time!" Ben yelled as the officer left.

He hit the bars again, shouting into the darkness until his throat burned and his eyes felt heavy. Remi was in danger, and he couldn't do anything. Ben slid down the bars to his knees, gently knocking his head against the iron. He balled his fists against his knees to keep them from shaking as he struggled to maintain some measure of collectedness.

If they wouldn't bring the inspector to him, he would draw the man out himself instead.

Ben sucked in a breath, and like a man unhinged, he jumped to his feet and grabbed the cot with all of his strength, throwing it. It took every ounce of his might, but when it hit the iron, it made the most awful, yet satisfying, sound. It bellowed down the hall, loud enough to alert all of the officers.

So he did it again.

And again.

He did it until his mind was incensed until there was nothing but blind rage to keep his muscles moving. If he stopped, he feared he would collapse from the enormous strain.

"Cease this at once!" The first officer, accompanied by another, banged on the bars again. Their voices were small in comparison to Ben's shouting, and when he threw the bed again, they nearly toppled to the floor.

"What's happening here?" The sound of the inspector's voice was enough to stop him. "Ben? What are you doing?"

Before his legs claimed him, Ben fell against the bars to keep himself standing. "You must let me out."

"What?" Marceau appeared incredulous. "Ben, I can't do that."

"You can," he huffed, "and you will."

The inspector leveled his gaze. "I can't."

"Madame Leone," he huffed again, trying to catch his breath. "Remi...she's in danger. Right now, right this second. I need to go to her."

His eyes widened a fraction. "How can you know?"

"It's her uncle. He's behind it all." Ben could feel his second wind coming on. "I need to go to her. Now!"

The inspector raised an eyebrow. "Do you have any proof of this?"

"Yes," Ben sputtered. "If you let me out and I get to her in time, I will give you proof. You have my word."

The inspector was silent for a moment longer, and then he was walking away. The other two officers followed him without another word.

"Her blood is on your hands!" Ben yelled, straining his already sore throat. "You coward! You're all cowards!"

Ben was on the ground again when keys clinked against his iron bars a few long moments later. He looked up, meeting the inspector's piercing eyes.

"I hope you'll spare me the guilt. I have a soft spot for Madame Leone," Marceau said.

The door of his cell opened wide, creaking in the dark of the *gaol*. After days locked up inside the small room, it felt good to step outside of his cage, but his relief was short-lived. He needed to get to Remi.

"Thank you," Ben said. "I will."

"Where will you go?" asked Marceau.

"Home," he said. "It's the only place I know she might be if he hasn't gotten to her yet."

Marceau nodded.

"If she's not there, then I'll…" He didn't want to think about the worst, let alone consider it. "I'll search the entire island until I find her."

"I will dispatch some of my men to the Cuvilyés's home and to your manor."

"And my footman?"

The inspector sighed. "I will bring him along. You'd best get a move on. I left my horse out front for you."

"Thank you," Ben said. "I'm forever grateful."

Ben started down the hall and stopped suddenly when the inspector called after him. "Monsieur? I need not remind you, do I?"

"Of what?"

"The law, sir! The law!" Marceau shouted.

Ben understood but knew he could not promise he would not hurt Arnaud. If a single hair was out of place on Remi's head, the man would pay dearly.

~

REMI

Remi stirred against the brush of a warm hand against her cheek.

The soft snaps and pops of the fire crackled in the background, the sound soothing her as she turned beneath the sheets. A pair of brown eyes watched her.

"Wake up, Remi."

"Ben?"

He smiled. "You're tired."

She agreed with a silent nod, a sob bubbling out of her. Sadness overcame her, and he pulled her close. "I feel broken."

"No," he said against her hair. "Bent, perhaps, but never broken."

"Why is this happening?"

Ben's hand ran soothingly down the length of her back. She felt wet, her clothes suddenly clinging to her body. The sound of the fire was replaced by the whipping winds of a cold storm raging overhead. They were a mess of tangled limbs, embraced by four dark walls with only one exit. A grave, a cell, another room she could not escape.

"Why does anything happen?"

"I don't know," she said.

"Will you give up?"

Remi shook her head lightly. "Part of me would like to."

"Do you know what will happen then if you do?" Ben's embrace hardened, and his hands stopped at her waist. She looked up into his eyes, now devoid of life. The fire in him extinguished. Her heart sank.

"You will die," she breathed. "And I will die."

"Is that what you want?" His lips moved, forming the words slowly.

Like Leith, his lips turned blue, and the impression of a rope deepened into a purple bruise around his throat.

"No."

"Then you must wake up."

As if on command, the sky above them opened up and rained down on them. The little space filled quickly with water, and when Remi breathed it in, she remembered: Elise was dead, Ben was not there, and she was in danger.

Her eyes flew open, the vision replaced by reality.

The grave was gone, as was Ben. The room was unrecognizable at first, becoming clearer as her eyes focused. Dim yellow lights hung overhead, and the damp air and dirt floor hinted at some sort of cellar or storage house. She felt like one of the bodies that Ben had stored, only unopened and still alive. She moved a fraction, and it set her body ablaze with pain. She winced.

Whatever drug he'd used on her had not worn off completely yet.

"I'm surprised you're awake."

Arnaud appeared around a corner, dragging something heavy with him. With a groan, he heaved the weight of his baggage, slamming it into the spot opposite Remi with a hard thud. Her throat tightened, and she pressed her dry lips together in an effort to contain her fear.

"I would have let her go," Arnaud said, nodding his head toward Sylvie's crumpled and broken body, "but she left me with little choice."

"What?" The question came out strangled, but he must have anticipated her reaction.

"Your maid is—well, *was*—a hysterical thing." There was an edge of humor to his voice. "Did she tell you everything? She said she kept it a secret, but I couldn't be sure, could I?"

"What are you talking about?" But then Remi stiffened. Sylvie *had* confided in her before running away. She admitted to her part in delivering the letters on Hugo's behalf.

"Ah, there it is," Arnaud pressed his lips together. "You *do* know something."

Remi was silent.

"Did she tell you about Edgar? How she helped me with the body?" His eyes lingered on Sylvie before he approached her mangled body and knelt before it. He extended a hand to her hair and brushed it gently as if she were a sleeping child instead of a corpse. "Stitched up the old fool after I was done, then cleaned up his blood. She was incredibly thorough."

Remi stifled a sob. It wasn't any wonder that she ran away. She had too many secrets for someone to bear.

"Then there was the matter of Hugo's letters," he chuckled. "I told him it was a fool's errand, that he stood no chance at wooing you. Still, he pursued you anyway. Poor Sylvie. Caught up in all of the muck."

Her uncle's eyes turned to her, and in the dim light of the cellar, every line on his wicked face made him more monster than man. It was an expression she recognized—the same look her father had worn the night he confronted her mother. Madness consumed him.

A man she'd known to be benevolent and loving, suddenly a heartless killer.

"For a time, she was useful," he taunted, grabbing a fistful of Sylvie's hair as he pulled her into an upright position. "But I don't like to leave behind loose ends."

Sylvie's slacked jaw hung awkwardly to one side, dry blood crusted around her lips. Remi's uncle stood and dragged the corpse closer, forcing the dead girl's face into Remi's. She felt helpless as he mocked her. "You should have heard her scream."

Remi closed her eyes, warm tears streaming down her cheeks. She didn't want to think about how her friend had suffered. Sylvie was too sweet to deserve such treatment. It was unthinkable that her uncle was capable of killing another person, yet he'd admitted to two deaths already.

"Unfortunate, I know, but necessary all the same," he said, bored, as Sylvie's body thumped to the ground again. "Your precious Ben will pay the price for me, though. And you'll be here, just the same as Sylvie."

"You wouldn't." Terror gripped her. *Does he mean to kill me?*

Arnaud's hand wrapped around Remi's arm and pulled her up with a sharp tug. She cried out, her eyes forced open from the pain.

"I would, Remi. I absolutely would."

Remi bit her lip.

"My brother should have done you the same way he did that director," Arnaud snarled. "Instead, he sent you to me. And what a miserable undertaking it was."

"He *paid* you," she spat in his face. It had not been kindness that guided her uncle but the promise of money. "How miserable could you be?"

"Very, Remi! He planned to stop paying me, so I had to convince him to let you marry. But I see my error now." He grasped her chin and tilted it back. "I let you live without rules. My brother always said that you would ruin us. I was a fool not to listen."

"I was married!" Remi's eyes watered. "You were rid of me! Why would you ruin that?"

"Why?" A manic expression overtook her uncle. His grip on her chin tightened. "Why, you ask? Because that lousy old fool tricked me!"

She was quiet for a moment, shocked. Finally, she asked, "You figured it out?"

He shoved her back, hard. "Of course I did. He made all of these asinine excuses the moment the money was withdrawn. It was the last of your dowry and my brother's allowance combined—you can imagine how angry I was to realize it was all for show."

"So you killed him?"

He scoffed. "He crossed me, Remi."

Tears ran fresh down her cheeks. To think that Edgar would risk so much for so little. What was the return on his ruse? What could he have gained for tricking her uncle out of money? He must have had good intentions. He must not have known how it would all fall around him, no matter how clever he thought himself.

"Everything has been on the verge of collapse for years, Remi," her uncle sneered. "Elise was an expensive child, as you know, and despite my efforts to repair our situation, I have been unsuccessful. The Leone girl was a start, but she failed. No money, just lies."

Remi nearly choked—whatever warmth she had left sapped from her skin.

"You don't mean Ben's sister?" Her lips quivered.

"She was at my every beck-and-call. That girl, if I had asked her to, would have thrown herself from the moors regardless of if I'd pushed her." Arnaud's eyes danced as though he took joy in the memory of the girl's death.

"You monster," Remi spat.

Arnaud simply shrugged, unbothered by the insult or her vitriol.

Poor Soleil, she thought. Her heart ached for Ben and for her own loss. Arnaud had treated her well, loved her even, and yet the man before her was not the one who had raised her.

"My reputation would have been ruined," he said.

"Better ruined than someone else dead," Remi said, her voice filled with disgust equal to what she felt in her heart.

"Nothing has gone right," he seethed between gritted teeth. "But I intend to fix that. With both you and the other Leone gone, I'll inherit what's left of your property." Arnaud grabbed at her hair and held it tightly. "And I'll tear that wretched manor down myself when I do. I'll turn over every worthless cent of that land to some money-hungry bastard, too, if it means my luck is restored."

His fist tightened, and she yelped. He raised his hand against her but failed to strike a blow.

Remi fell to the ground as Arnaud was shoved backward by an unseen force. Free of his grasp, Remi tumbled forward, the side of her face connecting with the packed dirt floor. Bile rose from the back of her throat and spilled from her mouth onto the floor. She coughed, rolling onto her back as another figure joined the fray.

"Lay another hand on her and I'll kill you."

Hugo! Remi's eyes landed on the crazed redhead. Sweat spilled down his brow as he shook with unbridled rage.

"She's mine," Hugo snarled, pulling a silver revolver from his breeches. "You said she was mine."

He has a gun, Remi thought in a panic. Part of her was relieved by the sight of it, but in Hugo's hands, it was inherently more dangerous.

"Put that away, you fool," Arnaud said as he nurtured his jaw. With the men distracted by each other, Remi worked faster on the rope around her wrists until it became loose enough to slip her hands through.

"I should have never agreed to this!" Hugo exclaimed, the rattle of the gun in his hands louder than Remi's racing heart. "You should have married her off to me, not the old bastard."

"We can make new arrangements," Arnaud said as he started forward slowly, hands raised. "Remi is unmarried now, a widow, and my daughter is dead. With her inheritance…"

"What?" Hugo asked, his handle on the gun faltering slightly. "That wasn't part of the plan."

"Elise? Of course, it was part of the plan," her uncle said. "How else was I meant to procure Remi for you? You'll have twice the riches with her."

Remi lifted herself carefully enough not to be noticed, her gaze transfixed on the gun. If Hugo shot her uncle, he would come for her next. His lies faded into the background as his words sunk in. Did Hugo not know about Elise? If he didn't, that meant he'd had no hand in her death. Without thinking, Remi screamed, "He's lying to you, Hugo! There is no money."

Arnaud's expression grew crazed. He lunged at Hugo while the other man was left dumbfounded, knocking the revolver from his hands. It hit the ground near Sylvie's discarded corpse and lay in the dirt while the two men threw fists and curses at one another.

Remi crawled toward it, and once her fingers had a hold on its grip, she jumped to her feet and ran.

THE CEMETERY

BEN

*B*en's legs and feet burned by the time he made it up the hill to the manor. His breath came to him in ragged puffs, and the air stung when it hit his lungs. Night was closing in and a storm followed him the entire way home; he was drenched in rain before sweat had even touched his brow. Dripping wet, he flew into the foyer of the manor and called out for Remi.

Silence.

Ben called for her again as thunder drowned out his shouting.

"She's not here." He pressed the heels of his hands to his eyes and breathed in deeply.

The study, he thought. *Check the study. Maybe she's left a clue.*

The chances were slim, but he hurried down the hall regardless. Outside, the rain picked up and pounded against the glass. Ben could hardly see at first, but a flash of lightning lit the room long enough for him to notice that the rug in the center of the room had been pulled back. In the spot where his father's prized moth had been displayed, a trap door had been revealed.

He dropped to his knees and looked into the darkness.

"How many more secrets are you keeping?" He asked aloud, thinking of his father. Thunder rumbled in reply.

It was too dark to see where it went, or how deep it was. He scrambled to his feet and ran to the kitchen, turning out every cabinet until he found an old lamp. There were stores of oil and he managed to replace enough for a flame to hold.

Ben ran back through the kitchen, colliding with Jacques and nearly dropping the lantern.

"Hells," Jacques swore.

Ben must have looked awful, judging by Jacques's reaction, but he thought Jacques looked worse. Bruises ran along his jaw and dry blood crusted on his brow.

"Make haste, Jacques." Ben pushed past him to the study, clearing the darkness with his golden light. "I assume Marceau told you where to find me?"

"He did."

"Did he also tell you that Remi is missing? That her uncle is behind it all?" Ben set the lamp down beside the hole in the floor and gestured to it. "And this...well, I've just found this, but I suspect Remi had something to do with its discovery."

"Do you intend to go in?" Jacques asked.

"Yes."

"Are you certain she's down there?"

Ben breathed out slowly. "No, I'm not. But I don't know where else to look, and she's in danger."

"Then I'll come with you." Jacques appeared skeptical, but he did not argue.

"No, my friend." Ben placed both hands on Jacques' shoulders and lightly squeezed them. "The inspector will be here soon with the *gens d'armes*. Wait here for me."

"Is this wise?"

But Ben was already dangling his feet in the hole, finding a foothold on a ladder against its side. He pressed his heel against it, and it held his weight without breaking. "My gut is telling me I'll find her on the other side of this tunnel."

Jacques nodded. "I trust your instincts."

Ben nodded, turning his body as he pressed into the side and climbed down. He held out his hand for the lamp and Jacques passed it over. The hole was not as deep as he'd thought, and once his feet touched the earth, a long stretch of darkness waited beyond. The hair on the back of his neck stood up straight and gooseflesh pimpled his arms. He shivered.

Ben.

A cool breeze brushed against his cheek, and in it, he swore he heard Remi's voice calling his name.

"Whatever is leading me," he lifted the lantern high, illuminating what he could of the tunnel, "I hope it brings me to you."

Without another moment's hesitation, Ben chased down the shadows, swallowing them whole with the light swinging in his hand. With any luck, Remi would be waiting at the end—*alive.*

REMI

All Remi knew was that it was dark and raining.

She had been wrong about their whereabouts, as the cellar led upstairs to a dilapidated house. She'd never seen it before; it was nestled far back in the woods. The perfect place to hide. Remi's heart ached for Sylvie, who had been dragged there only to die alone. For as long as she lived, Remi would never forget the way her uncle tossed the young girl aside.

Rain soaked through her dress and her hair clung to her skin. She'd been running for what felt like hours, though little time had passed. The gun was slick in her hand, but she held it with a vise-like grip.

She rested against a tree to catch her breath.

"Remi!"

Her heart skipped in her chest.

"You little bitch! Where are you hiding?"

She covered her mouth to suppress a gasp. He sounded close. *How much space have I put between us?*

He called again, his voice growing louder. Remi shook with fear. She couldn't see in the dark, past the trees, or through the rain dripping in her eyes. They were in a heavily wooded part of the island, and she had no inkling of where they might be.

A flash of lightning lit up the sky.

Something fluttered in the distance, the glancing light dancing off their beating wings.

Moths? She wondered.

Another flash of lightning revealed more than just moths. A few feet away, standing between two trees, was Edgar. His white eyes sparkled in the dark, and the shimmering outline of his body was bright enough for her to see him amongst the brush.

Her uncle's voice was louder still, but seeing Edgar spurred her on.

Follow Edgar, she told herself. *Follow the moths.*

Remi grabbed her skirt and picked up her feet, following Edgar as closely as she could. He faded in and out of sight, always reappearing further ahead whenever she drew close. With her uncle at her back, he was the only thing that she could trust.

"I see you!"

A rock hurled past Remi's head, and she ducked sideways. Her shoulder slammed into a tree, but she righted her footing and moved faster.

"Please stop this!" she begged through ragged breaths.

"This is your doing!" Her uncle ignored her. "You have been a pox on my family for too long, you miserable bitch."

Then you shouldn't have taken me in, she wanted to say, but she couldn't. It hurt to think about them; when she did, it only reminded her of her father—the man who had thrown her away.

Now his brother pursued her, ready to spill her blood for the sake of nothing. There would be no value in her death, but that hardly mattered to him. He was responsible for everything, and because of his madness, she'd lost Elise and countless others.

Ben's smile came to mind.

"He'll die too!" Arnaud cried as if reading her mind.

She choked on a sob but kept moving. Edgar was still there,

guiding her through the woods. All she had to do was keep her feet moving and she would make it. By some miracle, she would survive—she had to. Her uncle wouldn't get away with what he'd done, she'd make sure of it.

Keep running.

Mud caked her feet, pulling at her boots with each step.

Run, run, run.

Something hard hit her ankle, toppling her over as she fell onto her elbows. The gun flew from her hand, a few inches out of reach. Reaching for it, she looked back at the object that had tripped her and was shocked to find a headstone popping out of the ground. Her eyes adjusted to the darkness, and more silhouettes like the stone she had tripped on became clearer.

"The cemetery," she breathed, scrambling to her feet.

Edgar waited, watching her with his moths fluttering about his head.

Two more familiar faces joined him—Leith and Elise.

Remi's heart clenched tightly in her chest. They were there somehow, urging her on. She should have been afraid, but their white eyes and ethereal presence comforted her. She spurred herself forward, her ankle throbbing from its collision with the stone. Arnaud was behind her somewhere, his breathing as loud as hers. He grew weary from chasing her.

Further in, the trees started to thin.

The rain had picked up, and the wind was stronger than before. Her dress was soaked through, and her teeth chattered. Edgar, Leith, and Elise were waiting, moving gracefully across the cemetery. But then, without warning, they were gone. Remi panicked and hurried her pace. It wasn't long before the Leone family mausoleum came into view.

"Thank you," she whispered to herself.

The moths that had been circling Edgar's head were gone, save for one lone creature that beat its wings gently as it rested on the handle of the gate outside the mausoleum door.

"Remi! Remi, get back here!"

She turned sharply on her injured foot and winced at the pain. Hobbling to the mausoleum, she did not stop until the smooth granite was underhand. She pulled at the handle, hoping that the gate was unlocked, and sighed with relief when the handle turned freely in her hand. Remi felt tears forming as Arnaud's angry shouts closed in.

She used all of her strength, still holding the gun and pulled the gate open. She balanced against the frame, falling forward into waiting arms as the doors widened.

"Shh." A voice whispered, hands gripping her arms as she was dragged inside.

The doors closed with a soft click, and darkness consumed her. Outside, she heard her uncle. "Remi! I know where you are. I'll find you!"

"Are you hurt?"

Twisting in her captor's arms, she recognized the voice. A strained cry left her chest, his name distorted as she rasped, "Ben! How are you here?"

"Try to keep your voice down," he whispered. She felt his hands run up and down her waist, feeling her arms until his hand found the gun still gripped in her shaking fingers. "A gun?"

"Yes…" she breathed. "Hugo had it…they fought, and I stole it."

In the dark, she heard Ben chuckle, though it sounded humorless to her ears. "You are unfailingly clever."

A knock on the door. "Remi? Are you in there?"

Arnaud had found them.

He doesn't know that Ben is here, she thought suddenly.

"I can hear your heart racing, my darling niece," he sneered from the other side.

Ben leaned forward, his chest pressing into her.

"Give me the gun, Remi." His lips were warm against her cheek, brushing against her ear. His hand wrapped around the barrel of the gun and she released it. Ben moved her slowly, stepping in front of her to act as a shield.

When the mausoleum door opened, Remi closed her eyes.

Arnaud screamed her name one final time as the gun went off.

ANSWERS

BEN

The tunnel had been long, winding through the earth like a serpent.

Ben's lamp had ample enough light, but he hardly knew where he was going. It wasn't until the tunnel opened up that he realized he'd reached the end.

"What is all of this?"

He stumbled into an open space crammed with boxes and sheet-covered furniture. Too curious to stop himself, he snuck a quick peek into one of the boxes with his light. A flash of gold nearly blinded him. He reached inside, pulling out a solid gold candelabra. His jaw dropped.

"This can't be real."

He put the candelabra down and moved a sheet, uncovering a large oil painting and, beside it, a finely crafted marble bust. Ben could hardly believe his eyes. Treasure. It was *the* treasure. A man like Arnaud could live comfortably from the rewards each piece would no doubt provide him, or what money he could earn from a wealthier benefactor.

There was indeed gold, but he would never have guessed they had hidden an entire museum.

Now's not the time! Ben covered everything back up the best he could, planning to return for it later. *If* there was a later.

With his lamp in hand, Ben searched the rest of the area. Thankfully, there was a second chamber behind the storage, and at its core was a set of stone steps. Ben gave it a once over, confused by its operation.

"Where the hell does it lead?" His voice echoed back his own frustration. He scanned the room quickly, spotting a lone table to one side. Ben hurried to it, relieved to find a set of blueprints.

The drawings were of the pulley and the stairs. Something connected it, and if he was reading it right, then that meant turning the pulley would open the ceiling above the steps. Ben had come so far, and so he did not hesitate to do as the drawing suggested. His father always enjoyed building things, tinkering with them when he could. It was a pastime he thought his father had abandoned, but seeing the tunnel underground in his study, he wondered what else the late Edgar Leone had hidden.

What other surprises lie ahead?

Ben moved to the pulley and gripped the handle. He tried to turn it, winded after only three rotations, but the sound of gears moving spurred him on. Sweat dripped down his face into the damp collar of his shirt. He persisted, and when the ceiling above the steps opened and a mechanism clicked, locking it in place, he knew he'd been right to take the tunnel.

She's up there. I can feel it.

The steps were a short climb, opening up into a dark room. Once his eyes adjusted, he realized where he was standing. The mausoleum was a pleasant surprise, though shocking that the tunnel brought him there. He thought of Arthur Leone plotting out tunnels and passages to secure the safety of his family.

"Remi! Remi, get back here!"

Ben's attention turned to the door. Outside, someone had called for Remi. He heard the sound of scuffling, and the creak of iron as the gate opened. His chest tightened, his hands already prying open the second set of doors. A figure fell through, light and breathless. Her blonde hair was unmistakable, even in the darkness. Remi was alive; she was safe.

He thanked himself for leaving the gate unlocked the night they stole away his father's corpse.

"Shh," he warned, closing the doors behind her.

Muffled though he was, he could still hear Arnaud calling out for her. Remi was soaked, her breathing shallow and labored. He wondered how long she'd been running in the rain.

"Are you hurt?" he asked.

"Ben! How are you here?" The rawness in her trembling voice loosened the tight knot in his chest. He could have kissed her, he wanted to, but there was a madman stalking her outside. They were not yet safe.

"Try to keep your voice down." He felt along her body to her arms, if only to know she was unharmed. He felt cool metal in her hand, a remarkable discovery. "A gun?"

Through her rushed explanation, he heard, "Hugo" and "stole it."

"You are unfailingly clever." They had the upper hand with a weapon, and with him there, Arnaud would have no idea what he was walking into. *I'm going to marry her, I swear it.*

Arnaud called out again, closer than before. The mausoleum would be an obvious place to search, especially with their family name engraved along the top of the door. They had seconds before her uncle clambered into the unassuming space.

Ben leaned down, brushing Remi's cheek with his lips. "Give me the gun."

She relented and he moved her behind his body, shielding her from her uncle. Ben steadied himself and pulled back the hammer. It happened in a flash, within a breath, and the gun went off. Arnaud howled as he jerked from the impact, falling forward on the granite floor. Ben didn't wait. He grabbed Remi's hand and led her down the steps into the tunnel.

She winced at the bottom, collapsing from exhaustion.

"Is he dead?" She gasped.

"Don't worry about him," Ben said, studying her. In the lamplight, he could see the specks of mud on her skin and in her hair. "What's wrong with your leg?"

"It's my ankle," she frowned. "I tripped and twisted it."

She'd fallen somewhere in between where she'd been held and the mausoleum.

Above them, Arnaud groaned. Ben frowned and searched for the mechanism. After a moment, he found it and closed the tunnel off, lest Arnaud find the strength to pull himself down the stairs.

"Can you walk?" Ben turned his attention back to Remi.

"I fear I've spent myself running. It hurts terribly." She winced as she tried to put pressure on it.

Ben stopped her with a light touch before he took a moment to tuck the gun into the waistband of his trousers. "Take this."

He handed Remi the lamp from the table, then swept her off her feet. With her held tightly against his chest, he hastened down the tunnel, back toward the manor.

"Where are we?" Remi asked.

"Underground."

"But how?"

"You should know," he said. "You're the one who found its entrance."

She gasped. "The door in the study?"

He nodded. "You left it wide open. Thank you for that."

"But, you were behind bars the last time I saw you. How is this possible? Am I dreaming?" she asked.

Ben stifled a laugh. "You're not dreaming."

"Tell me. How did you escape?"

He glanced down at her, blinded at first by the lamp, though its glow was dimming as the wick had burned down. Her eyes, the ocean still in them, raged with a storm like the one outside.

"Inspector Marceau," Ben said. "I'll thank him properly once we're safe, but he let me out."

"Truly?"

"Yes. In fact, he's waiting for us at the end of the tunnel," Ben said. "Without him, I never would have made it to you in time."

"How did you know where to find me?" Remi asked.

"I didn't," Ben admitted. "It was a gut feeling. I followed the tunnel and it led me to you. It was a happy coincidence that it led to the mausoleum."

"I don't believe in coincidence. Not after everything I've seen tonight." She shivered in his arms and he squeezed her tighter.

"What do you mean?"

She closed her eyes and rested her head against him. "Would you believe me if I told you that your father showed me where to go tonight? All of them, actually. Leith and Elise, too."

"I would say," he said, glancing down at her peaceful face, "that my sister's ghost has haunted me long enough to believe that anything is possible."

They were quiet the rest of the way, eased by each other's presence. When their light came into view of the ladder he had first climbed down, Ben heard voices and feet shuffling against the hardwood.

"Monsieur! Come quick," someone said. "There's a light!"

Ben stopped at the base of the ladder, setting Remi down. She leaned against his side, passing the lamp to him as he held it up. Faces peered down at them, their features inscrutable.

"Here!" Ben heard someone call. "They're down here!"

"Help them up," someone else said.

Ben guided Remi to the ladder, lending her the light until she was safely at the top. He hobbled up after her, embraced by the warmth of the study. The *gens d'armes* were present, as was the inspector. He was speaking with Remi, who was sitting in one of the armchairs, her ankle already being looked at. Across the room, a fire had been started in the hearth. Martin fed it wood while Peter milled around the room, serving tea and small snacks. There were at least fifteen men in uniform alone.

"Good to see you're both alive." Guillaume pulled them up, helping Remi as she limped away from the opening in the floor.

"It was luck," Ben said. "Just…luck."

Luck and circumstance. If it wasn't for the tunnel, or the contraption in the mausoleum, Remi would have been lost.

"Monsieur Marceau would like a word." Jacques sidled up to Ben and led him through a small gathering to the man in question.

Immediately, Ben was thankful to see him. Their last encounter was tense, but with Arnaud the culprit, he hoped he wouldn't need to spend another night in the cell. "Your madman is at the end of the tunnel. I incapacitated him."

"I see you have a gun." Marceau nodded to the revolver still in the band of his trousers.

Ben pulled it out and handed it over. "It was dark, but I did shoot."

"Then we must apprehend him. Thank you for your aid." Marceau stroked his mustache. As he turned to leave, the inspector stopped and paced back to the two of them. His expression was hard as he addressed Ben. "We have plenty to discuss, but know this: it was a miracle that you were able to uncover the true culprit. I hope you will learn to dally less with the dead and leave justice to the men with authority like myself."

Ben nodded slowly. "I understand, Monsieur."

"Good." He said. "I am off for the moment, but I will return for you and Madame."

The inspector wasted no more time. He bellowed orders to the *gens d'armes* and ten of them went down into the tunnel, armed with lanterns to guide the way. For the time being, they were done with the madness. With luck, they would find Arnaud bleeding out, too weak to fight, and he would be detained.

"Are you well?" Jacques asked.

"Yes, thank you." Ben patted his friend on the shoulder. "I need a moment. Can you manage this crowd without me?"

Jacques nodded and joined the inspector. Ben approached Remi, who was consoling her aunt in the parlor. He had not seen Beline at first, but her presence wasn't unwelcome. He felt nothing but sympathy for the once loud and brazen woman.

"I am so glad that you're alive, Remi." Beline bawled, sinking her face into a handkerchief. "I don't know how much more my heart can take."

"Thank you, Tante Beline."

"Beline, why don't you come sit beside the fire with me?" Guillaume asked, shuffling her away toward the fire where Martin stood.

Ben knelt and looked up into Remi's face. There was a great deal of sadness in her, and yet she managed a smile. "Would you come with me?"

"To where?"

"To my sister's room."

$\sim$

BEN

No one paid Ben or Remi any mind as he scooped her into his arms again, carrying her into the hall and up the stairs. He stopped at his sister's door and set Remi right on her feet. The door creaked on its hinges, stirring the dust to life again as he opened it. It felt different to be there with Remi, to know that he had answers and could finally be at peace with her death.

"Why here?" Remi asked.

He led Remi to the bed, and she sat. She was silent, both in shock and awe.

"Your uncle told me something disturbing." Ben turned in a semi-circle around the room. The rain pattered against the windows, adding to the melancholy. Their night had been an endless fight against a perilous undercurrent. Now that they had weathered the worst of it, the storm had died down and with it, their constitution. Ben could feel his body tiring, but he felt restless still, and this could not wait until morning.

"What did he say?"

Sitting at his sister's writing desk, he ignored the scratched initials and opened the first drawer. He recalled the box inside the first drawer, recounting its plain façade, and his ignoring it for not standing out. When he and Jacques first searched, the box seemed normal, an inconspicuous thing. As he pulled it from the darkness, he realized how wrong he was.

Ben wiped away the thin film of dust from the lid as he set it in his lap. He could feel Remi's gaze, thoughtful as he waded through his confusion. "He said that Soleil had been in love with him. I thought it might have been nonsense, something to get a rise out of me, but I wanted to see for myself."

"And you think you might find what you're looking for in that box?"

"I'm not sure," Ben shrugged. "But I wonder if this is what Soleil was leading me to all those nights ago, and I was just too blind to see."

Remi's cool hands closed over his shaking one and regarded him with a kind smile. "Come over here to the bed. We'll sit together."

Ben let her lead him and sat at its stiff edge with her pressed into his side.

"If this is what your sister wanted for you," Remi gave his arm an encouraging squeeze, "then consider it closure. For the both of you."

"You're right." Ben lifted the lid and set it to the side.

Inside the box, there was a book of poetry with pressed flowers inside. Roses, lilies, and gypsophila—baby's breath. Pretty ribbons and strips of lace pressed together in neat coils, while bobs of thread milled around. Beneath the flowers, Ben found a pile of stacked envelopes and, seeing her name, extracted them from the box. Like him, she held her breath as they read the first letter.

Soleil,

Beautiful, clever, and endlessly curious…you are a poem, my love. I could speak your name throughout the ages and it would never grow old. With enough money, I would build you a castle. Will you meet me tomorrow night?

Yours,
Arnaud

Ben opened another and read:

Soleil,

Would that I could sing your name, proclaim to all that my love for you is as true as the ocean is blue. You are beauty defined, my dearest heart. Meet me tomorrow, a quarter after midnight. Let me praise your youth, let me show you how I have longed for you these last three days. I am a man starved of your affections and I crave you. I can only dream of the day when you have saved enough for us to escape—to elope and be together. Finally.

Yours,
Arnaud

Ben's heart sat in his throat. It was true then; his sister *had* been involved with Arnaud and none of them had known about it. Only, his father might have known, but it would be the last secret he took with him to the grave. He picked up another letter, shocked to see Arnaud's name on the post rather than Soleil's. He pulled out the letter addressed to Remi's uncle and swallowed.

"This one was from Soleil." He held it up.

"Read it," Remi said. Her patience, it seemed, was endless and he expected that she would sit with him all night if he asked her to.

Arnaud,

My heart is broken. You have left me in pieces, and I cannot keep from crying. Where did I go wrong? Did I ask too much of you? I only want to be with you. Please, please meet me at our spot. I will find more money if it means that you will be with me. Please, let me fix what I have broken.

Forever yours,
Soleil

At the bottom, a note had been scrawled in the corner: *No.*

Ben knew that it had been Arnaud, that he had returned her note without a second thought. He'd written her love letters, which she'd returned in kind, but when he'd broken her, he had left her with one word. It must have been after his final letter that he pushed her—*after* she threatened to tell Beline of his infidelity. Ben set the letters down at his feet, tucking his face into his hands. He ached for Soleil.

Remi's light fingers grazed the back of his neck as she drew him closer. She said nothing, only soothed him with mild hushes as her hands brushed back his dark hair. For a while, it seemed that all had gone still, that the night had stopped moving and they were stuck in the dark. But someone said their names, and Guillaume found them embracing on Soleil's bed.

"They found him," he said. "They found Arnaud."

"Alive?" Remi asked.

Guillaume grimaced. "Yes."

ARNAUD & HUGO

REMI

They would not be allowed to see him.

Remi was relieved, yet disappointed. After her uncle had been found in the cemetery, crawling on his belly in the mud like a wounded animal, he'd been locked up immediately. When asked about Hugo, Arnaud had given up the location of the abandoned house with little fight. As it turned out, the little house was the old groundskeeper's residence. It was left abandoned for a few years or more, making it the perfect location for Arnaud to hide. Giving it up was easy enough. If he was to suffer, then so would Hugo. He was discovered an hour or so later, nursing a broken arm and a sliced thigh. The altercation that Remi had used to escape was much worse than she'd imagined.

Inspector Marceau detained both men and was able to prove their guilt. There was no loyalty left among murderers, and for their crimes, they would hang.

"It was open and shut, as they say," Inspector Marceau said when he delivered a report to the manor a few days later.

The three of them—Remi, Ben, and the inspector—sat together in the parlor.

Remi eyed the documents carefully while Ben and Marceau

discussed the next steps. She could see that the report detailed everything: Remi's arranged marriage, the contract signed between Arnaud and Edgar, the proof of the stolen wine and its canceled purchase, and the men's confessions. Hugo had killed Leith in a fit of jealousy and rage and had admitted paying Sylvie to deliver his notes in secret without Remi ever knowing. Sylvie had paid a steep price for her own misdeeds; it was hard for Remi to feel anger towards the young girl.

"Your uncle fought, but once he discovered that we had wired his brother for the details of their agreement, he was willing to oblige."

Ben asked, "What did his brother have to say?"

"Only that Arnaud had been on the verge of insanity," Marceau demonstrated his exasperation with a grunt as he leaned back in his chair. "He claimed that Arnaud planned to murder Edgar Leone from the very beginning, even after their business concluded. Per your request, I asked after your sister—he claimed to know nothing of her passing, though tragic it must have been. Also, he said that Arnaud had promised to share whatever inheritance with him once the deed was done. Though I understand now that there was no true inheritance to be had, correct?"

"Correct," Ben said. "Just the land and this manor that has been in the family for generations."

"I see." Marceau closed his eyes for a short moment.

Remi had not thought much about the man at their first meeting, but he'd grown on her. "Monsieur," she said hesitantly. "Did my father make any mention of me?"

Marceau appeared thoughtful. "He only asked if you were well."

"Ah."

"I told him that you were in high spirits."

Remi thought it might help to know how her father felt if her brush with death had changed him—but she'd been wrong. Ben's hand fell to Remi's shoulder and he gave it a comforting squeeze.

"Will you be accompanying us to the docks?" Remi asked Marceau.

Beline and Guillaume had made plans to travel to the countryside immediately after Arnaud was detained. It would be a comfort for Beline to be with her extended family, and they would hopefully receive word beforehand, but they were leaving the Isle. With Elise's body preserved in a coffin, they planned to bury her far away from the Bleue. Ben and Remi had agreed to meet them, hoping to see Elise off with a final farewell.

"No, no. I would hate to intrude." Marceau hopped to his feet and Remi handed him the report. "Thank you for having me. A moment's respite from the darkness these last few days has done some good for my soul. It warms me to no end that you are alive, Madame Leone."

"Thank you," she said.

Marceau turned his sharp eyes to Ben. "Please accept my deepest apologies. I am happy to know you are innocent in all of this, though I would advise caution in the future. Disturbing a grave is a serious offense."

"As you've already said." Ben glowered.

"But I convinced my superiors that it was sanctioned," Marceau added, "if only to prove that the victim's deaths were indeed misinterpreted."

"That's kind of you."

The inspector crinkled his mustache and cleared his throat in reply. "Yes, well, I expect it's what your father would have said, were he here. He only ever had good things to say about his son, the doctor."

Remi watched Ben's eyes widen.

"Did you...did you know my father?"

"Please accept my apologies." Marceau bowed his head. "I could not risk anyone knowing the nature of my relationship with your family. In truth, I came here seeking answers myself. Your father and I had been writing to one another for more than a decade, off and on, about your family and its misfortunes. It started with your sister, in fact. He knew of me from the papers. I was shocked to learn that the Parisian news reached the Isle. I stopped receiving regular missives a few months ago, with the last being a wedding invitation.

"It was my intention to visit him after his wedding, but my timing could not have been worse. I arrived only a day before his death. I feel fortunate that I was in the right place at the right time to offer my services. Your father was owed as much justice as anyone: more so, as it turns out. I only wish I'd followed through sooner."

"I can hardly believe it," Ben said, stunned. "Is that why you were so willing to believe me?"

"In a manner of speaking," Marceau bristled. "I am a professional. I seek truth where the evidence leads."

"Of course. We never believed anything different, Monsieur," Remi added, touching a hand to Ben's back to steady him. He seemed genuinely astounded by the truth.

"Ah, well, since we are on the matter of your father," the inspector said, turning to Ben, "I nearly forgot. I found a letter addressed to you. It was taken from the maid's personal effects—among the other stolen trinkets. I thought it might be important."

From his pocket, Marceau produced a crinkled envelope. She had never seen it before, but the presentation widened Ben's eyes with recognition. He surged forward and took it from Marceau's proffered hands. He turned it thrice before folding it up and tucking it away inside his breast pocket.

"It is. Important, I mean," Ben said. "Thank you, Monsieur."

"I'll be off then." Marceau nodded his reply and then uttered a short farewell. Ben and Remi waited in the foyer to see him off. When he was gone, they called for Martin to bring their own carriage around. Beline and Guillaume would be waiting on them, and Remi did not want to keep them. Jacques brought it around a few moments later.

"I like him," Ben said as they settled onto the benches inside the cab. "Inspector Marceau, I mean."

Remi agreed. "Yes, he's very kind. I like his mustache."

"Does that mean I should grow one?" Ben chuckled.

"Not until you're very old," she said, taking his hands. The carriage was a decent size, but Ben's height and frame took up a majority of it. She hardly minded. Being trapped between Ben and a hard spot had become a favorite position.

He smirked. "I've heard that a mustache is an altogether different experience for women."

"I love you just as you are." Despite herself, she blushed at the insinuation. It was difficult enough to keep her hands to herself during the day, which said nothing for her restraint at night. She could only imagine what a mustache would do to her poor nerves.

Ben smiled knowingly, and, to tease her, licked his lips. He laughed when she turned her face to her hands. They should have disguised their affections better and waited until the worst of it had been dealt with. They'd tried—sleeping in different rooms the first night had done little to quell their desires. It was Remi who had gone to Ben first, and she'd made her stay permanent—every morning, and every night since.

"I could kiss you," he said, reaching for her.

"Then kiss me."

It was simple and sweet—a gentle peck, a brush of his thumb along her chin to her cheek. They arrived at the docks shortly after, joining Guillaume and Beline inside the inn where they'd been staying. Neither of them appeared better than before, but it was to be expected. Beline had been struck by their losses, consumed by the death of her daughter and the impending hanging that waited for Arnaud. She was pale and out of sorts, but Guillaume ensured she had strength for the voyage.

He'd been a pillar for her to lean on as she grieved.

"You will write, won't you?" Remi asked Guillaume.

"Of course." He had secured himself a job with a tailor in a small town, allocating and purchasing fabrics, and eventually working his way up to an apprenticeship. But first, he would take Beline to her sister's home in the countryside. No one could blame her for wanting to leave, especially after her husband murdered their child.

"Take care of Elise," Remi said, embracing him.

She heard him stifle a sob as he said, "You know I will."

"Safe travels." Ben said, shaking his hand.

Guillaume returned the gesture with fervor and a slight smile. "Take care of Remi and keep her out of trouble. Madame Leone attracts it wherever she goes."

Remi felt a blush creep across her cheeks, startling when she felt

Ben's hand brush languidly along the length of her back. Her ankle throbbed with the rest of her. Thankfully, Beline interrupted as she took Remi's hands in her own.

"Will you walk with me to the boat?" she asked. "Elise is waiting."

Remi obliged her and tucked her aunt's arm into her own. They quietly beheld each other for the last time, their steps in sync as they walked along the dock. It would be difficult for her aunt, but the trip would be worthwhile. Staying would only further break her heart.

At least she has Guillaume, Remi thought as they boarded. Elise's coffin had not yet been brought to the lower deck, so she did not have to go far to seek out her cousin. Beline melted into tears at the sight of it and excused herself to the boat's small cabin. Remi sympathized. Her own tears were impossible to hold back; they fell down her cheeks, staining the fresh wood.

"I only hope you know how much I loved you," she told her cousin's coffin.

"I have no doubt that she did." Ben stood beside her, his presence comforting.

Remi looked into his dark eyes and wiped at her cheeks. In a hushed tone, she said quietly, "She was there that night. In the cemetery."

"You said as much, though I recall my father and Leith were present as well." He remembered her words as they walked through the tunnel. Perhaps she'd been half-asleep when she spoke, not that he could blame her. Running away from a madman intent on killing her would have been tiring, if not altogether terrifying.

"They were." Remi bobbed her head. "How curious that they were all there when I needed them."

"Perhaps they knew you were in trouble."

"I think so." Remi leaned into his side and he wrapped an arm around her shoulders. "Your father's fascination with moths helped a little, too. Though I could have done without his cryptic messages."

"Moths, you say?" Ben asked curiously. He recalled the display, toppled over on the floor where it once stood above the tunnel's entrance. "Is that how you found the trap door?"

"Partly," she admitted. "But it was your ancestors and those papers you had that brought me there. You teased about tunnels, and as it happens, you were right."

"Of course I was." Ben teased.

"There was a floor plan from the 1600s included in the documents." Remi nodded. "Arthur *had* built an extra room—the tunnel beneath the study."

"Mystery solved."

"Elise would have been thrilled." Remi smiled to herself, though the sadness that followed was painful to bear. With a few mournful tears, they parted from Elise's coffin as it was moved below. Remi embraced Guillaume and Beline one last time, and then she and Ben waved them off from the docks.

They withdrew to the carriage once again, followed by the somber emptiness that buried itself in Remi's heart.

Her family had been torn apart again.

"We can help them," Ben said to break the silence, "now that the family's fortune has been found."

When the carriage rolled into the cemetery and drifted past headstones, crawling back toward the Leone mausoleum, Remi found herself seated on the edge. It cheered her a little to know that a small part of Ben's family had been recovered. Passing through the tunnel in the dead of night would be different in the daylight, and she was eager to see it all with fresh eyes.

BEN

Ben studied the portraits and the sculptures as they were carried out of the passage through the mausoleum floor. It still astounded him that there was a moving contraption below, but he enjoyed the cleverness nonetheless. His sister would have found it amusing, too.

"The real work," Jacques grunted, hauling a large crate of silver goblets, "will be finding a way to get rid of all this junk."

"Junk?" Remi chirped, unveiling herself from behind a portrait resting against another pile of crates and chests. "It's all *treasure*."

"Of course it is." Jacques set the crate down, wincing at the sound of his back cracking.

It was the three of them, plus Paul and Martin, left to clean out the valuables. The latter had left with the carriage, hauling a second round of portraits and other odds and ends. It was too much of a task to take them through the tunnel and up the ladder into the study. Besides that, there was no light to guide them. It did work out, though. Martin would be bringing them lunch upon his return, and Ben was grateful for it.

They would be in the cemetery until well after supper, he suspected. It was a task they needed to complete by day's end so that his father's body could be returned and left undisturbed.

"We have our work cut out for us." Ben gestured toward the collecting items.

Remi touched his arm and shared a sweet smile. "We certainly do."

"We'll have to catalog and label everything," he said.

Jacques groaned.

Remi seemed excited by the idea. "Then we certainly won't be bored."

Ben nodded his agreement.

After everything, they wanted to make certain that the "treasure" his relatives had stolen and collected, would find their rightful homes. It would not hurt to have a pretty penny as some form of reward. In fact, it was almost necessary if they were to restore the family home.

"That reminds me," Ben reached into the breast pocket of his vest and produced the envelope that Lamotte first gave him, "I have a letter to read."

"You found it?" Jacques asked, shocked.

"Marceau returned it." Ben unfolded it carefully. "Our clever friend Sylvie stole this out from under me, it seems. May she rest in peace."

Remi sucked in a breath. "I wonder why."

"She must have been under instruction to take anything she noted of import," he said. "I can only imagine that she would have eventually handed it over to Arnaud."

Remi quieted. He did not have to guess at what she must have been thinking. If only Sylvie had opened up to them, they could have helped her escape her fate.

"Go on then," Remi whispered with a gentle touch on his arm.

Ben turned it over in his hands, once again, and for the final time, acknowledging his father's signature. Jacques and Remi waited as he broke the seal, practically on edge as he produced two pieces of paper.

"Is that a check?" Jacques asked.

Ben nodded wordlessly. His jaw nearly dropped. It was a check made out to Remi, with a sum that caught him completely by surprise. He passed it to her.

She was instantly worried. "What could this be for?"

Behind the check was a folded piece of paper. He unfolded it to a sea of sprawling words written in his father's unique hand.

Dearest Ben,

I am entrusting this note to you in the hopes that it will find its rightful owner, Mademoiselle Remi.

It is the total collection of sums from her uncle; the other half of her dowry, which he kept hidden from me, and extra from his allowance. I devised a hasty, reckless plan to expose his scheme to acquire funds that did not belong to him. My intention was to give her some semblance of freedom from the people who would have been rid of her for less.

Ben, if you are reading this, I hope that you will forgive an old man for his foolishness. I should never have sent you away. After your mother and your sister, I was desperate to keep you alive. My fears won out in the end. It was a cruel thing to do in the midst of your grieving. The failures are my own burden to bear, and I will carry them in life and well after. I am merely hopeful that this finds you in good health, and that you are home, where you belong.

Please tell Mademoiselle Remi that her company brought me joy. Because of her, our home had warmth again. I hope that she may shine a light in those old and darkened halls for many years.

With Undying Love,
Your Father

P.S. Please tell Lamotte that he has been instrumental, and an excellent friend.

When Ben finished the letter, he was surprised to find a weight lifted from his shoulders. He could feel the damage from the last sixteen years, spent far away from home, chipping away. It was an incredible relief.

"God rest Lamotte's soul," Jacques said, lowering his head in respect.

"Edgar shouldn't have." Remi sniffed. Her nose was red and tears brimmed in her eyes.

"But he did," Ben said.

Jacques crossed his arms. "Do you think he knew he might die pursuing Arnaud?"

"He might have."

His father's plan was bordering on mad, but he'd followed through on something he intended to finish. It was a short letter that brought solace, but it also left them wanting more. Ben would have liked to know about the valuables hidden under the mausoleum, and just how his father knew; how he'd found it soon enough to mention it in his will.

Or had he known all along and kept it a secret? He wondered.

"It was too good of him," Remi sniffed again.

Ben took the check from her shaking fingers and put it back in the envelope with the letter. Tucking it inside his jacket, he brought Remi into his arms. She folded around him.

"If you two are going to nestle up like a couple of lovebirds," Jacques groaned, "then I'll excuse myself. If you need me, I'll be dragging more dusty crates up the steps."

Ben chuckled.

"What do we do now?" Remi asked after a few comfortable, quiet moments.

"As you said, there is plenty to do."

She looked into his eyes, resting her chin softly against his chest. "I mean, what shall we do first?"

Ben purred, "We shall open a bottle of wine."

"And then?"

Ben leaned down, grazing his lips along her ear. He felt her shiver as his breath skirted across her neck. He nipped at her smooth skin and grinned when she jumped.

"Ben!" Remi's hands pressed to his shoulders, bracing herself against his sturdy build.

"The rest," he murmured, "we'll leave to the wine."

ACKNOWLEDGMENTS

This book was a labor of love for the last four years. I started writing during Covid and took a long break from it during the time after. I'm so glad I came back to this book and made it happen! I couldn't have done it without my amazing support system.

Thank you to my husband for being my biggest cheerleader. You pushed me to finish writing, you offered your input when I needed it most, and you were the first person to read it from conception to finished product. Thank you for all the encouragement, always.

Thank you to my author fam, Chantal Gadoury especially. We journeyed through the Shrike's woods together once, and writing that book with you helped me feel so much more confident in writing this piece. You're one of my best friends and favorite storytellers.

Finally, a huge thank you to the incredible beta readers who took a chance on a few chapters and then dove headfirst into this thriller. Your feedback and kind words meant everything to me!

This book is my love letter to the ones who dream about brooding love interests, haunted manors, and the damsels that run from them in the dead of night.

Thank you for reading!

A.M. Davis is an artist and an author from Ohio. She co-authored her first novel, The Shrike and the Shadows, a dark and twisted retelling of the classic tale Hansel & Gretel. By daylight, she is the marketing manager for an upscale resort. By night, she is seeking out her next story, playing video games, or imagining what new piece to draw and anguish over dramatically.

THANK YOU FOR READING

Thank you for reading *The Mourning of Leone Manor*. We deeply appreciate our readers, and are grateful for everyone who takes the time to leave us a review. If you're interested, please visit our website to find review links. Your reviews help small presses and indie authors thrive, and we appreciate your support.

Other Titles by Quill & Crow

The Quiet Stillness of Empty Houses

Eye of the Ouroboros

There Ought to be Shadows

www.ingramcontent.com/pod-product-compliance
Lightning Source LLC
Chambersburg PA
CBHW050800190726
48285CB00005B/1736